"N

He rolled them over swiftly, reversing their positions. Wrapping her hair around his fist, he began to kiss his way down her neck.

His heart thundered in his chest with a locomotive's fierce, ground-rattling force. Blood hummed under his skin. Nerves began firing faster, yet he didn't struggle to control the situation. No, with Kennedy's soft encouragements, he simply let go and followed where the moment led.

"You'll be the death of me, Kennedy Jefferson." He raised her hands over her head, his hands tracing down the soft undersides of her arms and down her sides, thumbs tracing the outer swells of her breasts.

"Dylan." His name was a tender plea from her lips.

THE IMMORTAL'S REDEMPTION

BY
KELLI IRELAND

Published in Great Britain 2015
by Mills & Boon, an imprint of Harlequin (UK) Limited,
Eton House, 18-24 Paradise Road, Richmond, Surrey, TW9 1SR

© 2015 Denise Tompkins

ISBN: 978-0-263-91799-4

89-1015

Harlequin (UK) Limited's policy is to use papers that are natural, renewable and recyclable products and made from wood grown in sustainable forests. The logging and manufacturing processes conform to the legal environmental regulations of the country of origin.

Printed and bound in Spain
by CPI, Barcelona

Kelli Ireland spent a decade as a name on a door in corporate America. Unexpectedly liberated by Fate's sense of humor, she chose to carpe the diem and pursue her passion for writing. A fan of happily-ever-afters, she found she loved being the puppet master for the most unlikely couples. Seeing them through the best and worst of each other while helping them survive the joys and disasters of falling in love? Best. Thing. Ever. Visit Kelli's website at www.kelliireland.com.

To Kate Hollister, author and fellow lover of
all things that go bump in the night.

Prologue

Scotland, 1718

A damp cold seeped into Dylan's bones. He and another young assassin had spent the night in the hillside cave again, waiting. It was the worst part of his job. He'd rather be active, engaged, whether in subterfuge or killing, because activity meant progress. Waiting meant…waiting. Nothing happened. The sun and moon chased horizons more slowly. And one could only prepare so much before the actions became habitual. And habit would get you killed.

Dylan flipped his kilt higher over his shoulders, his gaze locked on the sun's first softening of the eastern night sky. The Scottish laird of Clan McKay had made it a personal goal to see the Druids run out of his lands. He'd acted against the peaceful settlements with violence. It was about time the fat bastard met violence in return. He'd have to pass through this valley in order to reach the next Druidic keep. With a fair amount of certainty, Dylan was sure the man would never make it that far. It was, after all, his charge to ensure the laird didn't make it through this valley.

Dylan rolled onto his back and stared at the darkness above. The cave was deep enough he couldn't see the ceiling. Fine by him. Meant he didn't crack his egg when he stood up. He hooked an arm behind his head, pillowing it.

As far as headrests went, it wasn't bad. As far as beds went, the stone floor wasn't the worst he'd experienced. The cold, though. That was eating into him as he whiled away the hour before dawn with fanciful thoughts of the lass he'd last bedded. Bonnie little thing, blonde hair and all.

What had her name been?

Pebbles skittered down the hillside, the small sound amplified by the dark. A sigh breathed across the cave's mouth, soft and resigned.

Dylan reached for his smaller sword. The short sword hissed along its leather scabbard as he pulled it free. He clasped his dirk. Dark tartan made nary a sound as he flipped it back, disguising his broadsword. Rising to his feet like a phantom, he readied himself for any threat that might come against him.

"Gareth." The man's name was little more than an exhale between Dylan's lips. His companion didn't stir.

Dylan dared not speak louder. Instead, he moved to position himself between the cave mouth and the sleeping Druid.

"Rest easy, child of mine."

The feminine voice startled him, and he moved back a step. Shifting his dagger to an underhanded hold, he regained the ground he'd lost to surprise. Using darkness as another type of weapon, he sidled up to a small rock outcropping. It didn't hide him entirely, but it would give him an advantage if she tried to enter.

"Dylan."

The voice came from behind him and he whirled, sword and dagger raised. Both immediately clattered to the floor.

It was a rare man whose destiny was molded while he listened and watched. And for better or worse, Dylan was just such a man, for it was the goddess and Mother of All, Danu, who now stood before him, her face smooth and serene.

"We may speak at ease, for Gareth has been sent into deep slumber," she said, her voice as gentle as mist yet as powerful as lightning. "I must forewarn you, Dylan. There is a time coming, a time when you will rise to power and position, only to be tried in the greatest challenge you shall ever face."

"Why tell me now, Mother?" His voice cracked on the last word, and he blushed. He wanted her to see him as strong and capable, not a boy. Squaring his shoulders and taking a deep breath to emphasize the baritone he was developing, he asked again. "Why tell me now, Mother?"

She'd stroked his head then, and reality had gone soft. He'd seen a woman with a mane of black hair in a world that was not his own. Her eyes had been bluer than the shallows near the cliffs. Her mouth could only be considered wanton. She was the most stunning woman he'd seen, yet there had been something slightly off about her.

Danu removed her hand and reality snapped back into being, clear and stark.

Despite the fact Dylan had been trained to recall finite details, he couldn't remember anything that had gone on around her other than it hadn't made sense to him. "Who is she?" This time his voice did not break. Instead, it was heavy with reverence.

"She is your truth, the answer to your ultimate reckoning with an imprisoned god of the Shadow Realm. The wards that bind the gods there were not cast in a manner to make them infinite, and in your woman's time, they will begin to fail as Samhain draws ever closer."

Dylan's gaze shot to the goddess's. "Wait. What do you mean, *my* woman?"

"Do not question me. I risk the wrath of the All Father, Dagda, in coming to you now." Her words were soft but laced with power that burned along his skin. "You will find the woman and your truth within her. This will empower you to save not only mankind and the Druid race, but also the world as it will come to be. To fail and let the truth escape you will mean the release of the imprisoned gods. Chaos will reign as they seek to remake the universe as they would have had it, seating themselves as the supreme gods. Be assured that should you fail, Chaos will bring certain death. You will be the first to taste it, young assassin. In order to survive, you will be required to willingly lay either the truth or sufficient sacrifice upon the altar, to offer the lifeblood of faith to rebind the wards."

"What is sufficient sacrifice, should the truth not be found?"

"That is for you to discover. Begin seeking her in what will be a new world to you, Dylan, for she is the only one to hold the truth. You must find Kennedy Jefferson before all is lost. She holds within her the single truth you must reveal and accept."

Then she'd disappeared.

Chapter 1

County Clare, Ireland, Present Day

Dylan O'Shea leaned back, arms crossed, one booted foot pressed against the stone wall of the westernmost battlement. His gaze was locked on the storm brewing over the Atlantic. Violent winds drove sheets of rain across the Cliffs of Moher. The green of the grass echoed the peaks and valleys of the sea, where waves rose and crashed forward. He watched, unblinking, as lightning struck shallow water.

A sound not unlike a woman's sigh wove through the shrieking wind. He glanced up and shoved his drenched hair back, looking around. No one there, but he wasn't surprised. Still, the sound had his mind pulling up the image of a black-haired beauty with eyes bluer than the shallows near the cliffs and a mouth he couldn't help but consider wanton.

For three hundred years he'd searched for her on the goddess, Danu's, directive. Three hundred years he'd conjured her image during every empty night. Three hundred years he'd spent with that face, and he'd come to want her like he'd never wanted another. And now her time—*their* time—was coming. He knew it with the same certainty he knew this storm wasn't a natural occurrence. Not with the extremes he witnessed. No, the balance of the elements was already out of order. It left him uneasy, bordering violent, as he considered how the woman might fit into the threat that built on the air.

And if he knew the elemental balance was threatened, the Elder Council did, as well. It also meant it wouldn't be long before they sought him out, and it was about time. Idleness was driving him mad. Or, if he were dealing in honesty, madder.

As if summoned by his thoughts, one of the very men he'd been considering pushed through the iron-banded wooden door. "It's time," he said.

"Time." Dylan blinked slowly before turning his attention back to the sea. "It's a subjective topic, is it no'?"

"Stalling will do little but delay the inevitable."

"You engage me, of all people, with talk of delaying the inevitable?" The bite of his voice broke through the storm's fury, and the man in the doorway bristled.

"The Elder Council waits for no one, Assassin, not even you."

The slamming of the door would normally have made Dylan smile. Not today.

Shoving off the wall, he dropped his hand to the door latch when a whiff of citrus and heavy spice tickled his nose, the long-forgotten scent called up from memory with the same gut-churning effect as a roller coaster's first radical drop. Dylan froze. Rain still ran in rivers down his face, but the pelting he'd been taking faded. Uneasy, his free hand drifted to his dirk, fisting the handle.

"I would think you'd willingly, and wisely, speak to me without violence, Assassin." The musical lilt of her voice hadn't changed, not in three hundred years.

"You use my title but expect me to behave peaceably?" He let go of the door handle and turned toward the woman who stood untouched by the rain.

"And you, you won't use my name." She tucked long-fingered hands into the bell sleeves of her robes; at the same time she cocked her head to the side, openly considering him. It was the equivalent of calling him a coward, and he would suffer a lot of shit, but not that.

"A gracious welcome to you, Danu, Mother of All Things." Dylan's numb lips struggled with the formal greeting. His belly tightened, and he absently rubbed it as he considered the goddess. She hadn't shown herself to him other than that one night three centuries ago when she'd changed the course of his life.

Danu reached for him, dropping her hand when he stepped back. "You are still angry with me for delivering your solemn responsibility at such a young age."

Dylan's mouth opened and closed, his ability to speak lost in a turbulent sea of emotions. Barking out a laugh, he shook his head. "I've spent my life wondering if I'd dreamed the whole conversation, thinking myself mad at best."

"Yet you acted with faith, preparing yourself for the inevitability of death." She closed in on him, laying a hand against his near-frozen arm.

All he could think was that she was neither hot nor cold. Odd that he'd handled meeting her as a lad much better than he was handling this moment. "So I'll die, then, the last of your direct line to hold the position of Assassin, to wield justice as deemed fit by the gods."

Danu stroked his cheek. "It does not have to be so. You *must* find the truth of which I spoke that night and stop the goddess Cailleach from breaking the chains that bind. Until you have found the truth and made your decision, nothing is guaranteed." She smiled gently. "Man's free will is a factor that tends to skew even the gods' predictions."

Cailleach. The anger that always simmered so close to the surface of his consciousness flared. "Free will, is it? Then I'd have you go back and return mine to me. For I'm nothing if not a man. I'd be something other than what I've become because of your blessed intervention. You gave me nothing, nothing more than a vague promise that I'd perish if I didn't find this *truth* you referred to. Yet you delivered your jaunty news and disappeared, leaving me with nothing more than your charge. What the hell good has that done me, then?"

The goddess's hand stilled, then fell away, her face transforming. Gone was the compassion of only a moment before. In its place was a cold and deadly stare that told him precisely how far was too far to push her—and that he'd crossed that line with a running leap of the mouth. Damn if he'd back up or apologize or—

Dylan's back slammed onto the stone he'd been standing on moments before. Air knocked out of him, he wheezed in an effort to regain his breath.

Danu stood over him, glorious in her fury. "You will comport yourself with respect, Assassin. Furious or not, your time has come. You will discover the truth you lack before Samhain or you will damn mankind and the Druid race to the end of life as it's known. Extinction would be a kinder fate."

He slowly pushed himself to his feet. "Will you not give me more to go on than that? Or will you charge me to continue to search the world over with nothing more than faith?"

Her lips thinned. "Still you show such belligerence. My hope for victory fades with every word you utter." She stepped back, putting distance between them. "In order for all to survive, you will have the slimmest of opportunities— hours—to lay either the truth or yourself upon the altar. Regardless of your choice, the sacrifice must be made willingly."

He blinked rapidly. She'd failed to mention that little

fact the first time she'd come to him. Opening his mouth to speak, he realized he was again alone.

Fucking gods and their fickle demands.

Fighting to breathe normally, Dylan hauled the heavy door open and stepped inside, shaking the rain from his hair like a dog exiting a lake. He pushed the wet mass off his face then started down the spiral steps. There were one hundred forty-two treads to the bottom, and each one seemed to propel him forward faster and faster until he fought the urge to run. He *never* ran unless he was the one doing the chasing. Deliberately leaning back far enough he nearly ass-planted on the steps, he forced himself to move slower. The Assassin wasn't running, even from this.

Particularly from this.

He silently rounded the corner at step seventy-three when he heard methodical footsteps coming up the stairs. Whoever it was heard him a moment later and paused. Dylan's hand automatically went to the short sword at his back. He began to unsheath it, allowing the metal to rake against the scabbard in warning to whoever might think to surprise him.

"Put your weapon away."

The voice had Dylan's brows rising even as he let the sword slide back home.

Aylish rounded the corner and stopped three steps below Dylan. The height difference between the two was significant enough on the rare occasion the men were side by side, but now the Elder was forced to tilt his head back at an unnatural angle in order to meet Dylan's shrewd gaze.

The man looked older in the years since Dylan had last seen him. Considering the actual rate at which they, as Druids, aged, that it was noticeable at all said much. Fine lines speared out from the corners of Aylish's eyes, even as deep crevices ran alongside his mouth like cracks in the dry earth. They might have been smile lines if the man ever smiled, but in all Dylan's recollection, such events were rare. Silver strands of hair in the man's black mane reflected the little bit of light in the stairwell.

The Assassin cocked his head to the side and arched an insolent brow. "They sent you for me, did they?"

Aylish stood quietly and looked the giant man over before he spoke. "I'm the head of the Elder Council. No one sends me anywhere."

The surprise having passed, Dylan leaned against the curving stone wall and crossed his ankles, thumbs hooked in his jean pockets. "So you volunteered."

"You believe you're above my notice?"

"Certainly never above." The delivery was intentionally lazy and clearly irreverent.

"You'll do well to remember our traditions and the respect demanded of them, particularly as it relates to your Elders," Aylish bit out.

Dylan inclined his head. Pushing off the wall, he clasped his hands behind his back and spread his feet in a traditional at-rest position. "Forgive my impertinence. I meant no disrespect."

"You meant to press me until I snapped and, while I'm not proud of it, you've succeeded. And quickly. What was gained?"

Dylan chanced a glance at Aylish. "Nothing but personal satisfaction."

Aylish barked out a laugh, his bright grin melting the tension lines around his eyes and lips, the change reverting his appearance to that of a man in his early forties. "I rarely forget you're so direct, but when we've not dealt with each other in so long, it's easy to fall into the habits our brethren use to communicate."

"You dress up the fact that they stall and bicker then hem and haw like old women." Dylan held up a hand and shook his head before dropping back to the at-rest position, dipping his chin to the floor to hide his grin. "It's no wonder they draw straws to see who has to deal with me."

Aylish stepped closer. Reaching out, he laid a hand on Dylan's forearm. "You are our sword arm, our first line of defense against all comers, the shadow of death to those you hunt. It's no wonder they fear you more than a little."

Dylan's chin jerked up enough to meet Aylish's gaze. "Their collective power could end me. I'm not so foolish that I forget this simple fact." He silently cursed himself for admitting he considered his own end. It was soft, indulgent even, given his status and responsibility. He likely wouldn't have slipped if he hadn't just had the very same topic at the forefront of his mind and reinforced by the goddess.

Aylish dipped his chin fractionally and withdrew his hand. "Neither are they so foolish in their power as to forget that you are the potential salvation of our race."

"That answers why you're here." Dylan couldn't stop his lip from curling into a hard smile. "Danu came to me."

"When?" Aylish snapped.

He looked toward the rooftop. "Now. It's time. Either I discover the truth she charged me with finding or all of mankind falls." He arched a brow. "She offered an alternative."

"Tell me." The order was barked out.

"I can sacrifice myself in place of finding the gods' invisible truth, but even so there's only a slim window of opportunity in which it will make any difference."

Aylish reached out a second time only to let his hand drop to his side when Dylan stepped away. He turned to leave then surprising Dylan when he looked back and said, "It should never have come to this, blood of my blood, bone of my bone."

Dylan's whole body jerked at the sentimental address. He couldn't remember the last time Aylish had acknowledged him as such.

"The time for your charge is now. Our safeguards are breaking down, the Shadow Realm of Cailleach and her siblings pressing in. You can see it happening." Aylish raised his brows and tipped his head toward the storm raging outside.

"You blame the weather on a banished god's behavior?" Dylan curled the corner of his mouth up in a nasty smile. Looking out a small window in the battlement that faced the cliffs, his smile faded. A particularly vicious gust of wind blew ocean mist along the glass, and the smell of the sea—a source of life and, equally, death—assaulted him. And wasn't that what this was about? Life and death?

Aylish hesitated long enough Dylan was ready to throttle him. "The goddess Cailleach has chosen her physical host. The woman is in Atlanta, Georgia, in the United States."

Dylan's false calm broke, and he spun from the window to face the other man. A sick twisting in his gut nearly doubled him over. He fought the urge to grab his belly. "Why has no one told me?"

Aylish's shoulders drooped briefly, and he leaned against the stairwell wall for support. His head hung low, and he wouldn't look at Dylan as he answered. "Because we only just found out. The reports we're getting are disjointed at best. We believe the goddess is fighting to not only gain her freedom but to release Chaos, too."

Dylan's brows winged up sharply. "She's surely not so foolish as to believe she can control it. Chaos ultimately destroys everything. I don't accept it."

"What you accept or reject is irrelevant. There is only what is. Cailleach is pushing with incredible force against the spells which bind her. We're unsure from where she draws her power, but draw it she does." The Elder paused, watching Dylan through shrewd eyes. "You know what we require of you."

The burden of his role had never been so heavy, but he

would carry out his duty—find and eliminate the host. Vengeance was his dance partner, and the music was just beginning to play.

Dylan ran his hands through his hair and, to disguise their shaking, clutched his skull. "You would call on me now, make it an official matter of the Order and not the capricious gods."

"Mind your tongue. Our obligation is to serve the gods' purpose. They've not intervened, so this is for us to do. Eliminating Cailleach's chosen host and banishing the goddess to the Shadow Realm, where we will rebind her, is our only option. We must move, and now, on the woman Cailleach has chosen."

The hospital's antiseptic smell did nothing to diminish the sun's brilliance as it slowly rose over the window ledge at the end of the sterile hallway, and Kennedy Jefferson squinted. Autumn in Atlanta, Georgia, was beautiful, the air crisp and the skies a bright blue—unless a person sported a severe...what? Hangover? She searched her mind, ran her tongue over her teeth. No memories of drinking, no bitter aftertastes of alcohol or vomit. Instead, her eyes watered and shed emotionless tears as the sun continued to rise. Confusion muddled her thoughts, made them murky and disjointed. Unexplained fear wove through the fabric of her consciousness, out of place, a dark thread against a pale background.

Someone plowed into her. Terror made her clumsy as she fought to regain her balance.

"Sorry." The man's amused tone was totally unapologetic.

Dropping her gaze, she shuffled out of his way and sagged against the wall. Her purse slipped from the slight groove it had worn in her shoulder.

"Kennedy!"

Startled, she looked up to find a nurse charging toward her.

The woman slowed and then stopped, her assessing gaze sweeping over Kennedy. "You okay?"

"I don't think…"

Admit nothing, whispered a discordant voice.

Pressing her back to the wall, Kennedy looked around. "What did you say?"

The woman stopped short, brows drawing together. "I called your name."

"After that. What did you say after that?"

Pale brows relaxed over concerned eyes. "I asked if you were okay."

"Oh." Kennedy cleared her throat and, focusing, looked around. "So, I'm at the hospital?" Shaking her head, she held up a hand. "Sorry. I know I'm at the hospital. I work here. I mean, I'm here to work. As the director of nurses." She closed her eyes and tried again. "You seem shocked to see me."

The petite woman's shoes squeaked against recently waxed floors. "You didn't show up for drinks Saturday night, and you missed work yesterday."

Kennedy's eyes shot open. Denial burned across her tongue. "Not possible."

"No one's been able to reach you for something like three days." She yanked Kennedy into a fierce hug.

Three days. "I'm sick." The hoarse admission raked her throat with sharp tines. *No. Not sick. Worse than that.*

The nurse stepped back and tilted her chin up to accommodate the height difference between the two. "Seriously? Are you okay?"

There was that question again. Kennedy couldn't answer because she had no idea what had happened or what she'd done, no idea where she'd been. She hadn't had another blackout since… Friday night played through her mind. There'd been a bar. With bikers. A fight of some sort and she'd left in a cab. *The cab.* She'd been in the cab when she'd slipped off the precipice of consciousness.

The memory made her shiver. Hard.

"I need to get to work." The beep of monitors, calls of patients and steady rush of feet up and down the hall punctuated the soft words.

A tiny V formed between the other woman's brows. "I'm not sure you need to hit the floor if—"

"I need to work, to clear my head. I just…" Kennedy rolled her shoulders. "Grab me some scrubs and a patient care kit."

The woman chewed her bottom lip and looked Kennedy over.

"I'm not contagious." Of that much she was sure. When the woman still hesitated to move, Kennedy met her stare. "Don't force me to make it an order. Please."

"Okay." She shook her head when Kennedy opened her mouth. "Don't thank me. I'm not convinced I'm doing the right thing here." Shoving her hand in her shirt pocket, she fiddled with a pen. *Click. Click. Click.* "Room 4410 is open. Use the shower in there. I'll leave the scrubs on the counter." Her pager sounded, and she backed away.

Kennedy slipped into the vacant room, rushed through her shower, dressed then headed to her office. This job was all she had left in a world that seemed determined to see her follow in the footsteps of every woman in her family tree—footsteps that led to the intersection of Crazy Lane and Dead Before Forty Boulevard.

The constant beeping of cardiac monitors was driving Kennedy insane only forty-five minutes later. The clang of every slammed medical cabinet made her jump. Every alarm that sounded made her want to scream. Her neck prickled like someone was watching her. Strange memories invaded her thoughts, providing abstract snapshots of a life she couldn't recall living. A life that wasn't hers. Not anymore.

Elbows on the wide counter, forehead in her hands, she craved silence. The second she had it, though, she knew she'd give in to the exhaustion that dogged her. "Someone hook me up to a caffeine IV. Stat."

The nurse to her right laughed.

Kennedy looked over and tried to smile but couldn't. "Don't suppose you have a dollar, do you? I have to raid the vending machines before I lose my mind, but all I've got is a five."

The woman's grin faded as she studied Kennedy. "Girl, you look like someone beat you with a powder puff before putting your eye shadow on upside down."

"Huh?"

"Pasty face, dark circles under your eyes," she answered, digging a dollar from her pocket.

"Just tired." She accepted the money and turned away before the inevitable "what's wrong" question was asked. How the hell would she answer? *My life's falling apart, I'm disappearing in my own mind while I run around doing God knows what—and I'm scared I'm going to end up dead while my mind's on autopilot.*

Irritation rode her hard as she stormed into the employee breakroom. Her hands shook. Trying to force-feed the rumpled dollar bill into the recalcitrant vending machine made her long for a cutting torch. She'd take her time. Liberate bottles one at a time. Make the machine bleed quart after quart of whatever ran through its insides if the inanimate son of a bitch didn't give her caffeine *now*.

A large hand settled on her shoulder and she whipped around, fist connecting with ribs before she could stop herself.

"Ow!" Her best friend, Ethan, jumped back, clutching his side while eyeing her carefully.

"Sorry." The apology nearly stuck in her throat as she shook out her fist. The idea of hitting again was more gratifying than making sure she hadn't hurt him with her first swing. *That's not me.* Opening her mouth to ask if he was okay, the words turned to ash on her tongue. No matter how hard she tried, they wouldn't come.

Stumbling back in a rush to put distance between them, she tripped over a chair and did an ungraceful ass plant before sliding across the hard tile floor. "Damn maintenance! Is this the only place they get the wax and polish right?"

Ethan's gaze narrowed.

Kennedy could almost hear him ticking off marks on his checklist for mental instability, and the implication there was something wrong with her chafed. Even if it was accurate. It gave her fear a tangible foothold. Made it all too real.

Still sprawled on the floor, she glared up at him. "Stop looking at me like that." The unguarded hostility in the command forced her to close her eyes and take a deep breath. Undiluted anger simmered in her blood. *Not me, not me, not me*, she silently chanted.

A whir followed by the *thunk* of a plastic soda bottle being dispensed made her shoulders sag even as she opened her eyes.

Ethan extended a broad hand and hauled her to her feet, still eyeing her silently.

"You should've left me there and run for your life." Goose bumps decorated her arms, and she rubbed them briskly.

"I thought about it, but we both know you're only director of nurses until you can take over the world and make me your consort." He waggled his brows and offered a lopsided grin. "And everyone who's anyone knows you can't rule the world from the floor." He held out the bottle of Coke. "Caffeine."

Kennedy clenched her jaw shut and forced a close-lipped smile. "I suppose." *What in the world is* wrong *with me?*

Holding the soda as a bribe, Ethan pulled out a chair and sat. He toed a second chair away from the table and tilted the bottle toward it in invitation. "Scared me, disappearing like you did."

The urge to run kicked her adrenaline into overdrive. Fighting it, she sank into the proffered seat hard enough it slid back a few inches. "Caffeine first. Logical word exchange second."

"Caffeine *while* you explain." He handed over the bottle.

"If it helps, it scared me, too." The soft admission hung between them, the impetus to a conversation long overdue. Toying with the lid, she finally spun it off and took a deep pull. Ethan's silence made her shake her head as she picked at the bottle label. "Any other day you'd score me on depth and clarity."

"There's not a damn thing about this that I find funny."

His sharp tone made her look up. "That makes two of us." She took a second sip before setting the bottle on the table.

Raking a hand through his dark blond hair, he snagged the soda and took a sip. "Where've you been?"

"I can honestly say I don't know, but I'm pretty sure it's been a bad eighty-four hours."

He considered her, eyes guarded. "That's a long run of bad."

"Yeah." Adrenaline mixed with anxiety to form a wicked cocktail that spread through her with immediate effect. Breaths came faster. Heart pounded. Sweat prickled her nape. "I haven't been this screwed up since losing my dad and finding myself both devastated that he was gone but also horrifyingly relieved I could stop trying to please him while forever failing."

Ethan stood and moved behind her, laying a palm between her shoulders and rubbing tiny, soothing circles. "Slow down."

Panic folded in on itself and left her hollow, her skin too loose, her clothes too tight.

He gradually widened the circle. Heat emanated from his hand and spread through her at a lethargic pace.

Pervasive calm soothed the raw edges of her psyche. Her chin dipped forward. "I don't know what you're doing, but don't stop."

"It's nothing, really. Just touch."

"Whatever. I swear you've got magic hands."

His touch slowed further then stilled. "Tell me what's going on. You fell off the face of the earth. Didn't call. Didn't answer your cell. Scared me bad." Tense silence stretched between them, fragile as spun sugar.

If my life had a soundtrack, this moment would cue the dramatic orchestra piece.

Ethan pulled his hand away. "Something bad happened."

"What are you, psychic?" She twisted to look at him. "Because if you are, you should give all this up for the glamour of your own nine-hundred number."

He tucked a strand of hair behind her ear. "I'll cut you a good deal on my by-the-minute plan. Now stop trying to redirect the conversation and answer me. Where've you been?"

It was impossible to meet his open stare. "I don't know."

Fingers tightened against her jaw. "Come again?"

"I'm having blackouts." The words, nothing more than a whisper, yowled through her mind in desperation.

"You mean blackouts as in passing out and waking up, or episodes of fugue?"

"It's worse than fugue. I... I lose time, but always in short periods. Hours at most. Until last Friday anyway."

Wrapping her arms around her middle, she gripped her elbows and pulled tight. "I'm having violent thoughts, might even be getting violent while I'm out of it. I don't know." She forced herself to look at him.

His mouth worked wordlessly. He grabbed the soda and took a huge swallow. And choked. Waving her off, he wiped at his streaming eyes. "Violent how? Like *temper tantrum* violent, or *I'll cut you seventy-three different ways before I castrate you with a spork* violent?"

The hiss of the door's hydraulics saved her having to answer.

Kennedy shoved out of her seat and faced the nurse who hovered half in, half out of the break room. "You need me?"

"No. I mean, yes," he stammered. "A guy's out here asking for you."

"Asking for *me*?" Her stomach plummeted, hitting bottom hard enough to bounce.

Ethan cleared his throat. "Is he a cop?"

Glaring at him, she fought against the invisible vise tightening around her chest. "Why would you think he's a cop?"

"I, uh, sort of filed a missing person report."

"Oh, man. Okay." She bit her bottom lip. "I'll be right out."

The nurse said something over his shoulder as he left.

A deep, unfamiliar voice answered.

"I can't believe you involved the cops," she whispered, the words low and harsh.

Familiar, warm hands rested on her shoulders. "I'll explain that it was a simple misunderstanding."

"Sure." Yanking the door open, Kennedy stepped into the hallway only to stop so abruptly Ethan slammed into her. She hardly noticed.

The smell of the sea, with its salt-saturated air and rain-fueled storms, washed over her the moment she met the burning green gaze of the man waiting for her.

Chapter 2

Dylan O'Shea stopped breathing the moment the woman came into view. White noise wiped out all but the thundering sound of his heart in his ears as he felt every ounce of blood drain from his face. He hadn't been prepared. Not now. Not after so long spent looking for one face among millions over the centuries. He'd given up faith, and that's when the gods, with their arbitrary natures and impossible demands, struck.

Wide blue eyes were fringed in black lashes. Long hair, glossy as a raven's wing, curled loosely to the middle of her back. Porcelain skin flushed prettily. Tall but fine-boned, she couldn't weigh nine stone.

She pulled up short only to be driven several steps closer when the man following behind crashed into her.

Dylan hardly spared the guy a glance. Instead, with need flowing through his system like spirits after a night of revelry, he reached for her. He had to touch her, to know with certainty she was real. His hand cupped one side of her neck. One thumb moved of its own volition and tenderly stroked her jaw. Never in all his years had he wanted anything as badly as he craved this woman, body and soul. Desire choked on duty and left him struggling to breathe. *Don't demand this of me, Danu. Anything but this.*

"O-officer?" she stammered, the last of her soft color fading under his scrutiny. "May I help you?"

Her voice, sultry as sin with a smooth burn like fine

whiskey, rolled through him. He blinked slowly, fighting like mad to retrieve his scattered wits, and jerked his hand away. "Kennedy Jefferson?"

"Yes? That's me." She pressed her fist into her middle before absently gesturing to her companion. "This is Ethan. Ethan Kemp. He filed the report."

Dylan looked him over, entertained to find himself being equally scrutinized. "And who is Mr. Kemp to you, Ms. Jefferson?"

"A friend."

"Her *best* friend," Ethan amended, eyes narrowing.

"The distinction is duly noted." Dylan spread his feet and crossed his arms, ignoring the question.

"Your accent." She rubbed her forehead. "Where are you from?"

"Ireland." The admission was out before he thought about it. *Control. This is about control.* It seemed she'd wrested it away the moment she appeared. The idea that a woman could scramble his sensibilities with no effort galled him so badly, he forcibly pulled himself together with only brute strength of will. "I need to speak with you, Ms. Jefferson. In private." He hadn't intended to needle the other man. Had no interest in it, actually, as it would only waste effort and potentially complicate things, and Dylan was all about efficiency.

"You can speak to both of us since I'm the one who filed the report." Steel underscored the man's superficially congenial words. "Clearly it was a misunderstanding."

Dylan shifted his cold gaze to meet Ethan's heated one. "Then why was the report filed?"

"Like I said, it was a misunderstanding."

"Not good enough. I'd like details." He looked at the woman. "Do you want to give them to me, or shall I take my pound of flesh from your *best* friend?" Sure the exaggerated air quotes were another jab, but the guy was pissing him off.

"That won't be necessary." She ran a hand—a *trembling* hand—around the back of her neck.

Bingo. "Somewhere private, then." He swept out an arm. "Shall we?"

"I'll donate that pound of flesh. *I* filed the report, so *I'll* answer your questions." Ethan dropped an arm over the woman's shoulders and steered her down the hallway, dipping his face toward hers. "My office or yours?"

The woman looked up at him, brows furrowed. "Mine, I guess."

Dylan followed, silently weighing his options. There were several ways he could approach the situation, none of them ideal. Every scenario involved first dealing with her self-appointed guardian. *Friend.* Riiiiight. *Best* friend. He snorted.

She glanced back at him, teeth worrying her bottom lip.

He drew in a breath, opened his mouth to speak and stopped, jaw hanging open like an eejit's. A soft brush of vanilla wafted around him. Lavender wove its way through the dominant scent until the two were indistinguishable. His mind shut down as lust settled into the driver's seat. The click of her shoes on the tiled floors drew his gaze to her feet. "You always wear stilettos to work?" he asked softly.

"No." The response, quick and unguarded, returned color to her cheeks. She looked so vital in that moment. Alive. Innocent.

His lips thinned. *Can't be my concern.*

They took the elevator to the first floor. Tension wound around him as he followed the pair across the crowded lobby and through a lush and winding wing decorated with deep colors and saltwater fish tanks. The woman unlocked her office and stepped inside, Kemp hot on her heels. That left Dylan to follow on his own.

He did, letting the heavy door swing shut with an authoritative *whump*. Leaning against it, he surveyed the small room. The door was the only entrance. Or exit. *Excellent.*

Kemp pulled out the executive's chair on the far side of the desk and saw the woman seated before squaring off with Dylan. "I filed the missing person report. Since Kennedy's obviously not missing anymore, tell me what we need to do to close the file."

Dylan zeroed in on one word—*anymore*. He crossed his ankles and casually studied the toes of his boots. "Where were you, Ms. Jefferson?"

"Call me Kennedy. Please."

Not happening. Making this any more personal would destroy what little sense of self he retained. Lifting his chin, he peered at her through narrowed eyes. "Where'd you run off to…Ms. Jefferson?"

Her nostrils flared, eyes glittering. "I didn't run—"

"Truth." The barked command was all the louder for the heavy silence that followed.

A sultry laugh escaped her. "So demanding." She slapped a hand over her mouth. The voice that had come out of her mouth wasn't hers.

"Care to explain that little trick?" He watched her. Waited. When she didn't answer, he pushed off the door and slipped a hand behind his back to grip his primary weapon. "I asked you a question, Ms. Jefferson."

Those blue eyes were wide with undisguised fear. "I didn't mean to…that is, I… I'm…sorry." The last word was ground out.

"Accepted. Now, stop stalling and answer me." His arched brow issued a silent challenge to her burgeoning temper.

Kemp stepped up beside her. "You're badgering her like she's guilty of something."

Point to her BFF. He answered the man without looking away from the woman. "I won't leave without carrying out my duty."

Kemp dropped a hand on her shoulder and stared at him, considering. "I already told you the whole thing was a mistake. She was…"

"Sleeping," the woman blurted out. "Heavily."

Dylan knew his smile didn't reach the cold void of his eyes. "Heavy enough you didn't hear your phone when I called? My knocks at your door when I came by?"

She scrubbed her palms against her thighs. "Right."

He blinked slowly. "Sounds odd. Unnatural, even."

A raspy growl slipped between her lips.

Tightening his grip on his weapon, he shifted his weight to the balls of his feet.

The woman pressed the heels of her hands to her temples. "Not me, not me, not me," she whispered.

"Kennedy?" Running his hands down her arms, Kemp gripped her hands. "Talk to me, honey."

Fool. "I'm ready to finish this." Dylan knew the woman heard him when she darted a glance in his direction. Pupils enlarged, her chest heaved as he watched her fight to regain control.

"Noted," she said in that odd voice, dipping her chin sharply.

So he waited. Seconds turned into minutes. At no point did he relax his grip on his weapon.

Kemp shot him a hard look. "I'd appreciate it if we could finish this later."

Dylan's free hand fisted. "She and I haven't even started."

The woman looked up again, the blue of her irises all but gone. She stood with exaggerated care. "Why are you here?"

Gods, that voice. It reeked of violent deeds done in the dark. He fought to squash the urge to claw at his skin and dislodge her words, words that stuck to his skin like poison-tipped cockleburs. Never had he heard anything like it.

Stepping closer, she smiled. "And now it seems I've asked *you* a question. Hesitation won't be tolerated."

Kemp reached for her, trying to pull her back.

"This is between the woman and me. It has nothing to do with you," Dylan snapped. The man would back off or Dylan would be forced to divide his attentions, half on the woman and half on the Druidic arts to compel the man to leave. "If you have any sense of self-preservation, you'll back off."

"Back off, my ass." Kemp put himself between them, the woman at his back. "She matters to me."

May the gods save him from heroes. "More than your own life? Because if the answer's 'no'? Move. Now." He shoved Kemp aside and stepped into the woman's personal space. "I asked you to answer me, and more than once. I'm nigh done asking, woman."

Sweat beaded along her upper lip. Shadows moved in her eyes. "Don't…let me—" she bore down, panting through gritted teeth "—hurt anyone. Please."

With that, her eyes rolled back in her head and she collapsed.

Well, shit.

Head resting on her forearms, a safari-esque drumbeat pounded through Kennedy's brain over and over, her mental MP3 stuck on Repeat. Her head felt too full. Ethan rubbed her back, his warm hands turning her bones to Silly Putty. The mental drumming wound down to sporadic solo bursts when those magic hands slipped up her neck to massage her scalp. He chanted, voice so low she couldn't understand what he said. Twisting, she looked up to find his eyes closed and face totally relaxed. She took his hands in hers. Their warmth hadn't been imagined. Far from it. They were almost hot to the touch. *How? Why?*

"Better?" Ethan asked, interrupting her thoughts.

She settled back into his office chair. "Yeah." Digging an elastic band from her scrub pocket, she pulled her hair up into a thick, sloppy topknot. Her hands froze midway through the act. "Where's the Neanderthal?"

"Waiting outside."

"Think we can sneak out? I…" Fear strangled her and made her breath wheeze. "I need to talk to you. About what's been going on."

Ethan's gaze narrowed. "I'm up for a little spontaneous dissidence if you are. Put your head back down and give me a second to get rid of him." He slipped out the door.

Alone, her mind wandered. Thoughts crowded in, layering one over the other to form a collage of memories, some clear, others clouded. She poked at the unfamiliar images, trying to paint clearer pictures of places she thought she'd been, things she believed she'd done and, worse, violence she'd probably carried out.

Velvet-clad fingers swept through her mind, as visceral and malicious as anything she'd ever experienced. The intimate violation made her stomach knot up. Her vision fractured. Reality was suddenly painted with diluted watercolors. Squeezing her eyes closed and clutching her head, she gasped. Not okay. Not even *remotely* okay. "Stop it."

Low, angry hisses wicked along her skull. Her scalp tried to crawl down her face and escape the infinite voices trapped in the sound.

"Stop it," she repeated through gritted teeth.

"Stop what?"

The room snapped into focus. Somewhere nearby, a phone rang, the noise hammering her eardrums.

Ethan stood across the desk from her, a deep V carved between his brows. "What'd I do?"

"Nothing." She swallowed the bile that blistered her throat. "Is he gone?"

"Yeah. Off to get you a glass of water from the cafeteria."

A shaky breath escaped. "Okay. Let's get out of here."

Ethan hesitated. "We'll need to stay close. No way am I going to risk making this worse for you."

"I can't afford for things to get worse. We'll just go across the street to The Daily Grind, talk there."

"You're not worried about being overheard?"

Absently working loose tendrils of hair into the topknot, Kennedy shook her head. "We're regulars. I doubt anyone will pay us any attention."

"Let's go, then." Ethan peered out into the hall before gesturing her forward.

They walked hand in hand through the lobby, out the front door and across the street. A rush of warm air brushed over them as they stepped inside the coffee shop favored by hospital staff. The smells of fresh bread, cinnamon and ground coffee beans swirled around them. Cashiers took orders and baristas called out names. Fire crackled in the fireplace. Conversation buzzed, giving the café a distinct hive feel.

Ethan pulled his wallet and handed her a few bills. "Get me my usual while I grab a sofa." He took off, stalking the floor and looking for a group getting ready to bail. Kennedy watched him approach a couple packing their things. After a fast exchange, the couple left and Ethan flopped down on the leather seat. He sent her a thumbs-up and wide grin, making her smile absently in return.

"Lady, your order all ready?" The cashier, a small, short-tempered young woman cracked her gum as she waited on Kennedy to turn around.

"You'll address me with respect," Kennedy snarled.

The cashier popped her gum. "Your order, Your Highness."

Peripheral vision diminishing, something foreign rose in her, shoving at her will. She raised a trembling hand to her temple and whispered, "Not right now."

"Then step aside," the cashier spat, leaning around Kennedy to motion forward the next person in line.

"Not you, you idiot." The words were out before she could stop them. She lifted her gaze to the woman behind the counter and the woman gasped, stepping back a strong pace from the counter.

"I saw… I saw…" the woman sputtered.

"What? What did you see?" She ran her hands over her face, relieved to find nothing more than her own flesh and bone.

Still, the cashier kept backing away. She hit a rolling cart loaded with baked goods and sent it crashing into the wall. "Your eyes."

Fear lashed Kennedy's feet in place even as her pulse took flight. "Look, it was probably the light. Take my order and I'll get out of your hair." Kennedy's gaze darted around the coffee shop. "I need two chocolate mocha lattes, heavy on the cream, topped with whipped cream, and two croissants, warmed, butter on the side."

The cashier nodded and inched back to the register but still had to try three times to call the order as she rang it up.

Kennedy managed to pay without causing a scene, though the cashier refused to touch her when she handed over the money. Irrational anger flooded Kennedy. Who did the girl think she was to treat Kennedy like some type of pariah? She opened her mouth to demand an apology when the barista called her name. Spinning, she shouldered a stranger aside, grabbed the drinks and headed toward Ethan, desperation dogging her every step.

He'd understand. He'd help her get through this.

It seemed to take forever to reach him. Setting the cups on the little coffee table, she dropped onto the sofa and clutched her bag. The fine hairs on her neck stood up. *Someone was watching her.* She looked around but only saw curious glances in their direction. Nothing out of the ordinary.

Ethan grabbed his cup and blew across the lip. "What's going on, Kennedy?"

"This stays between us."

She could see a look of hurt tighten the corners of his eyes even as his brows drew down. "Always. It's always been that way."

"I know, I know." She buried her face in her hands. "I just… I needed to say it this time. I need to hear the promise. Words have power."

Ethan's cup clattered against the saucer. "Where'd you get that last sentiment?"

"No idea." She looked up. "Does it matter?"

"Depends. But I give you my solemn vow that I won't repeat this conversation." He watched her carefully, waiting for her to speak.

She let her attention drift to the fire. There was comfort in the blaze, something she'd never experienced before. Watching the gas flames as they rose and fell behind the fake logs seemed wrong, or inorganic at the very least.

Ethan broke her line of sight, and she shifted her attention back to him. Taking the cup he offered, she sipped. The drink was perfect, the bitterness of the coffee offsetting the sweet whipped cream and thick chocolate. Things like this made life seem better, even if only for the length of time it would take her to finish the drink.

"So spill it, Kennedy, and I'm not talking about the coffee."

"Right." She set the cup on the coffee table by her knee.

"About six months ago, I started having blackouts. At first they were really rare but, as time passed, they became more frequent." She waited for him to react, but he only nodded and gestured with his cup for her to continue. "Okay, so these blackouts have always been preceded by vision-reducing headaches."

"How fast is onset?"

His clinical approach stopped the encroaching panic, forcing her to think past it and answer his questions. "It begins peripherally, narrowing to tunnel vision before I lose sight altogether. I retain the ability to hear for—I'm guessing—approximately two minutes. My heart rate accelerates, but I attribute it to stress. Something in me shifts, like I'm harboring a different...this sounds so crazy." She shook her head and reached for her coffee cup, taking a scalding gulp.

"Don't edit this, Kennedy. I need to know exactly what's happening." Ethan's firm voice was more command than request.

"Look, this isn't easy." The heat from the cup seeped into her hands as she rolled it back and forth across her palms.

"Keep it clinical. If it's unexplainable, just do your best."

She snorted. "What, are you diagnosing me?"

"Consider this a free evaluation." He bumped her knee with his. "Go on."

Her voice dipped lower, and Ethan leaned in to listen. "When my hearing begins to fade, it's as if my will is being superseded by *something*, and then that entity's will pushes mine out of its way. I *feel it*, Ethan. I can tell my consciousness is being forced out of the way, but it's unstoppable. My will is shoved aside, and then I'm gone. I wake up in the strangest places having done some of the most inappropriate things—dancing nearly topless on a bar top to 'Tequila' at a biker bar was my most recent fete."

She paused and looked up to gauge his reaction. When his face remained neutral, she let loose the craziest idea. "I don't like light anymore. Darkness is more comfortable. I've even started living with my drapes closed all the time to avoid sunlight. I know it sounds crazy, but if I step into the shadows? It goes away. Ethan, I've got this creepy-ass feeling, like I've got some parasite sucking on me."

He ran his fingers through his hair several times as he considered her. When he finally spoke, his voice was sharp, his words clipped. "You're losing how much time per episode?"

Kennedy rolled her shoulders, trying to ignore the tension that had snuck back in. "It ranges. This last time was the worst. I lost days." Her voice trembled and she hated it, hated that whatever was happening was breaking her. She chewed on her bottom lip and looked anywhere but at him. When he touched her knee, she startled and sloshed coffee over the rim of the cup. It coursed down both sides of her hand and she cursed out of habit, hurrying to set the cup down. Mid-motion, she froze and slid her gaze to Ethan. "It doesn't burn."

He reached for her hand, taking the cup from her and setting it down before examining her hand. Though slightly pink, the skin was neither burned nor blistered. Ethan looked at her, his face a blank mask. But behind it, she thought she saw both fear and awe.

Taking her hand back, she mopped up the mess the best she could. "What?" she finally demanded. "Why are you staring?"

"Just waiting for the other shoe to drop."

Kennedy kept scrubbing at the table though the mess was long gone. "What makes you think there's another shoe?"

"Don't bullshit a bullshitter, Kennedy."

Pausing, she looked around the coffee shop. No one

was paying them any attention. Dropping the napkins, she clasped her hands together and leaned forward. "I had a second episode Friday night. It's never happened before. I was in the cab and then, next thing I know, I'm standing in the hallway on the fourth floor wondering what day it is—today." She lowered her voice even more. "I don't know what's happening, but I have this…this *knowledge* that I'm going to…" She swallowed hard and jumped when he took her hands.

"That you're going to what?" he asked, low and hard.

"I'm going to be responsible for a lot of death, Ethan. More than you can imagine."

Chapter 3

Dylan discreetly followed the pair across the lobby and briefly held off following them outside. Not once were they out of his line of sight. They might believe he was as gullible as a spring lamb born yesterday, but he knew the man, Ethan, had been looking to ditch him by sending him for a glass of water for the woman. *The woman. She wasn't simply* the woman *to him, but rather the* foretold *woman. Kennedy Jefferson.* The key to his survival lay somewhere within her. A hard shudder worked through him, and his fingertips burned. It was reactionary to clinch his hands in order to hide the show of magicks he couldn't regulate. Simply the thought of her challenged his control. Irritating, that particular tell, and not a small one at that. Made him feel like a fool on a righteous errand.

He watched as the two slipped inside the coffee shop before he stepped outside in silent pursuit. He stood in a group of strangers and waited for the crosswalk sign to turn. A wave of subtle power struck him, faint and scentless. If it had held a smell, or even a flavor, he'd have been able to identify the element to which it was bound, but the wave retreated far too quickly for him to gain a good hold on it.

Dylan moved quickly, undoing his cufflinks and pocketing them. The dirks up his sleeves and the gun at his back needed to be accessible without interference or delay. He hesitated—actually hesitated—outside the little coffee shop. Reconciling assignments where a gods-be-damned woman was the target had always been the hardest for him. But Kennedy Jefferson proved a whole different level of difficult. She'd haunted him for 300 years. Memories so clear they could have been recent versus centuries old swamped him. The goddess Danu's warning, issued in a dim Scottish cave three centuries ago, rolled about his mind. She had come to him and spoken of finding some immeasurable truth that would save not only mankind but the Druidic race, as well. To fail would result in the release of the imprisoned gods.

He'd pleaded with her, begged for more to go on than that. She'd considered him carefully before issuing him a name. "Begin seeking her in what will be a new world to you, Dylan, for she is the only one who holds the truth. You must find Kennedy Jefferson before all is lost. She has within her the single truth you must reveal and accept." And then Danu had disappeared.

The light changed, the crowd jostling him hard enough to knock some sense into him. He had no business bandying about with memories no more tangible than fairy tales. Instead, he searched the glass-fronted shop, located his target and shifted directions, slipping down first one side of the building, then around the back and up the other. There were exits fore and aft, as well as a handful of tiny windows. He couldn't watch them all. Shouldn't have to, though. She had no idea who he was or why he was here, so she wouldn't likely run. Not yet, anyway. Not unless Cailleach took the wheel, because that bitch had definitely recognized him.

Another brush of power skated over his skin with blades as sharp as knives. It had to be coming from the woman. No one else could harness that kind of power and keep it secreted, not from the men who'd done the background check on this mission. Hell, Dylan knew things about Kennedy Jefferson she'd likely hate—that her mother committed suicide when Kennedy was thirteen. That her father remarried when Kennedy was twenty-two and died of a massive heart attack last year, just days after her twenty-ninth birthday. That she'd been a combat medic in the army and went to college on the GI bill.

The only explanation for the power surge painted her as the source. Still, he needed confirmation. If someone with such undiluted strength had glommed on to her, the playing field had just changed.

Grabbing a newspaper, he pulled up a seat to one side of the shop's entrance. He could see her standing in line. *Perfect.*

The electric doors to the café swished open. Scents of coffee, baked goods and humanity were strong enough to mask all but the closest magicks, elemental or otherwise. *Damn it.* He needed to get a bead on the type of magick being wielded. Too many smells to contend with here. He'd have to step inside.

In the time it took him to dump his paper and move to the door, the woman had taken up with her companion on a sofa near the fire. Dark head bent forward, her lips moved rapidly. Every now and again she'd glance up, considering the man's response before carrying on. She looked over her shoulder once, gaze roaming the room. Those dark blue eyes stole his breath.

Kemp touched her leg and regained her attention before her gaze found Dylan. *Too bluidy bad.* He'd quite like to go ahead and call her out, to draw her out and end this here and now.

Dylan's power leaked inexplicably, coiling loosely around him. Before he could tamp it down, her companion's chin whipped up and turned toward him. Dark gray eyes were like storm-lashed seas, and Dylan knew for certain where the power he'd felt had come from. He could smell it now, the loam of damp earth, and knew only one brand of magick with such a distinctive scent. *Warlock.*

"Oh, son, ye've toyed with the wrong man," Dylan whispered, nodding his head in acknowledgment.

Kennedy's companion nodded back, never faltering. She must have misunderstood his movement as a suggestion to look to the doorway, because she stopped speaking midsentence and turned. Her mouth fell open.

He arched a brow at her and grinned, mouthing the words, "Your office. Now."

Her mouthed response had him smiling even wider.

The doors slid open and he stepped outside to wait. Over the years, he'd learned to pay attention to his instinct, and right now? That instinct was screaming she was about to take flight. The thrill of the chase had his blood pumping through his veins and, for the second time since he'd landed in Atlanta, he found himself feeling alive. It didn't slip his notice that both times he'd felt so invigorated, it involved the woman he'd just ordered to heel.

No, it didn't slip his notice at all.

"Hell," Ethan snarled, eyes focused somewhere behind her.

"What?" Kennedy turned in the direction of his stare. Her skin heated at the same time she broke out in goose bumps.

Dylan O'Shea smiled the darkest, most seductive smile she'd ever seen and mouthed three words. "Your office. Now."

"Oh, shit," she whispered.

"Kennedy? Look at me." Ethan reached out and grabbed her arm after Dylan left the building. When he tugged, she turned to face him. "We've got to get out of here."

She reached for her coffee cup, her hand shaking so badly she abandoned the effort. "I can't just leave, Ethan.

The cop obviously knows we skipped out. I can only avoid his questions so long before he hauls me in for a more formal sit-down."

"I'm not screwing around." His voice struck her like a lash and made her flinch. He grabbed her wrist and squeezed hard enough she gasped. "And he's not a cop. Not even close."

"What's with you? You're hurting me." She yanked on his grip, but he didn't let go. "And what do you mean he's not a cop?"

"Sorry. Look, I recognize him. I should have realized it before now. I…" He let her go and ran both hands through his hair. "He's dangerous, Kennedy. More dangerous than you can possibly imagine."

A quick glance around proved the man had disappeared. The way she struggled to sit still, the feeling of eyes boring into her back, said he was watching them. "What's going on?"

"Have to get to my car." Ethan stood and scanned the coffee shop. "It's the only chance." He stood and yanked her to her feet.

"Hey!"

"Quiet," he whispered, gaze darting around.

Tension wound its way up her spine in lazy spirals, tightening and strangling as it went. "You're scaring me."

"Yeah? Good. Better scared and alive than naive and dead."

Dead. "You've gone over the edge. The guy said he's a cop." Dread followed tension's weaving pattern up her back. "What if I hurt someone, Ethan? What if I did something horrible and that's why he's here?"

"He never once said he was a cop, Kennedy. We assumed. But he's not. He's a…the…*not* a cop. Forget it. I've got to get you out of here." Arm around her shoulders, he steered her to the back of the coffee shop.

"Get me out of here?" she parroted.

Ignoring her, he stopped outside the restroom and glanced around. "Go inside. Lock the door, count to thirty and then shimmy out the window. Head to your car. I want you to drive a hundred miles east, then a hundred miles south. Make credit card purchases. Call in a hotel reservation somewhere in North Carolina, somewhere you could get to today. Buy a plane ticket somewhere across country, but don't go to the airport. He'll be watching. Probably your house, too." He pulled his hair. "Then I want you to come back here and meet me at my house at nine tonight. It'll give me time to figure out how to get you out of this."

"This? This *what*? You're acting crazier than me. Why in the world do I have to leave through the bathroom window?" She looked back. "He's not even here."

"Yeah, he is. Just because you can't see him doesn't mean I can't sense him."

"I'm going to lose it if you don't tell me what's going on."

He pulled her to a stop outside the bathroom door. "I can't. Not right now. Just…if you've ever trusted me, please do as I say. I'm going to redirect his attention, make him think I'm helping you out a different window. In the meantime, you crawl out this one and run. Get to your car and drive like the devil's arrived and brought hell with him."

Goose bumps stole over her skin and she shivered. "A little overdramatic, don't you think?"

"No. I don't."

And with that, he pushed her into the bathroom and shut the door.

Kennedy stumbled into Ethan's house a few minutes before nine, exhausted. Ethan had freaked her out. His fear had leeched straight through her, and she'd carried it with her everywhere she'd been today, from the outlet mall for clothes to the computer café to every gas station. That fear had eventually bled off, though, the adrenaline unsustainable. Now, wandering through his dark house, it was back. Tendrils wound around her legs like a thorny climbing rose. She wasn't sure what to do. The sting of tears caught her off guard, and she blew out a hard breath.

"What's happening to me?" she whispered in the darkness.

A hand clamped over her mouth tightly, and she was dragged back into a hard body.

She fought like a mad woman, biting, kicking, scratching—everything she'd learned in the army.

Just as she'd maneuvered to flip her assailant over her shoulder, he shouted, "Calm down!"

Nostrils alternately flaring and sucking almost closed as she struggled to get enough air, she stopped fighting.

"I'm letting you go."

Hands slipped away and she spun, knee connecting with a denim-clad groin.

"Oompf!" Ethan doubled over and couldn't contain the groan that escaped him. "Damn it, Kennedy. You just scrambled my eggs."

Chest heaving, she took in the shadowy form of her best friend. "Damn *you*, Ethan! You leave me with directions to run and then return before shoving me into a freaking public restroom, show up here in the dark and finally, truly, scare the crap out of me. What'd you expect me to do? Say *thanks*?"

"Keep it down." He propped his hands on his knees and slowly worked his way to standing.

She rubbed her lips, tasting blood. *Mine or his?* Spinning on her heel, she stalked into the kitchen, leaning against the counter. "I decided I'm not doing this, going along with your apparent *he's dangerous* theory just because I trust you. And I do. Trust you, that is. It's just…

"This is out of control, Ethan. Climbing out public bathroom windows and dodging Dumpsters and one very large rat to get to my car isn't reasonable. I'm bruised, scraped up and scared. Living like this isn't an option. Personnel made it clear last time I missed work that my job was in jeopardy. After this latest stunt? No way. It'll cost me, and being the director of nursing is who I *am*, Ethan. I'm not willing to give that up."

He stepped close and wrapped her in his arms, the hug tight and long. "I'm sorry."

"Me, too, though I'm still not exactly sure what happened." She tilted her head back and he kissed her on the forehead. "Thanks."

"You're my girl. How else would I greet you?"

"Want a beer?" She opened the fridge and retrieved a bottle, offering it over her shoulder.

"Nope. I'm driving."

She twisted the top off the bottle and took a long pull, the hoppy flavor making her taste buds curl a little, before turning toward Ethan with slow deliberation. "Driving?"

"We're getting out of here."

"Clearly, you didn't hear me. I'm not going anywhere."

Ignoring her, he spun away and, wraith-like, slipped through the dark house.

She rolled her shoulders and leaned a hip against the counter. It took a minute for her to gather her wits about her before following him down the hall and into his bedroom. When she reached for the light, he grabbed her wrist.

"Lights need to stay out."

"What? Why?"

"I would imagine we're okay, but I don't want to tempt the Fates. The, uh, guy from earlier could be around," he muttered.

"The cop that's apparently not a cop." She considered him carefully. "You realize that every word out of your mouth makes you sound like you're the one in need of the psych eval, right?"

The ensuing silence said volumes. When he finally spoke, his voice was low, hard in a way she'd never heard it before. "You'll owe me an apology when this is all said and done."

She knew she should say something to smooth ruffled feathers, but she couldn't bring herself to do it. Instead, she carefully lowered herself to the floor and sipped her beer, watching as he packed a small bag.

"You have no idea how much trouble you're in. Why is this guy gunning for you? What have you done?"

She coughed and sputtered, wiping her mouth with the back of her hand. "Gunning for *me*? You make me sound like I'm an animal and it's open season. And as for what I've done? That would be a big, fat *nothing*. Not that I remember."

Ethan shifted. A slight split in the curtains let in the glow from the streetlight and made his gray eyes appear nearly lifeless. "You have no idea what you've gotten yourself into with him."

"Then explain it to me." Derision dripped from each word, and while she wasn't proud of herself, she really feared Ethan had experienced some kind of mental break.

His eyes narrowed. "I ought to, if only to prove you're screwed. But I'm going to try to talk you into leaving first."

"I told you—I'm not leaving."

"You've got to get out of town. Your only chance is to start a new life somewhere else."

"Not happening." Tracing the rim of the bottle, she considered Ethan. "Who is he, E? I kept thinking about him this afternoon, and I have this feeling I've seen him before. It's like part of me recognizes him, but it's the part of me that isn't *me*. Does that make any sense?"

Ethan stopped breathing.

Something was right on the edge of her consciousness, something big, but it wouldn't materialize. The harder she chased it, the more like smoke it became, sifting through her fingers with every grab, spreading thinner and thinner until there was nothing left to seize. "I don't know how else to explain it, but I know I'm not afraid of him."

"Well, if there is some *other* part to you, she's an idiot."

A deep growl slipped through her lips.

She stood slowly, fighting an unexpected wave of vertigo. "No. I mean it. Explain."

Ethan's chin hitched up and his eyes darkened. A small smile played at one corner of his mouth, and he watched her with disturbing intensity. "You want to know? Think before you answer, because once you know? There's no undoing it."

She stared at the sliver of light, thinking. Several long minutes passed before she found her answer and was able to look up at him.

The glint of determination on Ethan's face was so familiar she hardly considered it significant. He was a playful person, true, but he had a steel core almost everyone missed.

He crossed his arms. "Well?"

"I want to know."

A strange quiet took hold of him as he settled into himself, and she watched it happen with growing anticipation.

"You're sure?" he asked once more.

Tension spread through her in stops and starts, dragging frayed nerves along for the ride. "Just say it," she snapped out.

"Fine," he answered in kind. "I'm a warlock—magick-practicing and everything."

She broke into a full grin. When he did nothing but stare at her with a totally straight face, her grin began to fade. "Ethan—"

"Nope. That's not the end of it." He dragged a hand down the front of his face. "I knew I'd seen Dylan O'Shea before but couldn't remember where. He came to a coven I was involved in at the time, and he was looking for someone."

"A coven, as in a bunch of witches with black cats and brooms and cauldrons." Shaking her head, she tried not to laugh. "That's rich, Ethan."

"I'm not a—" He paused, trying to find a way to explain. "Dylan O'Shea is an actual living, breathing Druid. What's worse? He's their Assassin. And they only let that dog off the chain when they've got a real problem."

"That's not funny." The words were filled with disbelief.

"No, it's not."

She shook her head. "You're trying to scare me into compliance, but it's not going to work."

Ethan tapped his chin for a second then smiled, but it was far from a happy sight. "Trust me." A command, not a question.

Kennedy opened her mouth to answer but could only wheeze. Her hand went to her throat in a panic.

"Easy, honey. I took your voice."

He leaned forward, hand outstretched, and she scrambled back from him. The backs of her knees hit the bed and she dropped to the mattress, hand still at her throat. *This isn't real.*

"Hey. It's me. Same guy I've always been."

When Ethan reached for her throat, she leaned back.

"It's easier for me to return what I took if I'm touching you."

Tension devolved to violent shaking, but she let him come closer.

He passed his hand down the column of her throat and whispered a few unintelligible words.

Her throat tickled for a second and she cleared it. "Holy shit," she said softly, the curse filled with both fear and awe.

"That about sums it up." Ethan didn't look happy.

"I'm not saying you're right, but if you are, why has Dylan been *let off the chain*?"

"I don't know why, but he's here—" His head snapped up. Sidling up to the window, he shifted the curtain aside. "Goddess preserve us. He really is. He's here."

Chapter 4

Dylan crouched in the bushes outside Ethan's house. There were no lights on inside, but a red, new-model muscle car sat in the driveway. Given the earthy scent he picked up from the perimeter and the brush of power he'd felt moments ago, it had to be the warlock's.

He rubbed his hands down cargo-clad thighs. His face paint was oily, his shoulder holsters chafed and his scalp was tight. Nothing felt right about this. The need to unfurl his own magick, to feel out the house, skated down his arms and burned his fingertips. Reality shifted, blurring his hands. *What the hell?* Something was messing with his control, ramping up his tenuous hold on the aether.

Ever volatile, his magick didn't come only when called, like some elemental lapdog he commanded to heel. Aether demanded more recognition than that. If he didn't exercise the magick regularly, it forced his hand. He'd leak power in a steady drip, drip, drip. Then he'd blow. Surroundings would be fundamentally changed. From the animate to the inanimate, nothing was safe.

The breeze shifted, and the woman's scent flirted with his senses—lavender and vanilla. Yet underlying that was something dark, a faint smell as pungent as burned hair that tainted her natural fragrance. It hadn't been there earlier. The warlock's green, earthy smell confused things.

He refocused on the house as a shadow moved by a window, one that was decidedly too tall to be...*her*. His chest ached and he cursed long and low. She was his mark. Nothing more, nothing less. He'd carry out his duties as he always had—with cold precision.

The warlock scanned the bushes where Dylan hid.

He wondered for a moment if Ethan could sense his magick. If he could, he'd be more of a contender than Dylan had originally given him credit for. The Assassin in him almost wished for that. His need to take back the control he'd lost this morning in letting the woman get away made him slightly reckless.

The curtains shut abruptly, and he had the distinct sense his wish was about to come true. He did a quick physical inventory of his weapons—short sword, daggers, gun, taser, garrotes, injectable sedation, smoke grenades, tear gas, extra bullets, both plastic and steel cuffs. It was all there. Sidling up to the front door, he used the deep porch shadows to hide and wait.

No one emerged.

Slinking around the side of the house, he scaled the fence and dropped into the backyard. Dylan slipped closer to the house. French doors on the lower patio were the most logical means of entry, but he'd likely be forced to work his way upstairs at some point. Being trapped in a stairwell with a warlock flinging elemental magicks at him would put him on the defensive, and Dylan didn't operate that way.

He took the steps to the deck, edging up to the glass slider. Going to one knee, he peered around the corner. Few adversaries expected a man his size to come in low.

Unfurling his magick, he let it flood the house like smoke, filling every crevice, nook and cranny. They were there. The feel of them tickled his overstimulated senses. Her scent moved through him, unleashing an altogether different kind of desire in him. *Damn her. Damn her for mixing this up.*

Need coiled in him like a giant snake, and he cursed her under his breath. It was as if she'd bewitched him. From the moment he'd seen her the first time in his dreams, he'd wanted her. The reality of the woman was far more potent, fueling an irrational desire that called to him to toss duty aside, go to her and forget both obligation and honor.

Dylan pulled back and thumped his temple hard with the heel of one hand. He'd never failed an assignment, and this wouldn't be his first. Whatever truth he'd been warned so long ago to find in the woman would have to come second to his responsibilities and, if necessary, his life.

Shaking his head to clear the hazy craving that was her siren's song, he reached slowly for the door handle. It unlocked with a simple mental push. The resounding *snick* in the oppressive, stormy atmosphere announced his location as effectively as if he'd rung the front bell.

He let the door whisper open.

The first attack came as he crossed the threshold. A short incantation followed by streams of light as bright as the sun. They struck him full in the chest and launched him backward so hard he hit the second-story deck railing. He nearly went over.

A short, female shout of alarm pulled him upright.

Then the damn warlock struck again.

This time Dylan did go over the rail. He managed to tuck and roll into the landing, missing the concrete pad by inches. Not that the grass was that much softer, but at least he didn't break anything that would keep him out of the fight.

Dylan shoved to his feet and raced to the fence, vaulting it without slowing down. He rounded the house and smashed through the front door in time to see Ethan haul Kennedy down a long hallway. He started after them, his pace leisurely. He waved a hand at the front door. *"Chomh luath agus a scoir, anois chuimhne. Oscailte do cheann ach mé."* Once an exit, now a memory. Where the door had been was now solid wall.

Casting a hand toward a window, he murmured, *"Phána gloine balla bpríosún, beidh tú a oscailt le haghaidh aon cheann ach mé."* Glass pane to prison wall, you'll open for none but me.

A slow smile spread across his face. His eyes grew hooded as he recalled the door downstairs had been glass, as well.

They were trapped.

The sound of Ethan's vehement cursing reached him. "He's blocked the windows."

It might have been cruel, but Dylan chuckled. "You're caught in a gambit of your own making, warlock. This ends now."

"You can't have her." Ethan stepped into the hallway. A burst of black flame raced Dylan's way.

Dylan let his power free, watched it roil in his palms. It consumed the blaze, changing it to water that splashed at his feet. He wiped his hands on his pants. "Playing dirty, is it not, using black fire against an enemy?"

Even in the poor light, Dylan could see Ethan's face go ashen. "It's not possible."

"What's not possible?"

"No one controls the aether." The words were heavy. "It's not predictable."

Dylan shrugged. "Amend that to no one you've ever *known*, and you've got it right. And as for not being predictable? Neither am I."

Dylan's bitter, cold voice left a thick rime over Kennedy's skin.

Ethan stepped back and pulled her behind his body. "You're not taking her, you pile of Irish sheep shit."

"No? Seems we're not of an accord, then." That silky

voice, laced with promised violence and pain, bled through the dark.

Ethan shuffled backward, herding her toward the bedroom. "Go. Lock the door."

"No."

"What?" His hoarse whisper grated across the air.

Her voice was so steady it surprised her. "I'm not going down without at least throwing a punch." Stepping around him, she faced Dylan.

Lightning illuminated the Assassin from behind. She might not have been able to pick him out of the dark without that blinding flash. When his eyes began to luminesce, she stepped toward him. "Don't do this."

He snorted. "You don't think to plead, certainly."

She swallowed so hard she knew he heard it. "If you'll tell me what it is you think I've done, I'll undo it."

His lips thinned. "Ye canna undo this."

"There has to be a way. I don't even know why you're here." *This is a nightmare. God, please let me wake up.* She forced her legs, which were numb with fear, to move forward another step.

The planes and angles of Dylan's face seemed harsher in the next lightning flash. He spread his feet and let his hands relax at his sides as he considered her. "It's not my place to explain justice, only deliver it."

"If you kill me, it's murder, not justice." She pressed the heels of her hands to her temples and shook her head before looking up at him, knowing her eyes were wild with desperation. "I've done nothing!"

He looked her up and down. "You've truly no idea," he said softly.

"None," she answered in kind.

Cursing in another language, he never took his eyes off her. "I'll give you the truth. Nothing more. I've been sent to cast out the goddess, Cailleach, who possesses you, and rebind her to the Shadow Realm."

A bark of crazed, near-hysterical laughter escaped. "Cast a goddess out? How?"

"The only way. I'll be taking your head first, heart second, so she canna reincarnate."

"No!" Ethan shouted, grabbing her arm and yanking her back.

Darkness pulled her under so fast she never had the chance to warn them. She fought to stay alert. Shoving, kicking, scrabbling, she managed to maintain a precarious foothold in the now. The moment she realized what she'd done, she stilled, terrified to disrupt her tenuous hold on reality.

The world looked different. She could see Dylan through the dark, though he still resembled her worst nightmare...and greatest temptation. Lust flooded her, and it took a moment to realize it wasn't hers alone. *What the...* Whoever had a hold of her wanted him. Bad. Images and ideas, both hers and whatever consumed her, crashed through her mind. They collided and separated so quickly she struggled to keep from merging with those of her parasite. The creature's—goddess's?—thoughts were wild, unhinged, even.

Kennedy heard herself speak, words that weren't hers breeching the darkness. "I grow tired of this byplay. We all know it will get us nowhere." The voice was huskier than Kennedy's, similar yet dissimilar.

"No one invited you to the party, you fruitcake." Ethan sounded like he'd moved closer, but it was no longer a matter of turning around or reaching back to simply see.

She'd become a passenger in her own body.

"Kennedy, I know you can hear me. Get your ass back here."

She saw her hand rise. Unintelligible words erupted

from her mouth. With the flick of a hand, a huge crash sounded close behind her. Kennedy fought the urge to scream as her feet turned without her directive. She wanted to rail against the sycophant that had co-opted her body.

Ethan lay crumpled on the floor, the drywall at the end of the hall concave where he'd impacted. Blood ran through his blond hair and trailed down his forehead in a broad stripe.

Dylan's voice drew her joint attentions. "Was that truly necessary, Cailleach?" He was casual, his brogue nearly absent. "He's hardly worth the effort."

Clearly, Cailleach didn't feel the same. "He's an annoyance the woman and I haven't the time to deal with."

Dylan's left eye twitched. "Is she aware of you?"

Her hitchhiker waited silently. Kennedy experienced the being's distinct interest—the kind of interest a woman has when the strongest motivator is desire for something or someone. A single word passed through Kennedy's consciousness. *Consort.* Cailleach pushed against her, harder this time, and Kennedy held her ground. Her lips curled up even as she pressed a hand against her temple. "The little mortal thinks to fight me. Should I destroy her?"

Panic left an acrid taste hovering at the back of her throat. Her heart skipped a beat before taking up a rhythm appropriate for a fast, dirty salsa.

"She doesn't believe you're really here to kill us. Should I crush her hope now and explain who you are, what you're capable of, Assassin? Or should I let you have the honors?"

This isn't happening. None of this is happening.

The discordant voice chuckled, low and rough. "Oops. Seems she heard me."

Dylan watched her with dispassionate eyes that gave away nothing. When he finally spoke, his voice made the hair on the back of her neck rise. "What she is or isn't aware of means little so long as the assignment is carried out. Say what you will. All you're doing is tormenting her before the inevitable end."

In the stillness, Kennedy's emotions began to fray. *I'm just another kill. My blood on his hands means nothing to him.*

True, answered Cailleach. The goddess seemed to take over her body and move it accordingly. She now mimicked Dylan's position, leaning Kennedy's body against the hallway wall.

Dylan's phone buzzed in his pocket once then quit.

"Shouldn't you answer that?" She smiled and traced fingers over Kennedy's nipples, back and forth until they stood erect beneath her camisole. It was a ghostly sensation, wrong on every level. "No? Fine. I have an arrangement to propose. I'll need a consort, Assassin. This body could be yours for the taking." She held out her hand to him.

She's pimping me out?

His lip curled. Leaning against the wall, he gave no indication of his intent. "I could do better with a Dublin streetwalker."

"*Bastun,*" she spat out. "You desire her. I know you do."

Dylan shoved off the wall and shouted, *"De réir Danu, I éileamh an bhean is mo chuid féin!"*

At the same time, Cailleach screamed, *"Do chroí damanta go luaith!"*

Power ripped through Kennedy with the force of a thousand joules. She screamed, strategically cleaved apart only to be slammed back together once the magick left Cailleach's hands.

Hurled magicks collided midair, creating a burst of blue-black flames that wound together intimately, climbing to the ceiling and spreading out. A shockwave rocked the room and percussed their ears. The glass doors and windows held.

Dylan dove forward, knocking her to the ground.

Cailleach snarled. A brutal swipe to his wrist left it bleeding and his hand limp. Claws curled, she shredded his shirt and ripped a dagger from its sheath, the tip slicing into his forearm. Scrambling to her feet, she clasped the knife as she moved in to plunge it into Dylan's back.

He rolled away at the last moment and Cailleach stumbled. Kennedy didn't know whether to cheer or scream. Both emotions fought for a foothold on the tiny ledge where her remaining sanity perched.

Dylan drew his sword, the blade scraping against the scabbard with the hiss of metal against metal.

Magicks silently unfurled around them. His own softened and twisted everything it touched so he appeared to move through ever-shifting surroundings. Cailleach's dark magick swirled around her feet, as dense as Dylan's was fluid. The fine black mist widened even as it drifted up her legs, twining around them like some great cat.

Tendrils of the goddess's magick bled through Kennedy's consciousness. She struggled to dislodge the sticky, invasive tentacles that seemed determined to dismantle her, one painful, spearing jab at a time.

Cailleach laughed and began to retreat. "We'll save this for another day. I find I enjoy sparring with you."

Darkness threatened to swamp Kennedy, a pervasive sense of nothingness—an absolute void she was powerless against.

Cailleach faced the Assassin.

Kennedy watched as Dylan hesitated. The surety of a decision made skipped through his eyes just before he shoved his damaged hand in his pocket and pulled a syringe, flicking the cap off. He charged forward. Slamming into them, he drove them into the wall. They hit hard enough that Kennedy experienced the breathlessness of impact.

Dylan's body pressed into hers. Their hearts thundered

against each other, the stormy rhythm hammering her awareness. She experienced a brief connection with him, intimate in the silence of her mind.

His arms shoved under hers, the needle digging into the soft area between her collarbone and armpit. Dull, aching pain quickly spread as he dug the needle in all the way to the shank. He slid his short sword up between her breasts. The guard came to rest against her sternum as the tip pierced the soft underside of her jaw.

Kennedy arched her neck away from the threat and cracked her skull against his chin. A scream lodged in her throat, but she was too terrified to move as she found herself faced with two attackers—one a physical assailant, the other an emotional terrorist. The shock that he'd drawn blood, had actually acted against her without consideration that it was *her*—*her* body, *her* trapped inside—snipped her last thread of hope that this was all a bad dream.

"I can end this right now," he said, panting in her ear.

"You won't," Cailleach purred. Every word drove that soft spot under her tongue onto his blade. "You may want to slay my mortal host, but you won't. Not yet. You'll seek to bind my immortal soul on Samhain, and your *honor* won't settle for less."

He kicked her feet apart, wrapping a foot around her ankle to keep her off balance. "You mean nothing to me, Crone."

"No, but for some reason? She does."

Kennedy's heart stumbled, and she felt Cailleach's smile.

"She's the means to your end." Dylan pressed the sword point deeper, splitting her skin wide. "You'd be an utter fool to bank your eternity on any more than that."

And just like that, the goddess was gone, and Kennedy was falling against the sword with no idea what scared her more—the cut of the blade or the brutal emptiness of the Assassin's words.

Chapter 5

Dylan depressed the syringe's plunger hard and fast. It was the woman's voice that cried out in pain even as the goddess tried to curse him, her words misshapen by the drug's impact. Unfazed, he dropped his blade and rode her to her knees, holding her there with his good hand as the drug worked through her system.

Smoke boiled around him and filled his lungs. He looked up. *Dagda's balls. The collision of black magicks.* Ethan's house was burning down around them.

The calculating part of his mind said to leave the woman and let her be recorded as a casualty of the fire. There would be no inquiry.

But it was the other part of him, unfamiliar and unwelcome, that demanded he discover the truth about the woman. Smoke thickened around him as he looked at her, crumpled on the floor. Violence flooded him. He despised indecision, despised being cornered and forced to choose between two impossibilities. Throwing his head back, he roared his fury to the heavens. How could he, for even a moment, believe he had a choice?

What he was going to offer her was no kinder a fate, but he couldn't leave her to die this way.

Sweeping her up, Dylan rushed to where the front door had been, flinging magicks ahead of him to fold the wall open. Racing across the lawn, he reached the warlock's sports car and dumped her unceremoniously in the passenger side. Her eyes tried to track, but she couldn't make them focus. With the dose he'd given her, she'd be out for hours.

Her mouth worked slowly, and she tried to speak around a tongue that felt too large for her mouth. "Muh…" She blinked slowly. "Muh…"

"Easy. You've a good while before your time comes."

"Eth…an." She licked her lips. "Get… Eth…"

Ethan. She was trying to say the warlock's name.

Under any other circumstance he would have left the man as a casualty, yet it was clear she wanted him saved. Pain struck his chest hard and fast. He'd not be entering a burning building on the whim of his mark. Of course, the man might have knowledge the Order could use in managing the woman until Samhain.

Not like you to lie to yourself, his subconscious whispered. *You go back in there, you'll know exactly why you're doing it and it's not for information. It's for the woman's peace of mind.*

Kennedy continued to fight to say the warlock's name, the short sound coming further and further apart as she sunk into unconsciousness.

Danu's prophecy was driving him mad, if he'd even think of returning to the house. It was the only logical reason he could accept that explained the connection he had with this woman, his concern for her well-being. She was his mark, not his heart mate. Yet inside, before she'd collapsed, he'd felt their hearts beat together, their rhythmic parallel a shock. He'd experienced the taste of her fear and known a moment of complete confusion. The combination of events had thrown him off so much that he'd discarded his blade for fear he'd inadvertently cut her.

Never, in his hundreds of years, had he experienced such need for a woman. Danu's prophecy had said nothing of this, had spoken only of finding his truth in her, but not that it would cost him emotionally. He couldn't afford to *feel*. A lifetime spent avoiding wasted emotion left him certain that wasn't part of his personal absolution in this matter. Still...

With a low, heartfelt curse, he sprinted back across the lawn and into the blazing house. Finding the man and hoisting his unconscious form over his shoulder in a fireman's carry, Dylan ran for the car, slid the driver's seat forward and hoisted Ethan into the backseat.

Kennedy had nearly rolled off the front seat, and he had to resituate her before he could get out of there. He leaned the seat back and buckled her in. A few words of simple magick and the engine rumbled to life and he roared out of the driveway.

Sirens sounded in the distance. Neighbors were in their yards, no doubt initially drawn by the epic boom he and Cailleach had caused when their curses collided. One of his ears was still bleeding, and he needed to get the pilot on the phone.

He and Cailleach... He hadn't cursed her. No, he'd claimed rights to the woman when he'd yelled, *"De réir Danu, I éileamh an bhean is mo chuid féin!"* By Danu, I claim the woman as my own! So foolish. But he couldn't ignore the thrill that heated his blood at the ancient declaration. *Yet she's not only mortal and bound to die, she's also bound to do so by my hand.* Dylan pounded his fist on the steering wheel. Danu had charged him with finding some critical truth that would save the world from the course it was on. What could he possibly learn in eleven days?

Because that was all the time he had left before the Order would rebind Cailleach. And it was Kennedy's lifeblood Dylan would spill to seal the wards.

Kennedy. He couldn't think of her in terms of a name, only an assignment. Anything more would tear at the fragile sense he had that she was somehow more, that Danu had entrusted her to him not as a means to the Council's end, but as the only means to prevent his own.

He tore down the street, unconcerned with witnesses at this point. If he had to wipe minds, he'd wipe minds, but getting to the airport was his primary priority. He grabbed the facial wipes he'd stuck in one pocket and began scrubbing the black grease paint off his face. There was a franticness to his motions he didn't initially recognize. When he did, he threw the fouled wipe onto the floor with a curse. *An adrenaline cocktail with a straight anxiety chaser.* Ever since the woman had opened the door at the hospital, the mix had been a steady rush through his veins. Not once in his history as the Order's Assassin had he doubted his ability to carry out a job. But tonight, for the first time in his long life, he'd hesitated.

Fire trucks and police cars raced by as he made his way out of the neighborhood. No one looked at him twice with the fire's fascinating devastation.

Dylan turned onto the highway and accelerated as fast as he dared. Digging out his cell, he called Gareth. The phone rang four times before the other man answered.

"H'lo?" He yawned, then grunted as he presumably stretched.

"Get up."

His voice changed from sleepy to alert in an instant. "Dylan? What have you got?"

"I've *got* a heavily sedated woman and a wounded warlock in a stolen car. I'm headed to the airport. Call ahead and tell them I'm coming. I've ruptured my right eardrum, can't hear well enough to ensure they repeat the orders right."

"I've got a pen. Go ahead."

Dylan relaxed a fraction. "I can't have a flight plan filed, so grease those wheels. Send two of the local lads down to the hangar to…help. The warlock will be at the airport, so—"

"The hell I will," Ethan slurred from the backseat, forcing himself to sit up. He tipped over, hit his head on the door panel and was out again.

"The warlock?" Gareth prompted.

"Make sure someone looks at him. He needs medical care and will undoubtedly need more before this is over. Stubborn Yank." Dylan looked at the woman slumped in her seat. "Have Flaugherty meet us at the other end. Riordan, too. The woman is going to need a bit of medical attention herself."

"You knock her around?"

"Piss off." The possessive snarl crawled out like a beast from a dark cave. *Gods be damned.* He needed to be done with this job, done with *her.* "Just do your job, Gareth. No questions."

"Sure, though you seem a wee bit protective over a woman you're going to eliminate." He paused. "Wait. You're bringing her here? To the Nest?"

Dylan's shoulders tightened until he thought his skin might split. Ignoring Gareth's questioning prod, Dylan said, "You're not to tell Aylish I'm returning with her. I'll handle that myself."

Gareth's silence was heavy despite the miles between the men.

"Your vow, Gareth."

"You're asking me to go against the Council." He muttered something unflattering. "You're my best friend, mate, and I trust you with my back in any war. I figure this is just that. You've got my silence." The sound of Gareth rubbing his morning whiskers reached Dylan's less damaged ear. "Gotta ask it, though, man. Is it worth it?" He paused. "Is she?"

"She's the one, Gareth. She's the one Danu foretold."

Dylan answered Gareth the only way he knew how. With the truth. The man had been with him when Danu had appeared, though the other man had been fast asleep. He alone knew of the prophecy and Dylan's charge.

"Fecking hell." Not even the mediocre cell connection could hide Gareth's quiet concern.

Dylan drove in silence, the other man content to wait until the Assassin chose to speak. What an amazing fool and even better friend. "I've got no clue what to do with her, but I'll need her close to discern the goddess's truth."

"Would be bloody lovely if the gods would see fit to give you a bit more time, no?" Gareth spat. "I'll make the arrangements at the airport. Call if you need me."

He thumbed his phone off. There were so many things he needed to do to make this next step possible, but likely the first on the agenda was to notify Aylish. Steeling himself for the conversation was harder than Dylan had imagined.

His fingers were stiff as he dialed, forcing him to make corrections more than once. He didn't want Aylish to hear anything from him that might betray his confusion. The weight of that long-suppressed emotion was like a fist around his lungs. He forced himself to slow his breathing. What did he have to hide? He'd done nothing the Order hadn't charged him to do, pulling the goddess closer and restraining her by any means necessary. Of course, he highly doubted Aylish would agree that *any means necessary* included securing Cailleach in the heart of the Order's operations. What Dylan least wanted to discuss was his hesitation in the use of additional force against the woman when the goddess betrayed her accelerating strengths. Aylish was no fool. He'd demand an accounting for the Assassin's hesitation.

He hit Call and waited a while for the overseas connection.

It was six in the morning there, but Aylish still answered, sounding as if he'd expected Dylan's call. "Assassin. What news?"

"Cailleach is both weaker and stronger than we antici-pated. She rose tonight, and we had our second conversa-tion and first true confrontation, this one involving black magick. She's not a rival to underestimate, not in any way, prior to Samhain." He waited. When Aylish remained si-lent, he went on. "She claims she can rise enough to engage in the host's activities and be aware of her surroundings, without fully manifesting."

"You allowed that to happen without taking appropriate defensive measures?" Aylish's brusque tone betrayed both his disapproval and his fury with admirable efficiency.

Dylan's mind fell through time, and he was suddenly a child again. He'd longed for this man's approval, craved it like a drowning man would air—desperate, hungry, fierce—but it never came. He'd learned to steel himself against the disappointments. Centuries. He'd had centu-ries to stop blindly and foolishly expecting even one word of recognition. Yet the wanting never abated. It galled the hell out of him that he was reduced to enforcing the same emotional safeguards now that he had then.

"Assassin? Has the connection been lost?"

Almost permanently. Assassin, and never *son*. Dylan forced himself to relax his grip on the phone before an-swering. "The connection is fine. I was thinking."

"I'll be calling another meeting with the Elders today. Is there anything else you feel I should pass on?"

The urge to consult him about Danu's ages-old dream pounded at him, but pride kept him silent. He'd not go run-ning to his father now if he hadn't then. "Yes. When Cail-leach possessed the host today, she partially manifested, changing the host's hands into her own."

Aylish interrupted, cursing violently enough that Dylan

raised his brows. "Kill the woman now. We cannot risk Cailleach regaining additional strengths in this plane."

Dylan gripped the phone case so hard the plastic and metal creaked in protest. "If we kill her now, we'll have little time to find her new host before Samhain. We'll have better luck securing the current host and controlling the outcome on Samhain per our original plan."

"Your orders are to end her now. I will call the Elders together and prepare the ritual to identify Cailleach's next host. The moment she rises, we'll dispatch you. Return home and await your next orders."

The disconnecting click was sharp. Silence yawned in the absence of conversation. *Kill her now.* A glance at the woman revealed her eyes were only partially closed, her breaths a bit shallow.

Realization dawned on him, a sort of sunrise of consciousness. Danu had told him this woman held his single hope to survive. He need only find this mysterious truth. And if identifying that truth would save his life, greedy as it seemed, he had good reason *not* to kill her yet. Until his blade fell, nothing was decided.

Gods save me, am I truly taking her home? And after that directive from Aylish?

Yes. Yes, he was.

Dylan took the off-ramp to the airport's private runway entrance and mindlessly followed the dark road. A right turn pointed him toward the airport's private hangars. He slowed his approach to the gated entrance. The magickal push it took to wake Ethan was second nature, and Dylan watched as the man's eyes fluttered open.

"Ow," Ethan groaned, gripping his head.

Dylan didn't bother to hide his grin in the rearview mirror. "Sit up. You're going to help keep your *best friend* from being questioned."

He watched the warlock grip his head, hands coming away bloodied. "What happened?"

"Cailleach. I explained what she'd do if she rose, but apparently you're more a visual, hands-on learner." He reached over and sat Kennedy upright. "I want you to lean her seat back and wad that jacket up. Prop her head on it against the frame."

The reply from the backseat was surly at best, disrespectful at worst. "Why?"

"Because I'm going to tell the guard she's sleeping, and you're going to go along."

"Why?"

"Do you really want to do this right now?" Silence. "Lean the damned seat back. Now." The whir of the electric motor buzzed, a low-level hum of angry insects against his damaged ear.

Ethan placed the jacket between her head and the car, gently arranging her hair. "Close your eyes, find some rest," he murmured, laying his fingers against her temple.

The tingle of magick in the car was the only thing odd about her closing her unfocused eyes with a sigh.

Dylan's heart lurched at the sight of her so relaxed. With skin like alabaster, hair as dark as night and a mouth made for sin, she looked like a fallen angel. He couldn't stop glancing at her as he drove. His body quickened against his will.

"Damn it to the ninth level of hell!" He pounded the steering wheel with his fist. "Not only am I caught in an emotional bog, but I'm maudlin with it, as well. Might as well retire and take up competitive knitting."

"You knit?"

"Piss off, warlock." Dylan rolled the window down and tried not to glare at the gate guard.

The standard night watchman, a burly fellow who took his job seriously if his starched uniform and buzz cut were any indicators, lumbered out of the gatehouse. "You have a pilot ID or flight plan?" The portly man hitched up his belt and retrieved his flashlight, shining it into the car. "Lady got a problem?" His gaze skipped back and forth between Dylan and the warlock so fast Dylan wondered if the man observed any detail at all.

"No problem other than she's sleeping." Dylan's quiet resonance commanded the man's attention. "I'm running late, so if you don't mind…" He jerked his chin toward the gate arm in an attempt to get the man to move away.

"She don't look like she's sleeping." He shone the light into Kennedy's face.

Dylan snapped. Grabbing the flashlight, he removed it from the man's pudgy fingers in one deft move. "She won't be if you keep harassing her." He removed the batteries and handed the light back. "Open the gate before I call the tower for your supervisor's name." For effect, he pulled out his cell.

"Asshole."

The muttered insult only made Dylan grin. "It won't be the last time I'm called that and worse." Staring at the man, he murmured, "*De réir mo uacht, tú nach cuimhin liom.*" By my will, you remember me not.

The security guard's face went blank.

Dylan pulled straight into hangar C-1. A midsized Learjet sat, the pilot lounging against the step railing as he chatted up a brunette flight attendant. Parking at the base of the stairs, passenger side to the plane, Dylan met Ethan's gaze in the rearview mirror. "Scoot over."

Ethan opened his eyes and whistled, long and low. "Your people know how to travel."

"You need to stay here." Dylan shut the car off and got out, not surprised when the warlock did the same. "I said 'stay.'"

"I'm not your lapdog, Assassin."

"That's fair." He opened the passenger door and undid the woman's seat belt. He pulled her out of the car and settled her over one shoulder, her dangling hands gently brushing his ass. With her settled, he turned back to Ethan. "I asked, and you'd have fared better if you'd listened."

Ethan opened his mouth to argue, but stopped when Dylan grinned. "What?"

Dylan raised a hand, his fingers blurring before he called fire to their tips. "I'll not kill you, because it would…distress her." It irritated him to realize his actions were, in large part, due to what she would likely think of him. "But you're not coming with us." He saw the moment it all clicked for the man.

Ethan's eyes widened and he took a step back. "You aren't taking her, you sheep-loving, skirt-wearing, mud-drinking son of a bitch."

"Now *that's* a fair curse," Dylan said, smiling.

Ethan reclaimed that step and more as he rushed Dylan.

The murmur of his voice disappeared in the depth of the hangar. *"Bí go fóill."* Be still.

The warlock froze, teetering precariously midstep.

"Duillín ar shiúl, titim níos tapúla. Lig codladh éilíonn tú go dtí go bhriseann an ghrian a slumber." Slip away, fall faster. Let sleep claim you until the sun breaks her slumber.

The warlock crumpled, his head bouncing off the concrete.

"Poor bloke. That's going to leave a wee bit of a mark, I'd imagine." Dylan toed Ethan and flipped him over, wincing at the knot already forming on the man's forehead. "You'll have a wicked headache, no doubt. You shouldna have disparaged the Guinness."

Turning, he carried Kennedy to the plane. Looking back, he watched as the warlock's car—driven by his men, the backseat once again occupied by the warlock—pulled away from the hangar.

Something in the cabin chirped, and Paul jogged up the steps, sliding past Dylan and into the cockpit to slip on his headset. "L1-DEC, Captain Duffy." He glanced back into the cabin, his gaze landing on Dylan's. He pulled the headset off. "We need to get in the air, sir. Immediately." Paul called out for his cocaptain, Angus, with a sharp shout as he began to fire up the plane. "The FAA seems to have noticed our abrupt change in flight plans."

"Meaning?" Dylan asked as he slid Kennedy into a seat.

"Our fuel order was flagged because it came in after our flight plan was canceled."

Could nothing go easily tonight?

Buckling his sedated companion in, Dylan pulled the steps up as the two men put the plan in motion. The flight attendant had stepped to an office across the hangar for some unknown reason and started running toward the plane. "Leave her," Dylan ordered as he shut and locked the door.

The plane started out of the hangar as the security patrol pulled in, lights flashing.

Dylan peered out the front window. "Faster, mates. Those flashing lights don't mean you've won a prize at bingo."

Accelerating, Paul and Angus didn't flinch when the FAA officers moved their cars into the plane's path in an effort to block it. Instead, the pilots powered forward, forcing a standoff. Security pulled out of the way, and the jet continued to gain momentum.

"Have a seat, sir. We're jumping the line."

The cabin pressurized, and Dylan's ruptured eardrum screamed.

"This is L1-DEC requesting an open runway immediately." Paul listened and grinned. "We'll be making our way straight ahead. Many thanks, Tower."

The jet accelerated, never slowing as it took a slight turn. The engines opened up. Dylan was thrown to the floor as they raced down the runway and took to the air. He pulled himself up to the window's edge and looked down on the FAA's security patrol, their strobe lights growing smaller and smaller before disappearing as the plane climbed into the cloud cover.

Dylan gained his feet and moved into the chair next to Kennedy. "Let's hit international airspace as fast as possible, gents." He looked over at her. The snakes that had been roiling in his gut settled. He'd made it out of the country with her, but one question loomed.

What now?

Chapter 6

Kennedy's head rang like church bells prior to Mass. But instead of ringing fifteen times, they just kept gonging. Then she opened her eyes to the setting sun's brilliant kaleidoscope. It seared her eyes, and the largest bell in her head boomed its objection. "I'm gonna puke."

The car came to a quick stop, her seat belt locking up and pressing against her throat. It only hurried the process along. She fumbled for the door handle and fell out, landing on her knees in wet grass. Hands held her hair back as she retched until she knew there was nothing left in her except those things that were permanently attached. Eyes closed, she shook in the damp, chilly air. Her clinical mind told her she shouldn't be so weak.

"Are ye done, then? We've a ways to go yet."

Trembling muscles locked up with fear. Everything moved with a hazy, slow-motion effect as she turned her head.

Dylan O'Shea knelt on one knee beside her, her dark hair fisted in his grip. "Did you hear me?"

"I'm not going anywhere with you." The words were raspy, her throat raw. Grabbing her hair, she pulled. Hard.

He let go.

She toppled over, landing in the very edge of her vomit. Rolling away, she kicked back, knocking him off balance enough that he was forced to grab the car or land on his ass. She scrambled to her feet like a drunk, weaving before she fell forward. Gravel dug into her palms and knees.

Nothing would move right, though, including her thoughts. *Drugged. I've been drugged.* It might have helped to shake her head, but she had no desire to strike up the church bells again. And struggling to rise was pointless. Even if she got up, she clearly couldn't run. Her best effort had been as effective as using cooked noodles for stilts.

Hot hands grabbed her by the upper arms and hauled her against a rock-solid abdomen. His grip tightened briefly and then she was off her feet, tucked up close to that hard chest. She curled into him, the smell of salt-heavy air and a faint hint of smoke unfurling around her like an invisible cloak.

"Warm."

His arms tightened. "Aye, I suppose I am. Particularly to you."

She pushed against him until he relaxed his hold. Then she allowed her fuzzy mind a breather. Reality softened, overlaid with a dreamlike quality she quite preferred.

When he slid her across the backseat, she listed into the door and propped herself in the small space between the door and seat. A slamming door sounded far away. Then the car's engine came to life, followed almost immediately by small bumps and a gentle hum. They were on their way again. "You're waking up a wee bit too much for my tastes. I'll go easier on you this time." Dylan's warm, heavy arm wrapped around her, and he snugged her up tight to his hard body.

A sharp stick made her flinch. "Thamn ith," she slurred.

"This will help you relax and enjoy the last—"

His words grew distorted like a record playing at the wrong speed. Darkness crept in, pulling her under. Fear dug icy fingers into her chest, and she grabbed blindly for his hand.

Dylan grasped the proffered forearm and slid his grasp down to instead hold her hand. Boneless, she slid into his side, and he caught her as she tipped forward. Intent on setting her back in her seat and fixing her seat belt, he couldn't hide his surprise when she wouldn't let go of his hand. Even heavily sedated, she had a death grip on him. Her soft but capable hand looked so small in his. He held on to her as tightly as she did him.

A frown tugged at the corners of his mouth. "Bluidy hell. Next stop for you really *is* competitive knitting, man."

He let his head fall back and simply watched the world pass by. *Home.* He was home.

The weather had turned colder even in the short time he'd been gone. A sliver of the volatile gray sea could be seen to his right. The wind blowing off the tempestuous waters was frigid. He'd known he was home when his bollocks had drawn up into his throat with the first gust of wind. There was no place like Ireland.

Time warped and slowed, until he sat, fully aware of his surroundings and the fact nothing, and no one but him, seemed to breathe. He slid one hand toward his boot but was quickly rebuked with a soft "tsk." Dylan whipped toward the noise and found Danu, goddess and mother of the Tuatha De, sitting with Kennedy's feet in her lap. He wanted to snap at the goddess, to demand she account for withholding her counsel until it was nigh time to carry out his duties. But when he opened his mouth, only air escaped.

"It seemed reasonable I remove your voice, lest you allow your heart to overrule your mind in conversational regards and say something you'd come to regret." The goddess ran one hand up and down Kennedy's shin. "I know you're angry with me, Dylan." She blinked slowly at the fury he felt displayed on his face. "Perhaps I should have rendered you vegetative, for your face speaks volumes."

His nostrils flared.

She grinned. "I've no idea why this amuses me so. Apologies." With a wave of her hand, his throat relaxed.

"You would come to me now, when time works against my every effort, and what? Advise me on the invisible truth this mortal woman holds for me?" The bite of his words echoed throughout the car. "I've sought your wisdom again and again, yet you've left me with nothing but vagueness and the burden of incomprehensible knowledge."

"Mind yourself." The warning couldn't have been clearer. "She is, indeed, your burden." The goddess looked at his mark, the woman slumbering so heavily across the backseat. "She, however, is also your only chance at salvation. Obviously you felt strong enough in my warning that you elected to withhold her dispatch. In doing so, you elected to bring the Crone into the heart of the Order and put them at risk to the last man. Where is the wisdom in that?" Danu's gaze burned into his as she awaited his answer. When he offered no response, she closed her eyes and gave a short nod. "I'll have the truth from you. What did you seek to gain in delaying what you've already deemed inevitable?"

Possibilities.

The one-word answer was thrown forward by his subconscious without consideration.

Danu's face softened from that of warrior goddess to mother and nurturer. "You find it a flaw that you seek to exhaust all options to reveal the truth instead of steadfastly carrying out your assignment. I, however, find hope in you for the first time in many years. You are more than the sum of your deeds, Dylan O'Shea. I leave you this—do not allow perceived transgressions to create blinders where none need exist."

The scenery was suddenly speeding by, the transition from inertia to rapid forward momentum as disconcerting as the time Gareth had convinced him he had to try an American roller coaster. Dylan looked toward the sea. Several kilometers passed in silence before he realized he'd begun stroking his charge's hair. No, not his charge. Kennedy. She had become someone to him long before Danu's visit. He'd just been too thickheaded to acknowledge it. And now? What changed now that he could call her by name? What right did he have to seek any type of possibility, particularly with her?

The easy answer, mate? None.

Still, he couldn't help but wish for one night, a single eve in which he might slake this boggling lust he held for her. Only her. *Only Kennedy.* Never had a woman affected him so. It chafed to find himself nearly led about by his cock now of all times.

A cell phone rang in the front seat. The driver answered, tone crisp. "Flaugherty." He listened. "Yes, sir. I have him and he's brought—"

Dylan lunged forward and ripped the phone out of Flaugherty's hand.

The driver jerked the wheel, the car nearly ending up in the ditch.

The overreaction told Dylan the young man wouldn't ever make it through the Assassins' Program. His reflexes lacked control while his mind was too easily influenced by external stimuli. "Eyes on the road." He lifted the phone to his ear and waited.

"I can hear you breathing."

Yet another way I seem to have failed you, Da. I continue to breathe. "Do I apologize or go without my supper?"

"Mind yourself, Assassin." Aylish's own breath was short. "The storm is rising again, and the candle the Council lit as a representative of the hag's lifeline still burns. The flame should have been extinguished prior to your return. Cailleach's host isn't dead."

Dylan took a deep breath and lifted his face to the car's roof, imagining the smell and energy of the sea. "Are we or are we not charged by the Father, Dagda, and the Mother, Danu, to preserve life, respect the forces that flow into the creativity and art of living in order to find understanding and wisdom and to discover *awen*, our own divine knowledge?"

"We are," his father answered cautiously. "But part of that is to follow the rules set forth by the Father—"

"And the Mother," Dylan interjected. "She came to me, Aylish. My responsibilities lie with finding a hidden truth the woman carries."

"Aye, the truth that she's Cailleach's host. It's clear, Assassin, that you've allowed yourself to become led astray in this matter. I thought better of you."

Dylan bristled. "Then take it up with Danu, Elder, as I'll be following her directive as we're meant to do, honoring my Druidic oath to respond to any given situation with the wisdom garnered by the eons of generations to walk before us. I'll use my gods-given common sense to follow Danu's order before yours, old man. It's the right way of things."

"And if the gods have told me otherwise?" his father asked in a low, dangerous tone.

"If they fight amongst themselves, it makes all the more sense to do as common sense dictates." Dylan looked down at Kennedy's face, flushed with warmth and sleep. "We lose nothing in keeping the woman alive a few days longer."

"All that is well and good. I'd ask, however, what you've done with her." The absence of inflection in his words said the head of the Elder Council was treading a fine line between anger and rage. "The Elder Council searched the North American continent. She's not there."

Dylan ground his teeth together so hard his jaws hurt. "No, she's not."

"Why?" It wasn't curiosity that had the man asking. Curiosity had never sounded so harsh.

"Because she's with me." He hung up on the ensuing silence, unwilling to engage the Elder over the phone when he'd be home in less than fifteen minutes.

So much for the element of surprise. He should have known better where Aylish was concerned.

Time to plan an offensive strategy and hope to Dante's nine levels of hell it was somehow enough.

Raised voices reeled Kennedy up from the depths of unconsciousness like a mindlessly landed trout. She tried to speak, but her mouth was filled with cotton so thick someone should be along to harvest it anytime. Trying to swallow confirmed her salivary glands weren't working.

She tried again, cracking an eye open at the same time. "No spit."

Where was *she?* "Spit," she repeated, this time with more force. Neither man acknowledged her. They were too busy chest thumping like gorillas at the zoo. "Whose banana's bigger?"

That got their attention.

A man who looked suspiciously like Dylan glanced over at her with absolute malice. "What the feckin' hell is she blatherin' aboot?"

Dylan's hands clenched into fists the size of Thor's hammer. "Show a little respect, Elder or no'."

The other man stared at Dylan as if he'd lost his mind. "Respect, is it? You've respected none but yourself for the last two centuries. And now that the reincarnation is aboot tae happen, ye demand respect? No. No, Dylan. Ye doona bring a parasitic host here, of all places, and demand respect ye've not given in far too long."

"Where's here?" Kennedy tried to sit up but her muscles were too relaxed. Somewhere close, someone giggled. Oh, wait. That was her. *Whatever.*

Dylan closed his eyes and sighed.

"*What* did she joost say? *Where's here*, is it?" The man drilled a finger into Dylan's chest. "Ye've kidnapped her, have ye no'?"

Dylan pushed into the man's finger, forcing him to move it or break it. "Aye. I did. It's part of me plan. Ye think I'd act without one?" His right fist flexed.

Kennedy tried to sit up again, to no avail. "You." She managed to point at the smaller Dylan. "He's devious and maybe violent."

He ignored her. "Did ye truly think it through?"

Dylan stared down at the subjectively smaller man. "Aye, I did."

The other Dylan looked over the bigger Dylan through narrowed eyes. "Is she more to ye, then?"

"She's naught but the means to the end of my assignment." Her Dylan had relaxed his hands and taken on an unnatural stillness.

Then the other Dylan spoke, his words driving adrenaline through her system so hard it ate at the vestiges of the most recent drug. "So ye mean tae kill the bitch here?"

Dylan coldcocked the subjectively smaller man, laying him out on the cold stone floor. "Donna talk aboot her tha' way, auld man, da or no'." Her Dylan shook his hand out. "Strikin' ye wasna part o' me plan."

Kennedy looked back and forth between the two men. *Dad?* "What *plan*?"

Ignoring her, he stared down at the man on the floor for what felt like hours before he offered the man a hand and hauled him to his feet. Dylan didn't look at Kennedy when he made the overdue introduction. "This is my da. Name's Aylish O'Shea. He's normally smarter than to stick his head up his arse in front o' guests. He's the head o' the Elder Council for the Order."

The stranger rubbed at the knot on his jaw that promised to bruise. He didn't acknowledge Dylan's introduction but instead turned to her. The look of intensity on the stranger's face wasn't a surprise, but his words were. "Welcome to Ireland, Kennedy Jefferson."

Dylan had helped her to her feet. He'd refused to look at her, yet insisted on keeping his arm around her waist for support. She'd been dumbfounded at the almost courteous gesture and, judging by the looks of every other man they'd passed, she wasn't alone.

He'd led her up the stairs, supporting the majority of her weight as her muscles trembled and refused to work. A misty haze still clouded her thoughts. It was going to take a while to get the drug—drugs?—out of her system. If he'd tell her what they were, she might be able to request the counteractive drug. She huffed. Fat chance he'd afford her more than a grunt, just as he'd done when she asked if they were actually in Ireland and again when she'd asked where they were going.

Dylan's fingers dug into her waist, and he tucked her in tighter to his side as a remarkably handsome man approached.

Wearing faded jeans, a cream-colored sweater with the sleeves pushed up forearms ropey with muscle and battered work boots, he appeared to be in his late twenties. His skin was tan enough to leave a faint white line at his wrist where his military-looking watch had shifted. He stood a couple inches shorter than Dylan but still several inches taller than her. Hair the color of honey was traced through with both darker and lighter strands. And even though he had the face of a model and the body of a ripped personal trainer, it was his eyes that demanded her focus. They were a light, bright blue. Faint creases at the corners of those merry eyes said he smiled a lot and, sure enough, he did just that as he came closer. A deep dimple accentuated the curve of his lips and gave him a look of delighted mischief she wagered could turn to sultry sin given half a chance.

When he spoke, his deep voice made Kennedy sigh. "Good to have you back, mate. Did you meet Aylish in the foyer?"

"Aye." Dylan shook his head. "We exchanged words."

The man seemed neither impressed nor surprised. "Over you bringing her to the Nest?"

Dylan lifted a shoulder in a lazy shrug. "They entrust me to carry out my assignments as I see fit. If they want to start telling me how to do the job, they'll need to find a new Assassin."

Kennedy couldn't help but recognize—sans violence— the similarities between Dylan's relationship with his father and the one she'd held with hers. Neither child seemed able to please their respective paternal parent no matter what choice they made. She regretted she'd never resolved that with her own father. Perhaps Dylan could, though. She twitched at the memory of his fist plowing into his father's face and reconsidered even as Dylan's hand tightened a fraction more. Much tighter and he'd be massaging her liver.

Dylan slid his palm to her lower back and urged her forward a step. "Gareth, this is Kennedy Jefferson."

Gareth's smile widened and revealed a row of perfect teeth. "I'd assumed, as you've never brought another woman into the Nest."

She ignored the way Dylan's hand had wadded her shirt up in his grip.

"I'm Gareth Brennan, Dylan's second-in-command here at the Assassin's Nest. It's nice to meet you." He looked her over carefully, and she fought the urge to look away. "So you're hauling that bitch Cailleach around, yeah?"

Her vision tunneled and she shook her head wildly. "Don't. It's nice to meet you, Gareth, but don't. If you insult me, or her, she…" Kennedy pressed the heels of her hands to her temples hard.

"Kennedy?" Dylan's smooth, deep voice provided an anchor in the storm of her sudden fear.

"You can't taunt or tease." She focused on taking smooth, regulated breaths, and struggled against the rage that fought to strangle her.

"Who? You mean Caill—"

"Don't call her that!" Kennedy rubbed her temples, trying to soothe the shuddering sensations away. "You can't use her true name. Call her… Maxine."

Dylan rubbed a hand between her shoulder blades. "Calling the bitch by name tends to bring her to the surface. None of us want that."

Gareth's blue eyes had darkened. "My sincere apologies, Ms. Jefferson."

"Now, me? You can call *me* Kennedy." She met his eyes, knowing she couldn't disguise the fear in her own. "Apparently, none of it will be an issue much longer anyway."

Dylan jerked against her back whcrc he held her shirt.

The stark realization that passed over Gareth's face would have been comedic in almost any other situation. His gaze darted to Dylan. "You don't mean to…" He trailed off, stopping himself before he finished the sentence with "kill her."

She was sure of it.

"We'll discuss it once she's settled." Dylan gently pressed forward to start her walking again.

Gareth nodded and stepped aside. "I'll see you soon, Kennedy."

Her mumbled response was automatic. "Nice to meet you."

Dylan directed her to another flight of stairs and she balked. "My legs aren't going to manage much more. By stair number three, I'm going to have to sit down." That she sounded petulant would normally have bothered her, but she was beyond feeling much. Instead, she found herself fighting to recover the time she'd lost. *How long?*

She yelped, instinctively throwing her arms around Dylan's neck when he scooped her up and started up the stairs. "What are you doing?"

"You said you couldn't manage. This is the last set of stairs, so I'll manage for both of us."

"Where are you taking me?"

He opened his mouth to answer her then snapped it shut.

"Look, I assume any dungeons would be below ground. We're in some type of big-ass building that for all intents and purposes seems like a castle. I know it's called the Nest and everyone here knows you." Her brain hurt. "Do you live here?"

Muscles knotted at the back of his jaw as he clenched his teeth. Nostrils flaring, he only nodded.

"Okay."

He looked down at her, gaze sharp. "That's it? *Okay*?"

She didn't answer, just pulled her arms from his neck and rested her head on his shoulder. Holding it up was simply too much effort. His heart beat strong and steady beneath her ear, fueling in her a deep apathy.

The last thing she remembered was his voice rumbling softly beneath her ear, but the words didn't mean anything.

She was too far gone to care.

Dylan hesitated at the door to his personal suite of rooms. The door opened at his murmured command, and the smell of home settled over him like a benediction—

smoke overlaid with leather, all with an undertone of whiskey. It didn't change the path he'd chosen to take on the flight from Atlanta to Shannon. Knowing what lay ahead of him meant dread had dogged his heels from the moment the decision had been made. When he'd met Aylish in the foyer, he'd nearly confessed, nearly sought counsel from his da. Yet now, with Kennedy in his arms, he found himself experiencing a swift pinprick to the heart, something that threatened to manifest as hope. There was no danger of bleeding to death, yet it didn't stop the acute pain.

He'd follow through and see if it brought him any closer to the truth Danu demanded he find. Because if he was honest with himself? He had little to live for but no desire to die.

So he'd defy respect for the living as he had with nearly every assignment. He'd barter with the goddess, seek to gain her trust by pretending interest in her offer of becoming her consort. This would afford him insight into her purpose, her short-term plans and her ultimate goals. He would feign interest in her no matter how ill the thought made him, because he intended to survive the gods' attempts to break out of the Shadow Realm at any cost. Besides, it wasn't as if he was a man who could legitimately claim it offended his morals. He had so few left it was nigh laughable.

Stepping into the room, he gently toed the arched wood-and-iron door closed. Everything was just as he'd left it. The small office through the doorway to his right was filled to overflowing with books, maps and small items he'd collected in his travels—flotsam that made him mistakenly appear sentimental. He'd taken his laptop with him, but his PC sat to one corner of the desk. The large monitor was canted so visitors couldn't see its face.

He stepped farther into the main living area and, with a deep sigh, looked it over carefully. A wide flat-screen television hung on the same wall that afforded the doorway to the office. Two leather sofas, old end tables and an equally old coffee table made up all the furniture in the room. No pictures decorated the walls, but the family crest, matted with a piece of the family tartan and framed in ornately carved walnut, hung beside the door. A series of three windows, each eight feet tall and four feet wide, were spaced evenly across the back wall. In front of the right window was a professional telescope. An Oriental rug was the only carpet in the entire suite. Stone floors were both uneven and cold. He hadn't ever given comfort a thought before, instead relying on the functional and pragmatic. It had served him well. That he wondered what Kennedy would think when she woke surprised as much as irritated him.

Frustration piqued, he strode through the wide double doors to his left that had been left open. His bedroom was another study in practicality. A large armoire held a second television while a highboy housed any clothes he wasn't able to hang in his closet. A duplicate set of the living-area windows framed the best view he had of the Cliffs of Moher. He moved to the center window like a falling meteorite drawn by Earth's gravitational pull. This, *this* was his place.

Closing his eyes, he drew a deep breath. The salty air settled at the back of his throat and he swallowed, savoring its slight tang.

The woman in his arms shifted and sighed. Guilt cloaked his shoulders, an unfamiliar and unwelcome weight. Turning away from the window, he moved toward his one indulgence: his bed. Two nightstands flanked the custom mattress. Wider and longer than a traditional king-size bed, it was plush. A thick, overstuffed pillow top created loft. The tall box spring lent the bed additional height. He'd made the mahogany sleigh bed to fit, taking time to hand-carve the intricate Celtic designs on the headboard and footboard. Untainted by his life, it was his one point of pride, this bed. This was the one place he could sleep and truly rest, where he didn't hold himself in a state of suspended animation as he waited for Death's card to be dealt him.

Holding Kennedy closer to his body, he freed one hand and flipped the brocade comforter back. He tossed his extra pillows aside and paused. She was the first woman he'd ever have in this bed. That she'd also be the last didn't escape him. The pinprick to the heart was sharper this time, and he thought he actually bled.

Dylan shook his head, his words low and tinged with uncharacteristic humor. "You're definitely slipping, man."

He'd never brought a woman here, into his home. There were places for hire that catered to his preference for one-night stands. Even then, it had been ages since he'd allowed himself to take pleasure in a woman, let alone her company. And now Kennedy lay, her hair fanned across his pillow, the first, and last, woman who would ever occupy his bed. Never again could he allow this type of intimacy, and that was what this was. Her presence, seeing her in a bed he'd made with his own two hands, was a relentless hammering against a heart gone to stone. He had no interest in intimacies, only in getting the job done expeditiously. She would not break him from his duty, could not save him from his fate.

Taking his time as he laid her down, he didn't look too closely at her. It seemed prudent given his strange state of mind. Instead, he focused on getting her shoes off and the covers pulled up around her shoulders. Then his gaze betrayed him, sliding to her face. It was her dark hair that did it, a shadowy nimbus spread across dark green sheets.

"Bonnie lass." He picked up a wayward curl and rubbed it between his fingertips. Her familiar scent wafted up from her, and his cock throbbed at the idea of his pillow smelling of lavender and vanilla, his sheets smelling of their desire after he loved her body. "Foolish man," he whispered.

Cailleach had been silent since he'd drugged Kennedy. He needed the goddess to throw off the sedation and rise if his plan had a chance of working. As much as he admittedly hated to deal with Cailleach, there was only one surefire way to find out.

He moved so he stood at Kennedy's shoulder. Extending both hands, palms down, he hovered one over her head and the other over her belly. Aether wove through his fingers. Here in his place, with the sea at his back, he drew on his magick. It raced through him like a hellish fever.

"Iarraim ar an bandia, Danu, seo a chosaint bean a hóstach ar an ceann dhíbir a dtugtar Cailleach. Éirigh liom, Cailleach. Freagair mo thoghairm, Bend do mo thoil agus ní sin a dhéanamh díobháil. Come, bandia na Ríochta Scáth, go mb' fhéidir go mbeadh mé tú a cheistiú." I call on the goddess, Danu, to protect this woman who hosts the banished one known as Cailleach. Rise to me, Cailleach. Answer my summons, bend to my will and harm none in doing so. Come, goddess of the Shadow Realm, that I might question you.

The host's eyes popped open.

He dropped his hands to his sides.

She looked about wildly, her attention finally coming to rest on Dylan. Her gaze narrowed. "What purpose have you for summoning me, boy?" She tried to push herself up, but the drugs were still impeding the host's body. "And why can't I move freely?"

"I think we've established I'm not a mere boy, Crone. As to why you can't move, I had to subdue your host after you grew a wee bit rowdy at the warlock's house." He arched a brow, affecting an insolence that would, without a doubt, irritate the hell out of her. It worked.

"Consider your actions lest you incur my wrath." Her voice was an echo of a thousand screams.

The hair on Dylan's arms stood up. "We need to talk."

She clenched her jaw, and her lips thinned. With sloppy movements, she drew a hand from beneath the covers. Undeniable surprise crossed her face when she glanced down and found her own clawed hand. Her decision to hide their offensive appearance was broadcast in her eyes before she took action. "The time for talking is well past, don't you think?"

"I believe there's plenty we've yet to discuss. You thought to use your magicks against me when I'd not provoked you."

She grinned and then laughed, the humor never reaching the cold depths of her eyes. "You didn't provoke me? Your recollection and mine vary greatly."

"Do you want to hear my offer, Crone?" He lifted a hand and casually inspected his nails.

"Speak."

He glanced at her sharply. "You'll afford me respect or I'll not only rescind my offer but I'll end this now."

She only stared at him.

"You want a consort." He kept his face blank as her eyes widened and she licked her lips. That he was about to do this only proved how far his mind had tumbled down the slippery slope of wanting. "I'm willing to consider your request."

"What do you require of me? Name it and we'll see if we might strike an accord."

She answered too quickly, and it gave him the distinct upper hand. It revealed that she was not only anxious, but also willing to bargain in order to get what she wanted. Him.

His low, controlled response didn't come easily. "First,

I want the surety you'll not now, not ever, force the host to have her body used by me. If I choose to take her, she'll be wholly agreeable."

"It will be my body, and I'm entirely willing." Her eyes grew hooded, and she looked him over suggestively. "In fact, I'd take you now, would you have me."

Bile rose in his throat. He ignored it. "Even so, until you're fully reincarnated, she's the right to say whether or not she wishes me to use her body for my pleasure. It's not open for debate." His words were short and harsh when she opened her mouth to argue.

Her interest cooled. "You won't speak to me as such when you're my consort. Understood?" When he didn't answer, she blinked once, slowly. "Your second condition, Assassin?"

"I want you to remain out of her consciousness when she's in my private presence. I will not have you impersonate her as a means of seducing me. Again, not now and not ever. This is non-negotiable. If I sense you, the deal is off."

"It means much to you that I remain secluded in the Shadow Realm while you're alone with her. Why would you so limit my early enjoyment of your bed play if you truly choose to serve me after my reincarnation?" Cailleach scrutinized his face for any hint of a lie.

He gave her none. "If you're in her consciousness, the choice is not hers."

"I'll agree, but with my own condition."

He crossed his arms over his chest. "Which is?"

"Should you end up seducing the lass on your own, you'll summon me. I'll know of the progress between the two of you so I can confirm that you still desire her, and will be fully 'amenable' when I completely manifest. I'll need to ensure you're the type of lover I desire. If for any reason you rescind your offer or betray my trust, it will mean war between us—me and my siblings—and every last one of your people." She licked her lips suggestively. "I'll want your word on the matter."

He didn't hesitate. "Done."

"Then, by all means, let me be the first to honor the negotiation." The host's eyes closed, and a shuddering breath left her body.

Dylan leaned forward and cupped a hand over Kennedy's nose, relieved when he felt her draw her next breath. The goal had been to buy time before Cailleach's reincarnation in order for him to find Danu's truth. But there was a catch. One he was sure the dark goddess was aware of, but one he couldn't change with all the magicks in the world. He wanted Kennedy in the way a man wants a woman, when the want becomes something more akin to craving, and the craving evolves to need. But he wouldn't take her without her consent.

Something in him clicked like a lock's tumbler falling into place.

Whatever the truth, he'd uncover it and stop this madness before he entirely lost control of the situation. And with Cailleach's agreement to remain in the Shadow Realm while he was alone with the host, he'd bought them both a stay...if not from temptation, certainly from death.

One couldn't ask for much more than that.

Chapter 7

Skin at the nape of her neck prickling, the sensation of being watched grew stronger as Kennedy cracked one eye. Lying on her side, she faced a stunning view of cliffs and sea.

Ireland. The man, Dylan's father, had welcomed her to Ireland.

A rush of renewed surprise and curiosity prompted her to move lethargic muscles. Tangled sheets and heavy blankets ensnared her, thwarting attempts to push herself to sitting. Finally, she leaned against the headboard, panting and sweaty as any prize fighter after eight rounds.

Cold air caressed her sweat-slicked skin, and she scrambled to pull at least the sheet up over her naked body. *How had she ended up without clothes? Had her parasite forced her to—*

Movement registered at the corner of the room. Kennedy jerked her head to the right to confront whoever stared at her. Her lips parted and a small "oh" escaped as a half-hidden figure, more shadow than man in the semi-darkness, unfolded from a chair and moved toward her.

The Assassin.

The urge to flee evaporated, replaced with a different kind of instinct altogether.

Dark brown hair fell several inches past his shoulders, the slight wave giving him a cultivated yet careless look. Her gaze traveled down the deep V of his linen shirt to appreciate the heavily muscled chest and hint of rippled abs. She tried to swallow, but her throat constricted. He wore leather pants that laced in lieu of a zipper. Pushing up a bit higher, she continued her perusal and found him barefoot. Yep, just that linen shirt and the leather pants. With laces.

He stopped short of the bed and watched her with narrowed, cautious eyes. "I can fix that."

"The fact that I'm naked or that I'm hungover?" She struggled to get her hands to move and fold the covers back properly. "I'm a nurse. Tell me what you gave me, and I should be able to tell you how to undo it."

"Phenobarbital."

Slogging through her mind proved an exhausting exercise. She wanted to give up and opened her mouth to do just that. What came out, though, had nothing to do with raising the mental white flag. "Sodium bicarbonate." The answer had apparently been lying in wait.

He closed the distance to the bed and, from the nightstand, retrieved a glass filled with milky-looking water. "Bottoms up." Lifting the glass to her lips with one hand, he cupped the back of her head with the other.

She worked not to gag as she swallowed the gritty drink. He'd mixed it strong. When she'd taken all she could, she turned her head away. Goose bumps rose when cold water escaped the rim of the glass and ran down her chin and neck.

Without a word, he disappeared through a doorway only to emerge seconds later with a towel and fresh glass of clear water. He lifted the new glass to her mouth. "Small sips."

It disconcerted her to find him staring so intently. She turned her attention to the task of getting the water down. Self-conscious, she couldn't manage much. "Thank you."

He took the glass back. "You're welcome. You can have more in thirty minutes."

"Right. Slow intake." She took her pulse, estimating everything. Seemed like things were coming back online, slow but sure. Lifting her chin, she narrowed her eyes and looked the veritable stranger over again. He sat on the edge of the bed next to her, one knee up, one foot on the floor, and everything she'd thought to say to him took flight.

He eased forward and touched her cheek, his fingertip light as the brush of a burning ember against cold skin. Tracing the path the dribbled water had taken, his touch was gentle, tender even. He paused at her collarbone, his finger tracing the hollow where the water had collected.

She found herself wishing for a turtleneck. And a parka. And a scarf. As it was, the sheet left him a generous expanse of bare skin to work with.

He leaned forward and brushed his lips over the tender area where her neck curved into her shoulder.

She looked up at him, brows furrowing. "What are you doing?"

"Touching you. Nothing more than touching you, Kennedy." He traced his fingertip lower.

"With your lips?" she demanded.

He didn't answer, just met her gaze without blinking.

"Well, don't." She flopped back on the bed. She wanted to drag his hand with her even as she wanted to bite that damnably seductive finger off at the first joint. "Given the little I remember, you went from killer to killer-kidnapper in the space of one very messed-up evening. Anything else I need to know, seeing as I'm naked?"

"It was necessary for your safety," he said stiffly. "And nothing's happened you haven't consented to."

"I asked you to take my clothes off?" she demanded.

"Fair. Nothing *else* has happened you didn't ask me for."

"What did I ask you for? Specifically." The quiet weight of her words seemed to register with the behemoth of a man standing at her side.

"I'd not take anything from you that you weren't willing to give, lass."

"Right. Oh, wait. That *can't* be right, oh great and mighty Ass."

"Ass?"

"It's short for Assassin. You know, a nickname." She smiled and batted her eyelashes. "So since you're not in the practice of taking things from me without my consent, how about giving me my life back? I'll even make it easier so you can take this in small steps. Let's start with clothes. Give them back. Then you can get me the hell out of here." Her chin quivered, and she hated herself for the brief show of vulnerability. "Get me home and we'll call it a wash. I'll forget I ever met you, and you can do the same."

"You'd write me off so easily?" he asked quietly.

She looked out the window at the stunning view. It took her a moment to summon the will to answer. When she did, her words were little more than a whisper. "I'd do my damnedest."

"It's not that simple." The hard-line in his voice couldn't be misinterpreted.

She didn't care. "This shouldn't be my responsibility, carrying this...this...*thing* around inside me. The last time the parasitic goddess rose? I fought her so hard, so damn hard. I held on with everything I was." She had to stop and master the urge to scream in remembered terror. "I fought, but it wasn't enough. *I* wasn't enough. And then? I heard *everything*—every damning word out of your mouth. I know you told her I meant nothing to you, that my death meant *nothing*. Then you cut me." Her hand drifted to the wound under her chin. "It gets hazy after that so, in the interest of keeping the replay short, I'll jump ahead to where you drugged me and hauled me to Ireland. You. *Ass*."

The Assassin stared down at her, clenching and unclenching his jaw as he started to speak and stopped himself repeatedly. Fury built until, unable to control it, he turned and hurled a ball of fire into the massive hearth built into the far stone wall. The flame hit the peat turf and it lit with a fierce *whoosh.* Even across the room the backwash of heat was intense. He turned and a fine line of sweat decorated the valley between his heavy pecs. "You heard what I wanted you to hear."

"Precisely. You. *Ass.*"

"Don't presume to understand, not my motives and *definitely* not me." He crossed his arms over his chest. "You heard what I wanted *her* to hear. Had I known you'd hung on, I'd have been more mindful with my words. And as for why things got hazy? You might think to ask yourself why I needed to drug you as I did."

"Why you had to..." Blood drained from her cheeks in a rush that left her lightheaded. "I lost time again. What happened? Did I hurt anyone?" Her hand shot out to grab his arm. "Ethan. Is he okay?"

"I made sure he had medical care before we left the airport." The giant man rubbed his upper lip. "Your *parasitic goddess* took umbrage with the fact he tried to stop you from scrapping with me. She undoubtedly left him with a concussion before we burned his house down."

The sound of the sea crashing against the cliffs grew louder, and she found herself with her feet on the floor and her head pushed between her knees.

"Deep breaths, lass."

Deft fingers massaged her neck as she fought to slow her breathing. "How did he get out?"

The Assassin sighed. "I went back in for him before the fire department arrived."

He'd saved Ethan? She rolled her eyes up. "Why?"

Color flooded his cheeks, and he wouldn't meet her eyes. "Didn't want you to suffer his loss."

His words to the crone sure as hell didn't match his actions or his reasons for saving Ethan. She wouldn't have suffered Ethan's loss long if his intent was to end this, this *thing* quickly. She wanted to believe him, needed to believe *in* him, but he'd given her no reason to. *Other than saving the most important person in your life so you wouldn't suffer.* But wasn't he letting her suffer by dragging this out? She shook her head. Raw emotion tunneled through her middle. Empty and wholly confused, a single thought made her breath catch. *If he'd been intent on killing me, he could have done it at any point while I was out.*

They continued to gaze at each other until she broke away, scrambling back under the covers and pulling them up even higher than before.

He moved to sit on the edge of the bed and rested a hand on her shoulder. "Kennedy—"

She shrugged his touch off. "Give me some time."

They sat that way for interminable minutes, she with her head resting on knees pulled tight to her chest and he perched on the edge of the bed.

"Why did you take my clothes off?" she whispered.

"I didn't want you to wake up without me here and run." He was staring at her when she glanced up sharply. "There are members of the Order who would see you dead regardless of—" he coughed and pulled his hair back from his face "—regardless."

"Regardless of what?" she pressed, desperate for some inkling that she mattered to these people as more than their sacrificial lamb. "Give me something. A single grain of hope in the endless sands of despair is worth the pearl it might become."

He considered her. "I'll make you a fair trade."

Her eyes narrowed. "Which is?"

A small smile pulled at one corner of his mouth, faint then gone. "Call me by my given name." He shifted on the bed, and the mattress sank, moving her toward him.

He reached for her at the same time she reached for him to maintain her balance. His eyes darkened. "Call me by name, and I'll give you the hope you hunger for."

She thought it odd he wanted his name from her, but, licking her lips, she took a deep breath. "Okay... Dylan."

The very air seemed to charge between them. His eyes luminesced. The storm outside grew more violent. Then she noticed his fingertips were warping, changing shape and blurring everything they touched. She slowly withdrew her hand.

Shaking his hands out, he drew a deep breath. "Apologies. My element, aether, is volatile. The nature of the times makes it more so." He met her gaze. "Kennedy."

Sheets tucked tight under her arms, she licked her lips again. His gaze shifted to watch her mouth, the sheer sexuality of the man unapologetically undisguised. She fidgeted, smoothing the edges of the sheet. "Hope, Dylan. That was the agreement."

"True." He moved with slow deliberation and took her hand, turning it over and bringing it to his lips. "I've an agreement with Cailleach that may save her rising in you."

"How?" she demanded, her hand instinctively wrapping around his and holding on with ferocity.

"She, ah, she..." He closed his eyes and took a deep breath. "Do you feel her at all in your subconscious now, lass?"

Kennedy dug through her mind and found it entirely silent. "No."

"She wants me as her consort when this is all said and done. In exchange, I'll not kill you."

"But I'm still lost," Kennedy said quietly, attempting to retrieve her hand.

Dylan held firm. "Not until all is said and done. I've convinced her to give me the remaining time before Samhain to...work out some issues. She's promised to remain out of your consciousness so long as you and I are alone together. That way she can't overtake your mind and force you to do anything you don't want to do." At her open-mouthed shock, his back straightened. "No matter what you might think of me, I'll not take a woman who doesn't want me in return, no matter the reason behind it."

"So you'd turn on your people?"

"No," he snapped. "But she'll not know as she's promised to refrain from breaking through your consciousness in order to give me the chance to…do what I need to do."

Eyes wide, Kennedy tried to make sense of what he was proposing. "If you don't want her rising while we're alone, should I make the leap that you're offering me a reprieve from her in exchange for…what? Time alone? With you?"

"It's an option, but so is keeping ye sedated as I attempt to find an alternate solution tae this mess." He tried to move away.

This time she held his hand, pulling it toward her and placing it palm down over her heart. A soft smile played at the corner of her lips. "Does your accent always get thicker when you're irritated?"

"Nay."

"Uh-huh." Slipping her fingers through his, she laced their hands together. "Thank you for trying to find a way to help me through this. I need time to think about time alone with you, though. It seems pretty clear that *time alone* is a euphemism for sex. Am I right?"

His eyelids lowered slightly. "Could be."

"I've never been one to bargain with my body, Dylan."

"Is that what you'd make of the deal I just struck with your proverbial devil? You think me a whore for doing the very same?" he demanded, yanking his hand back hard enough he nearly toppled her out of bed. "I was trying to spare you the crone's rising!"

"No, I—"

"Tread lightly, Ms. Jefferson," he said, voice cold. "I don't tolerate liars or thieves in my home."

Her face heated. "And if I had to fake passion? Would you punish me for that as some sort of lie?"

Face cloaked by the waterfall of his hair, his eyes glowed with intensity. "Trust me, lass. You'd no' be fakin' a damn thing."

Spinning on his heel, he stalked out of the room, slamming the door behind him.

Head reeling, Kennedy flopped back on the bank of pillows behind her. What had she done? She'd asked for hope. The last thing in the world she'd expected to get in return was a sexual proposition.

A sinking feeling in her stomach told her she'd not only looked that gift horse in the mouth, she'd also punched him in his soft spots by asking for time to consider. And wasn't that the oddest thing in all this mess?

She hadn't assumed anything about Dylan was soft.

Dylan stalked about his office, picking things up and setting them down, totally out of sorts. He'd thought the woman would appreciate a direct approach, a plan of action no matter the cost. He'd been wrong. She'd reacted as if bedding him was more unappealing than lying with, well, near anyone. The reaction stung. Badly. And that it affected him at all made him that much more furious.

How, then, should he have approached it? He wanted her. His solution proved a sound one that bought them time out of the crone's presence, time in which to discover each other, and for him to search her more deeply for Danu's truth. Where had he erred? Women were fickle creatures, to be sure.

The singular doubt he'd tried to avoid found voice and whispered through his thoughts. *She knows what I am, but only thinks she knows the blood that stains my hands. Even her paltry understanding of my past renders me truly repulsive to her, my centuries of obligation more abhorrent than she can tolerate.* The thought sickened him.

He retrieved a decanter of whiskey from one of many bookshelves and poured himself a solid three fingers, tossing it back. Normally, he'd relish the fine liquor's burn. Today, he felt nothing. Had he erred so badly, then?

"No," he said aloud, slamming his crystal highball glass down hard enough to hear the foot crack. That noise released some unacknowledged desire for violence. He spun and hurled the glass into the cold fireplace, crystal shattering into a thousand reflective shards. His position afforded him no mistakes. What he'd done was make an aggressive tactical maneuver to gain the upper hand. The woman simply wasn't accustomed to thinking in terms of the ultimate end game and the sacrifices it would take to ensure he came out on top.

Immediate erotic images of her beneath him, fingers digging into his shoulders as her hips rose to meet his thrusts, filled his mind. Perhaps a wiser choice of words was in store. Snorting, he grabbed the decanter and took a long pull directly from the bottle.

"If you fall into the bottle every time a woman turns down your charming advances, I would imagine you spend quite a bit of your annual income on liquor."

He swallowed slowly and lowered the decanter, setting it on his desk with ultimate care before turning to face the woman. His breath caught at the sight of her, wrapped in the sheet of his bed, her hair full and wild about her face. "You know nothing of me."

She arched a brow, fidgeting with the linen's stitching. Dark blue eyes considered him in the quickly fading light of day. "True. And yet still you expected me to flip the sheet back and offer you my body without hesitation."

Unnerved. He was unnerved. No doubt those insightful

eyes saw more than he meant them to see. That she could see through him so effortlessly disturbed him. Aye, it even irritated him. He closed his eyes and turned away. "What is it that bothers you about my solution? That it was practical instead of romantic? What's between us is a matter of your survival and mine, not pretty words and mooning eyes. Ye knew as much well before tonight."

All sound of her movement stilled. "My survival, yes. But why yours?"

Dylan pinched the bridge of his nose. "It's knowledge you don't need, so disregard it."

"Why are you so intent on shutting me out?" she demanded. "We're talking about my life and death like they're pawns on a universal chess board."

His chuckle was dark, even menacing, and it tainted what had been trying to gain a foothold between them. "You've the right of it there, lass. None of us are more than a piece on the gods' universal chess board, and they're ever maneuvering us to their advantage." He moved to the fireplace and tossed several bricks of peat on the grate before flicking his fingers at the turf and setting it alight. Then he looked over his shoulder at her, his eyes flat. "Some of us are just more expendable than others."

"Don't cop that attitude with me." There was steel under her normally dulcet tones.

The fire caught with a wee bit of encouragement. Standing, he turned to face the woman. The urge to strike out blinded him to anything but the need to protect himself from the threat she posed. "Ye think a tumble would make us what? More than what we were before? Nothing would change, Kennedy. I thought to buy you a wee bit more time, and may the gods pity the fool I've become. Danu herself charged me to see this through, and that's what I'll do. It's who I am." He held his palms out to her. "The blood of hundreds, even thousands, covers these hands. Wishing won't change my past or any of the choices I've made or have yet to make."

"If it's always been a matter of carrying out your obligation, fine. Why does it still have to be? Why do *I* have to be another casualty you burden yourself with? Surely there's a way to let go of what you are and carve out a different future for yourself."

He threw his head back and laughed, the humorless sound both bitter and mocking. "You think it's a matter of wishing for something different? I'm the Assassin until I'm taken out, either on an assignment or by my appointed replacement. Carve a little happiness out of that, *tú craos aisling bheag.*"

Kennedy's snarl was impossible to miss. "I never would have taken you for a victim, but clearly, circumstance has made you her bitch."

Centuries of maintaining a blank face kept him still despite the fact her words flayed his pride bloody. "I'm as much a victim as you are. You think I should choose another path, find one lined with daisies? Fine. I will—as soon as you realize what I proposed was just a fuck, a means to an end we'd both enjoy as we looked for alternatives." He saw when his words, crafted to hurt, struck home.

Skin the color of fresh cream took on a gray pallor. "So that's it. What it really comes down to is that you need to blow off a little steam and I'm handy." She tightened the sheet around her. Shaky legs wouldn't carry her fast but, propelled by her fury, they'd carry her far.

He opened his mouth to object to her leaving.

Her furious glare stopped him.

They stared at each other across an impossibly wide chasm of differences.

"How many days do I have left?" The broken hitch in her voice wrecked him.

"Kennedy—"

"How. Many. Days." Her lips trembled, and her eyes shone too bright in the firelight, but damn it all if she didn't keep her chin high and her tears at bay.

"Ten. Nine if you dismiss today."

"Might as well write today off as a total loss." She started forward, and he thought to block the door with magick, but nothing came to him.

Dylan panicked, anxious to reach out to her with words—any words—that would stop her from leaving him. But the gods chose that moment to strike him mute and magickally null. All he could do was watch her lift the iron latch on the door and walk through. Instead of slamming it in her wake, she pulled it closed with quiet surety. The click of the latch falling back into place was like a sword through his gut.

Burying his head in his hands, Dylan closed his eyes. What the hell had he just done?

Chapter 8

Kennedy let herself out of Dylan's suite. Unsteady on her feet, she was pretty sure it had nothing to do with the drugs and everything to do with the jackass in the bedroom behind her. A quick glance up and down the hallway showed it was empty. Charging from the bedroom in righteous fury had been satisfying until, wrapped in a sheet, she hit a public area. Now she'd give anything for pants, a shirt, even just underwear. *Vulnerability, thy catalyst is often stupidity.* Flipping a mental coin, she turned right and started shuffling along.

The wide hallway was lined with an aged Oriental runner so thin in places that the unrelieved cold emanating from the stonework seeped through and into her bare feet. Different types of weapons, a variety of tartans and the occasional gothic throne chair decorated the long passageway. Peat smoke infused both stone and rafters with an earthy, wild smell that teased her nose. The silence of the immense space filled her ears with a hushed white noise. Suits of armor became soulless men. Phantom footsteps haunted her—no matter they were her own. Cold like she'd never known crept through the castle, its invasive, spectral fingers unwelcome. She'd never been more out of place or alone.

Her fingers wouldn't be still. She picked at the edge of the sheet, wadding it in her fist only to smooth it out and repeat the process. Shutting her mind to Dylan's cruelty proved impossible. Every word replayed through her mind. Every exchanged look took on a hundred different possibilities, a thousand different meanings. He'd wanted her, wanted her reassurance, before things got out of hand. How had it gone so wrong?

Of course, it hadn't gone as wrong as it could have. She hadn't had sex with him, and the parasite she carried hadn't risen. Normally, that bitch was front and center when emotions ran high. Vague words, garbled as badly as a record played on the wrong speed, tried to sort themselves out. His voice and hers. But not hers. Kennedy pressed a fist to her stomach, but the fast, hard flip was unstoppable. She sank into the nearest chair, ignoring the belabored creak of springs and the waft of dust that rose around her like a shroud.

The more she thought about it, the more the memory formed. She closed her eyes and reached for it. The word "desire" repeated softly, but she couldn't grab more than that.

"C'mon, c'mon. You're right there, baby. Come to mama." Pressing the heel of her hand against her temple, she bore down and focused.

I need to ensure you're the type of lover I desire.

The words were so clear her head snapped up and she looked around. She was alone.

"I spoke those words. They came from me." The whispered admission was strained. Tears threatened. The driving emotion behind them burned out of control at the back of her throat. He knew she could fight to remain partially conscious. It could have just as well been her to say the words as it could've been the goddess. How could he tell the difference if Cailleach didn't want him to?

Indirect or not, had the whole thing been my fault? Or was it the reason he'd been so quick to dismiss me? Had

I somehow provoked Dylan? Was that why he was so intent on knowing I'd wanted it, wanted him?

And God help her, she had. She'd wanted him in the worst way.

The urge to go back and ask him, to demand he tell her the exact terms of the bargain he'd struck with the crazy bitch currently piggybacking on her soul, was strong. Pride kept her ass in the chair. A harsh laugh escaped her.

"Something funny?" The deep, dark voice cut through her mirth like a scalpel through rice paper.

Kennedy leaped from the chair and whirled toward the stranger. The cold, indifferent look in the unfamiliar man's eyes—eyes so light a blue they were almost colorless beneath his dark hair and darker eyebrows—had her staggering back. A faint five o'clock shadow defined a strong lower jaw. A small scar ran across his cheekbone, stopping directly underneath his lower eyelid. That silvery scar lent him a sinister air, although not nearly so much as his huge sword did.

Heaven help me, I wish that *were a euphemism.*

It wasn't.

"I'm Kennedy. Kennedy Jefferson. You're—" she cleared her throat and pounded on her chest "—one of Dylan's men. Right?" *Please say yes.*

"I know who you are, and I'm one of the Assassin's Arcanum." At her curious look, he blinked slowly, seeming to barely refrain from rolling his emotionless eyes. "*Arcanum* is an old word, meaning a remedy to troubles, so we're part of the elite force he uses to eliminate... threats, yes." He stared at her, eyes never wavering. "Regardless, you should be careful out here alone."

She fiddled with the sheet, tucking it tighter even as she spread her feet and waited for the stranger to act. He might kick her ass, but she'd get in a few good swings before going down. She was sick and tired of being threatened, manipulated, threatened, kidnapped, threatened and abandoned. If she'd drawn a line in the sand, this whole thing had launched her over it and into what felt like enemy territory. "Danger in the hallways—that what you're warning me of?"

"Take from the warning what you will." Never removing his gaze from her, he shrugged and started past her, careful not to touch her at all yet still passing close enough she felt the heat of his skin. He slipped down the stairs and out of sight.

She flopped back into the seat, fear rendering her boneless, her muscles useless. Curling up and wrapping the sheet around herself, she dropped her face into both hands.

Nine days. That's all the time she had to find a way to convince Dylan that killing her wasn't his best option. She had to wonder if nine days would be enough. If she'd had to bet on it? She'd have simply laid her money on the table and walked away.

She was pretty sure she knew how this was going to end.

Time ceased to mean anything in the dark passageway, Kennedy realized. The wind keened like a wounded lover, carrying with it the ocean's salt-infused scent of decay. At the end of the hall, a stained-glass window featuring a sword and coat of arms stood sentry over the night. It was little comfort and even less company. She shifted the sheet so she could tuck her feet under her.

The cold of the castle gradually crept into her hands and feet, turning the tips blue. What she wouldn't give to be home and away from this mess. She'd be more than willing to leave the goddess here when she left, too.

Ethan. Had his house truly burned? And if it had, what was he doing now? Where was he? Was he okay? Missing him created an ache that throbbed like a deep bruise, only it seated itself in her heart.

Her teeth began to chatter. She had to find some clothes and get out of here. Aching muscles protested their disuse when she stood by promptly dumping her forward. She landed in an unattractive heap of splayed limbs, a rumpled linen sheet and wild hair.

"Damn it all to hell," she shouted, pounding her fist on the wool runner.

Somewhere below, a door slammed. Footsteps sounded on the stairs as they pounded out a rapid-rhythm approach. Booted feet came into view at the same time a deep voice asked, "Kennedy?"

"Of course it couldn't be someone who had no idea who I am. I already did the stranger thing once tonight." She shoved violently at the mass of curls that blocked her view. "I swear I'm shaving my head."

"Sure and I think you'd cause Dylan a wee bit of distress if you did."

"Then get the shears," she snarled. Rolling onto her side, she looked up into the man's face. "Gareth, right?"

"At your service." He grinned, deep dimples emphasizing the smile lines around his mouth. A flush of color darkened his cheeks, and he shifted his gaze down the hall. "You're...hmm." He made a sweeping gesture over his pec.

Kennedy closed her eyes and prayed the gods would see fit to spare her nine more days of torture and humiliation. If they'd end her right then, it would save everyone a great deal of hassle. She looked down to find a breast partially exposed, the dusky crown of the areola peeking out. Yanking the sheet up, she blushed furiously. "Sorry. Just so you know, I don't normally wander bitter cold hallways in a sheet, flashing men I don't know."

"So you flash men, you do? Ones you know, that is?"

Her sharp response died on her tongue when she realized he was teasing her.

He considered her. "What did you mean you've done the *stranger thing once tonight*?"

Clutching the sheet, she shifted limbs gone numb from cold until she could see him better. "Some guy, dark hair, super light eyes, unfriendly. He came by to warn me off, I guess."

"That's Rowan. You'd do well to steer clear of him."

"Why? Isn't he a member of the Arcanum?" She pushed at her hair again and silently swore she was finding some shears.

"He's…yes. He's a member of the Arcanum, as are Niall and Kayden." Gareth shifted, shoving his hands in his pockets and rocking back and forth.

"But?" Kennedy prompted.

"Just give Rowan some space. He was the Assassin at one point. He resigned the post, gave it up to Dylan when he came of age." Gareth ran a hand through his hair before grinning down at her. "He's…never mind. It's not for me to tell." He extended a hand to her.

Accepting the proffered hand, she stood and promptly stumbled. Gareth caught her in his arms. She curled into him, reveling in the heat of his skin.

"Kennedy?" His husky voice made her look up. "This is a bad idea."

"You're warm."

"Aye, and you're Dylan's."

She stiffed and took a step back, trusting her frozen legs to hold her up. They did. Barely. "I'm not, and you'd be smart to strike that notion from your handsome head."

"Handsome, am I?" He grinned, but it didn't reach his eyes.

"You know you are. Charming, too. But Gareth?"

He arched a brow.

"I'm my own woman." The urge to beat on her chest and howl out her independence caught in her throat. A short, choked laugh escaped. "I'm losing it."

"It's the weather." He paused and looked her over. Running a hand over his hair, his biceps flexed. "And the fact you're wandering about in a sheet doesn't help as I'd imagine you're more than half frozen. That *bastún*. I can't believe he let you wander about like this."

"Don't worry." She looked away. "Cailleach didn't rise or anything."

Gareth reached out and stroked her bare arm. "Sweet, I didn't imagine she did or we'd all have known about it." His hand paused. "Though it's curious she's been so quiet."

"Dylan…" She chewed on her bottom lip and looked back toward Dylan's room.

"What did he do?"

Squaring her shoulders, she faced Gareth. "Talked to her. They came to a particular agreement. I remember part of it, but the words weren't mine."

Gareth looked her over carefully, leaving her profoundly exposed. He saw her, just her, and didn't seem to judge. The knowledge made her sag, physically and emotionally. As beautiful as Gareth was, the observation only cemented the fact that she wanted Dylan in a much more primal way. Her fundamental reaction to Gareth was much the same she'd had to Ethan—friendship, companionship and trust.

"I'm cold, alone and friendless. What would help me most is if you could fill those three voids, Gareth. I'm not after any more than that." She tilted her head back and looked at him. "Is that out of line?"

"I believe I can accomplish all three o' those things with no trouble. C'mon." Shifting to drop his arm over her shoulder, he turned her back the way she'd come.

"I'm experiencing extreme déjà vu."

"Traveled this hallway already, I know. But my rooms are next to his, so we'll have to go past his door."

Kennedy tucked the sheet tighter. "I can't deal with him tonight. No, I *won't* deal with him. I'm finished."

"I doubt that." His mumbled reply made Kennedy stiffen. "I'll explain in a minute. The hallways have ears around here."

The remark left Kennedy shaken. She'd been out here so long with no idea she could have been watched, or by whom. It made the dark hallway all the more ominous.

They passed Dylan's door, the silence behind it leaving her both defiant and defeated. Part of her wanted him to know she was fine without him. The other part of her wanted him to yank the door and haul her into his arms while he declared he wanted her—*her*—not the agreement with the goddess. Neither desire was reasonable, and it chafed her wounded pride.

"Here." He turned her toward the next door. After he passed a hand over the door, the lock clicked and he pushed it open, his hand slipping to her lower back to usher her inside.

Kennedy stepped into a suite of rooms that were remarkably different than Dylan's. Faded damask wallpaper covered the walls. In places, age had curled seams. Tall windows were adorned with silk drapes, and the fireplace had a stone mantel carved with ornate Celtic designs. Leather furniture, casually arranged, was complemented by heavy antique sidepieces—tables, overflowing bookshelves and a huge desk. His laptop sat, lid closed and highly out of place in the center of the coffee table.

Gareth moved into the room, keeping his gaze on her. He smiled softly. "Question?"

She nodded as she gravitated toward the warmth of the fire. "How can you have such cultured taste, love antiques, have incredible class and yet be such a close friend to the baboon next door?"

He shook his head and laughed. "He's not all bad, Kennedy." Moving behind a small wet bar, he held up a coffee cup. "Drink?"

"Coffee?"

He began to work behind the counter. "I was thinking something a little stronger—coffee with an Irish kick. Guaranteed to warm you straight to your toes."

The aroma of fresh ground beans reached her and she stifled a moan. "I've got narcotics in my system, so I should probably forgo." The admission hurt her. She needed that coffee.

"I wager you'll sleep it all off tonight." He mixed and poured. She sank down into the nearest club chair. The fire had warmed the leather, and that heat slowly seeped into her aching muscles.

Kennedy shut off the stained-glass lamp that sat on the table at her side. The light clink of a glass mug on a ceramic coaster drew her attention. The cream floating above her coffee surprised her. "This is Irish coffee?" She picked it up and sniffed. The cream smelled fresh, the coffee even fresher. Beneath that, the faint burn of whiskey was there.

"Try it before you cast it off." Gareth set his own glass mug down and strode out of the room, returning moments later with a large, velvet robe of deep blue. "You'll be more comfortable in this. You can either step into the jacks to change or I can hold it up and close my eyes while you pull it on and drop the sheet. Brought a thick pair of socks, too."

"What's a *jacks*?" She eyed him, waiting for the catch.

"Ah, for an American it would be the water closet, or restroom." He pointed the way he'd come. "It's through that door."

Her mouth quirked in a lopsided smile. "If you'll hold it up and close your eyes."

"I'm not thick. Dylan would have my balls for earmuffs if I was to gawk at you even a little while you're in the nip." He stepped forward with the robe held open and closed his eyes tight.

"I doubt he'd give a shit, to be perfectly honest. But thank you." Dropping the sheet was a mortifying experience, even if he wasn't looking. She was exposed in a very fundamental way, and it made her scramble to cover herself. The robe was made for Gareth, and he was a very big man. It swallowed her whole. Wrapping the tie around her waist, she looked over her shoulder.

True to his word, Gareth stood with his eyes closed and hands resting at his sides.

"You can open your eyes."

He did, blinking several times before picking up the socks he'd tossed on the table and handing them to her. "Have a seat, put those on and let's have a go at the craic."

"Excuse me?" Unfolding the socks, she sat in the chair and crossed her leg in order to reach her foot. A long expanse of leg was exposed no matter how she tried to adjust the robe. She gave up and pulled the socks on as fast as possible, rearranging the robe when she was done.

Gareth sank into a neighboring chair and propped his feet on the coffee table, eyes averted. "To *craic* is to chat about the happenings or, more accurately, the gossip. I thought we'd have a go at sorting this mess out."

"I see. Well, there's no mess. He intends to kill me in nine days or less. Seeing as I'm opposed to his plan, I intend to get the hell out of here and come up with a plan of my own." She picked up the mug absently, sipping the hot coffee through the thick cream. "Holy crap, this is good."

He grinned. "Takes an Irishman to make good Irish coffee, yeah?" He sipped his own drink. "So you believe he intends to kill you, then."

"He made it pretty clear before I left his room." A deep

flush spread up her neck, and she looked down into the coffee, dragging a finger through the frothy top. "Nothing happened between us, though. Just so you know."

He harrumphed, focusing on the first part of her statement. "So you exchanged words?"

She looked over at him, grateful he didn't stare at her with those intense blue eyes. They unnerved her. Measuring her words took a moment. "We did. It was civil. Then he got incredibly short and rude, so I asked why he was shutting me out."

Gareth grinned, but it was far from a friendly look. "Bet that set him off."

"That's a serious understatement. He…" She was appalled to find herself getting emotional over the man determined to kill her. *How fast could Stockholm Syndrome set in?* She took a long draw on her coffee, appreciating the warmth that spread through her limbs.

Gareth set his drink on the table, scooted to the edge of his seat and rested his forearms on his knees, letting his head hang low. "He didn't strike you?"

"No." The one-word answer was sharp.

"Then I'll not have to retaliate, so that's a relief." He turned to face her, his eyes piercing. "Do you know anything about Druids?"

"I know you're supposedly a peaceable religion, people revered as leaders for centuries." She worried her lower lip, twisting the mug in her hands.

"Longer. And as for peaceable? Most are. But there's a sect of the religion, called the Assassins, responsible for the safety and security of the Order. This keep is the central collecting point for all Assassins. It's called the Nest." His gaze narrowed. "You're not surprised."

The hot mug was burning her hands, but she couldn't seem to set it down. "No, not surprised. Some of this I know."

"From Ethan?"

She jerked around to face him. "What do you know about Ethan?"

He put a hand out to stop her. "I checked him out for Dylan and made sure he had medical assistance after you two took to the air."

Her shoulders slumped. "Then you don't know if he's okay?"

"Oh, he's fine. Had a concussion and felt like shit for a couple of days. He also had a couple of cracked ribs and was pretty bruised from the beat down Cailleach gave him, but it wasn't anything that won't heal." His leg bounced in a rapid rhythm, and he looked back at the fire. "Given his skill, I'd assume he's already fully recovered."

"How can you be certain?"

"I made sure he was okay. I figured you'd want to know."

"Thank you." The words were a hoarse whisper nearly consumed by the crackle of the flames.

"Ah, you're welcome." His skin had taken on a ruddy tone. "Slow down on the coffee. It'll catch up to you before long."

"I'm fine." Kennedy rose, the room tilted and she fought to gain her balance on legs gone soft with whiskey.

Gareth was up in a blink, moving to catch her before she fell.

She settled into the warm comfort of his arms, her sense of balance seriously impaired. Seeking to anchor herself in a room that spun, she wrapped her arms around his waist. "What the hell do you put in your coffee?"

"Just a little something to help you sleep, *a stór*." Gareth leaned back to take her in. "I suppose we should get you to bed."

Dylan had worked the harshest edge off his temper with the punching bag in his small personal gym before he went to look for Kennedy. She'd disappeared. Fear initially paralyzed him before he slowed down enough to think. She'd left his rooms without her clothes. The storm was brutal and she wasn't foolish. She wouldn't have gone out in it. Still, he'd gone down to the *Seomra Riachtanais*, the place both the Elders and the Assassins went to perform ritualistic magicks, to perform a spell of seeing. When he'd found no sign of her, he could only assume she'd holed up in the castle and returned to his room to get a good night's sleep. But sleep eluded him. He considered his options and thought going a few rounds with Gareth might do the trick. Dylan would even let the other man get in a few good hits before unloading the last of his temper on him.

Pausing outside Gareth's door, he heard the other man's voice. Likely on the phone, then. He let himself in quietly so as not to disturb the call, but it hadn't been a call he'd interrupted.

Kennedy stood in Gareth's arms, the man's fecking robe pooling about her feet. Eyes closed, she had relaxed into the man's embrace with a sigh.

Gareth looked enamored, his face a study of light and dark in the firelight. He'd rested his chin atop the woman's head with complete familiarity.

It was more than Dylan could take, a feud ending in, in…*this*. "Well, if this isn't fuck-all convenient."

They parted as if he'd thrust a blade between them.

Kennedy tripped over the hem of the robe and tottered before going down, her hip glancing off the edge of the heavy wooden coffee table. "Shon of a bish."

Gareth started for her at the same time Dylan charged him, fist hauling back. He hit Gareth in the ribs as the man turned toward him.

"What the bluidy hell is this?" Gareth shouted, moving around the sofa to the open floor.

"Ye had yer hands on her. That's out o' bounds, mate."

Dylan raised his fists and jabbed at Gareth, grinning when he blocked the punch.

Gareth responded to the swing with violence of his own, feinting right and swinging left to connect with Dylan's jaw. "Ye have no idea what ye joost witnessed, so bugger off."

Dylan backed up a few steps and shook his head to stave off the effects of the blow. Wiping the blood from his lip, he grinned slow and fierce. "I saw ye with yer arms around her. She's wearin' yer robe, and *my* sheet's puddled on the floor."

"Because ye left her," Gareth bellowed.

"Ye've got that wrong," Dylan answered softly. His answer ripped at him, and the unfamiliar jealousy that tangled his gut didn't sit well at all. "She left me."

Kennedy stood and gripped the back of the chair. "I left you because you're an ash…ash…ass." She tottered around the corner, trying to kick the long robe away. Tripping, she ended up on the floor again, one leg exposed to the hip. The glare she leveled at Dylan had him raising his brows in disbelief.

"Ye're fluthered." He couldn't help but smile, wincing as his split lip pulled.

"I don' know what *fluthered* means." Her words were slurred, her eyes unfocused.

And for some reason, this charmed the hell out of Dylan. A smile tugged at his lips. "Fluthered means you've had too much to drink."

"I only had coffee, thank you."

Her imperious, unfocused gaze was his undoing. He laughed, ignoring the aches from bruises already forming. "Gareth's Irish coffee will knock you on your arse."

Gareth stepped closer, his moves slow, his fists at the ready. "Are ye done effin' aboot?"

Dylan looked at his friend. He trusted Gareth, yet he'd

raged at the man for putting his hands on Kennedy. The emotions roiling about in him were eating him alive. He didn't have room for this, this and his duty. They crashed against each other like battering rams, each vying for his loyalty. But duty had always come first. Always. And now? Now he wasn't sure where it lay.

Trying to unseat the yoke of responsibility, he shrugged. "Aye. But you're no' tae touch her. She's unstable."

"Just a little…" She swayed unsteadily and grabbed the arm of the sofa, fighting to stand.

Dylan glanced at Gareth. "I'll take her to my rooms. She can sleep it off there."

That's when Kennedy flipped him off.

She staggered forward, eyes focused on him. "Go 'way."

Gareth caught her even as Dylan reached for her. "Look, man. She's completely pissed and doesn't know what she's about tonight. Let her sleep here and we'll sort this out tomorrow."

Dylan's shoulders stiffened, his fists tightened, but he nodded. There was nothing left tonight but to seek sleep and pray that Danu would see fit to offer guidance.

Chapter 9

A relentless beat pounded in Kennedy's head like a heavy-metal bass riff. One note, over and over, fed by the heartbeat that pulsed around her stomach. One eye opened and light blinded her. The bass tempo increased. She tried to swallow but her stomach objected to her efforts.

Gently, unsure she could map the path, she raised a hand to her forehead. "Oh, crap. I'm gonna die." That sentiment quickly changed as she shifted positions and nausea rolled through her. Opening her eyes, she frantically searched for the bathroom. Gareth had said something about it being in here. An arched doorway was her only choice. Sprinting that way, she hit the door with her shoulder and raced for the toilet. It was a near thing, but she made it.

Kennedy lost the little she had in her stomach. The heavy riff in her head pounded even louder, and she couldn't stifle a groan. "It was just fucking *coffee*."

"Irish coffee." Gareth's voice cut through her misery.

"You got me drunk." The accusation was made all the worse for the rasp in her voice.

"No, I told you to slow down while you were drinking the stuff like water."

A damp washrag appeared over her shoulder. "Thanks." Wiping her face, she stood, adjusted the robe she'd slept in and turned to face Gareth. Embarrassment flooded her cheeks even as her skull threatened to split wide open. "I don't suppose there's a magical cure for a hangover?"

"A small one." His lips quirked before one side curled up. "Meet me in the living room as soon as you're done in here, and I'll see what I can do for you." He started out of the room only to pause and look back. "I've a lad's trousers and a jumper for you. Boots may be a wee bit large, but they're close enough to your size you'll be able to walk."

"Thank you." She pushed as much sincerity into the words as she could. "I'll be out in a minute."

He nodded and left, shutting the door behind him.

Kennedy freshened up and got dressed in the clothes he'd provided.

The sweater was just large enough she had to roll the sleeves. Pulling her socks back on, she padded into the living room and gravitated straight to the fire. The club chair she'd occupied last night seemed to call to her, and she sank into the warm leather with a soft sigh. If she ever made it home she was selling her house and buying one with a fireplace.

Gareth moved into her field of view and sat on the sofa near her. "Ready to take a walk?"

"Walk?"

He reached behind the sofa and pulled a pair of battered leather boots and a heavy jacket. "It'll clear your head after I've done my bit, and we can finish last night's talk outside where no one will hear. It's none so bad out today."

She glanced out one of the windows and saw sunshine and fair skies. "It's beautiful."

"It's home."

She tugged on the boots, relieved they weren't horribly oversize. "Where'd you get the outfit?"

An unapologetic grin decorated his face. "We've young lads who are training to become Assassins. I raided their wardrobes."

"Remind me to send thank-you cards to those who are missing their britches."

He laughed and she winced at the sound. "Right. Sit back in the chair and relax. Pull your hair to one side if you don't mind."

She obeyed, closing her eyes and resting her hands in her lap.

"Deep breaths. Pay attention to my hands, not my words."

Strong fingers dug into the muscles of her neck. Starting low, almost below shoulder level, he moved from the center out and then up, working vertebrae by vertebrae. A soft groan escaped her when he hit a particularly tender spot. His voice took up a chant then, something soft and melodic that spoke to her, through her and reached for the center of all she was. She tensed. Gareth's fingers dug in harder, and she couldn't help but fall back into the rhythm of his movements, the sound of his voice and the sensation of self his hands evoked.

Reaching the top of her spine, he wrapped large hands around her head and dug his thumbs into the muscles at the base of her skull. Pain exploded through her brain, its intensity stealing every sensation—sight, sound, taste, touch, hearing. The crippling was raw, undiluted, that kind so rarely, if ever, experienced. Her body had no will. His hands supported her entire structure. The pain began to recede, normal light filtering through the stark, pure misery.

Those thumbs pressed deeper and another blinding round of pain overwhelmed her. She was reduced to the pounding of her heart, the rasp of her breath, the scent of the sea and the one constant—his voice.

Something shifted inside her, something that was both malicious and curious. At the same time, Gareth began to slowly withdraw the pressure of his thumbs. He used his fingertips to massage her head and gently coax her back toward the now.

She trembled as he guided her to lie back in the chair. His speech grew softer, then softer still, and his fingers moved toward her temples. Pressing gently, he whispered something so low she couldn't make it out before releasing her head in gradual steps.

Gareth moved around so he could see her, propping a hip on the sofa arm. "Better?"

"Unh." She opened her eyes and squinted at him. "You didn't tell me you were going to annihilate me, then put me back together with painstaking accuracy."

"In the name of self-preservation and friendship—mine with each of you—if you weren't put back together painstakingly accurate, Dylan would disregard that friendship and have my fecking arse." His solemn countenance made him appear ageless, as if he was beyond the reaches of time. "Magick comes with a price. Always. Healing's the worst of it because you're going against nature's timeline and speeding it up. You experience the intensity of healing on a much shorter timeline."

"Ethan said that, too—that magick had a price." She pushed herself up and touched her head.

"He was right. You'll be a wee bit tender for an hour or so, but the worst of it's passed."

"Thank you." Hair tumbled about her shoulders with wild abandon, and she frowned. Touching her scalp with tentative fingers, she managed to pull her hair up in a looped ponytail with only a single curse. She glanced at Gareth. "Don't suppose you'd have an extra pair of sunglasses?"

"Of course I do." He hopped off the sofa and jogged into the bedroom and back again before she could get her coat buttoned. "Here."

"Nice," she said, looking them over before sliding them on and pushing them up to rest on her head.

"Let's get out of here before someone, namely Dylan, comes looking for us. I'll tell you a bit about him before the day's through if you're willing to hear me out."

"I'm curious enough to accept that vague and poorly disguised bribe."

"Fair enough, seeing as it worked," he said, grinning. With a hand at her lower back, he guided her to the door and through it, down the hall and stairs, then outside through enormous wooden doors.

The brisk wind hit her face with an invisible slap that made her head jerk back. "I thought you said it was better today."

"Oh, aye, it is." He strolled forward, hands in his pockets.

It was only then that she realized he wore his coat unbuttoned. "You're insane," she said, jogging to catch up. "You'll freeze to death."

"Nah. It's none so cold as that. Winter will really hit in another three weeks, and we'll have snow and sleet with a wind so cold it freezes your marrow."

"Crazy Irishman," she muttered.

"American city girl," he countered, surprising a laugh out of her.

"True enough."

They wandered toward the edge of the sheer cliffs. Emerald, windswept grass grew to the edge and, in some places, down the face. A few smooth walkways offered a closer look at the waves crashing against the rocks, but Kennedy stopped short.

Gareth went on a few steps before stopping to look back. "Scared?" The teasing in his voice was evident.

"Hell, yes. One gust and I'm over the edge like some moronic tourist who wants to get that single picture that no one's ever been able to get, looks straight down and—"

"You needn't say anything more than you're afraid of heights, Kennedy."

"I…" She paused and looked at him, considering. "You know, if Dylan was half as intuitive as you are, I think things might have been different."

Gareth lifted his face to the sky and laughed long and loud.

"What?"

"Half as intuitive, is it?" His wide grin brought out his dimples. "Dylan's twice as intuitive as any of us. I swear his gut has an alert system like that color-coded defcon system your government uses."

She hunched her shoulders against a particularly strong gust of wind that brought with it the salty tang of the sea. *Dylan's scent.* Shaking her head, she said, "Look. If he were intuitive, don't you think he'd have thought before behaving like a moronic, overbearing, misogynistic, compassionless asshole?" She was almost yelling.

"I think—" Gareth walked back to her slowly "—that if he weren't so busy fighting an internal battle that involves oath versus desire, you'd have seen a different side of him altogether."

Every ounce of blood left her face. "He doesn't desire me. Not truly." The words were low yet fierce, and she doubted he'd heard her. Her expression had clearly said everything, though, given the intensity of Gareth's gaze.

"He's never cared for a woman. This is new territory for him, so you might go a bit easy as he navigates his way through the maze of emotions that come with falling in love."

She shook her head, the denial already forming on her lips. "No. He's at least thirty years old. Sometime in there he has to have loved *someone*."

Gareth stepped closer, lips thinning as his jaw muscles tightened. "I'm telling you he's never loved another—I, who have known him since we were bairns living next to each other's farms, I, who have walked into battle with him and bled by his side." He moved closer to her with every harsh word. "You think I'd *lie* about something like this?"

"No." She tucked her hands up in the sleeves of the

jacket and studied the ground at her feet, composing her next words carefully. She looked up and found him staring at her. "I have a hard time believing he cares for me as more than a means to an end."

Gareth's head snapped back as if he'd been hit. "Say that again."

Her brow furrowed. "The part about my being a means to an end?"

"It's you." He let go of her arm and grinned. "It's always been you. You're the reason he'll be strong enough to stop Cailleach."

"I have no idea what you're talking abou—" Pain struck her so hard that she doubled over and fought to breathe. Her vision didn't fade. It was simply gone, replaced by darkness more threatening than that of her worst nightmares.

Three-dimensional shadows moved through her blindness, hunched and twisted and wrong. The smell of decay and mildew and damp earth made her nose wrinkle at the offense. All of this combined was nothing compared to her fear of the thing that reveled in the dark, and it was coming. Her skin stretched and her fingers curled in on themselves as something too large for her skin clawed its way up from the depths of her soul, scaling her ribs and scraping across her sternum.

"Gareth," she said through gritted teeth. "Run."

Dylan rushed through breakfast. Internal excuses why he found himself in such a hurry flowed freely through his mind—he was hungry, she was his responsibility, Gareth was bound to want rid of her, she'd likely want her clothes back, Gareth would end up hopelessly enamored. That last thought had him shoving away from the table with enough force to both rattle place settings and draw curious glances.

Striding from the dining room, he nearly bowled Aylish over.

The Elder's jaw sported an impressive bruise. "We need to talk, Dylan." Aylish moved toward him, gaze never leaving Dylan's face. "There's much to say."

Emotional tumblers fell into place as he locked himself down. "This is neither the time nor place to sort out our differences. I'll accept the punishment deemed my due for striking the Elder, but I've more pressing issues at the moment." He looked back toward the stairs.

Aylish touched Dylan's arm and he jumped. His father withdrew his hand. "I'd have words with you now."

Dylan's abdominal muscles knotted, a painful jab above and to the right of his belly button. It stole his breath. His brows drew together. "I have to see to the woman. She's in Gareth's care at the moment and I…" His mouth turned down at the corners and damn if he could stop it. Clearing his throat, he forced himself to relax. "She's my responsibility."

"This evening, then, when you've settled things."

Sure his father mentioned settling things as a veiled reference to Kennedy's execution, Dylan's lips curled in a feral snarl. "I'll no' be taking care o' things in tha' manner for the moment." Not giving his father the opportunity to respond, Dylan turned and jogged across the enormous foyer. He took the wide stairs two at a time, turning right when he reached the top. Striding down the hallway with purpose, the only thing that mattered was reaching the woman. Her image had imprinted on his mind. Everywhere he looked he saw her, smelled whiffs of her scent and heard her laughter's echoes. He cursed in a creative combination of English and Irish. The sole lad Dylan encountered initially slowed his approach before scurrying past, head down, as he sought to put distance between himself and the Assassin. Reaching Gareth's suite, he started to open the door. Given the bout they'd had last night after his unannounced entrance, he let go of the handle and knocked. No one answered.

There was no more warning this time than the last. His lower belly cramped so hard he doubted it could have been any more painful had someone taken a set of vise grips to his intestines. Already doubled over, a sharp pain in his side made him jerk and take an involuntary step sideways. One hand went to his abs, the other pressing just above his waistband against his external obliques. "Oh, fecking hell."

"Assassin!"

The command in his father's voice forced him to gradually straighten and turn. "Not. Now."

"Gareth and the woman are on the cliffs. Cailleach's risen."

Chapter 10

Dylan exploded into action, pain be damned. He yanked a broadsword from a wall mounting and sprinted down the steps calling, "Send the Arcanum. Keep everyone else in the castle, and if ye've ever cared for me at all, ye'll leave the host be for the moment." The heavy oak doors opened for him before he got there, and he dashed outside without slowing. His legs pumped hard then harder as he covered the ground in giant strides, his lungs working like enormous bellows. Turf churned beneath his feet as he pushed himself against the wind. Every gust attempted to stall him. The winds fueled his inner demons. They whispered he wasn't strong—never strong enough to save those who mattered most. He fought harder for every step. Rounding the corner of the keep, Gareth and the woman came into view.

Cailleach had indeed risen. She'd taken Gareth's broadsword, leaving him with a single *sgian-achlais* in one hand. His other hand trembled as it hovered over his second *sgian-achlais*. The small knife had been buried to the hilt in his side. Blood from that wound, and several others, flowed freely. Gareth dodged a swing from Cailleach, stumbled and went to his knees.

"No!" Dylan's shout raced across the distance, a trailing haze of black magick pushing the command forward with furious intent. Cailleach turned at the same time the curse struck her in the shoulder. It spun her through the air before slamming her to the ground.

Gareth's pain-riddled gaze found Dylan. He said something, but the wind stole the words. The blond assassin dropped his wee blade and fell forward, propping himself up on his fist. His arm shook violently with the effort.

Time slowed. Every wave that battered the cliffs became a death knell booming in Dylan's head.

Gareth collapsed, hand knocked away from his wound when his chest hit the ground.

The reverberation of that impact echoed through Dylan. He loosed a battle cry even as the goddess stood over Gareth's prone form.

Cailleach's calculating stare focused on Dylan with singular intensity. She raised her sword and assumed a fighting stance.

Dylan swung his broadsword in a vertical circle at his side, rotating and loosening his wrist. Chest heaving, he slowed and adjusted his grip on the hilt. Gareth lay unmoving between them, hair strewn about his face. "You swore not to rise."

"When a warrior this lovely calls one's name repeatedly?" Weighted innuendo filled Cailleach's leer as she shed the heavy coat and toed off her boots. "You left him to seduce my host. I had no choice but to assume you had vacated her presence and, therefore, your presumed intent. Or perhaps I was wrong," she said, her smile feral, "and you've simply failed."

Dylan's pulse was a heavy drumbeat in his head, the tempo increasing.

"Nothing to say?" She toed Gareth hard. He didn't move.

"Nothing that will change the outcome." He moved forward.

Cailleach mirrored his action, walking around Gareth

until she was almost within Dylan's reach. "Then let's not delay the inevitable."

They came together, metal clashing as they swung the heavy blades with skill. The air darkened around them with black magicks the wind couldn't dispel. Every move was gauged to inflict maximum damage, every step and counterstep calculated to drive the opponent toward a less desirable position. The cliff rim loomed closer as they circled and slashed. Each deliberate strike drove the opponent's sword weight and killing edge toward the body's most vulnerable points. Grass withered and died beneath their feet as they drew on the elements, warping them into vile, unnatural powers.

Dylan pulled his dirk from its sheath, intent on claiming every advantage he could. If he could even briefly lock their swords at the hilt's notch, he could gut the goddess with the smaller blade. He kept Gareth in his peripheral vision, fighting to drive the goddess away from the wounded man. The realization that, despite the sounds of a sword fight, Gareth didn't move, nearly crippled Dylan.

Cailleach struck a particularly vicious blow, her eyes gleaming with manic light as he stumbled and fought to regain his balance. He'd underestimated her physical strength while still confined to her host's body. The goddess pushed him back with a sharp thrust that slid off his blade and sliced his upper arm.

Rage shrouded him in a hazy veil, and he barely registered the deep wound.

The residue of black magicks clogged his nostrils, combining to form a miasma through which they fought. Death's decay didn't smell worse. The thick atmosphere coated the inside of his nose and worked its way down the back of his throat. It wasn't nearly enough to stop him from adding to the vile brume. He threw hexes at Cailleach as they circled each other.

She reciprocated in kind, the conflict degenerating into the darkest one-on-one battle he'd ever fought.

The core of him bled from both curses he'd created and those he'd repelled. While he hadn't taken more than glancing blows, Cailleach's magicks still had to touch him in order for him to deflect them. A part of himself, however, a part he fought to keep locked away, thrived on the darkness. Quiet, sultry promises whispered through his mind—promises made by the magicks. Every malediction he invoked threatened to pull him under, to turn the tides of who he was and create in him a threat the Order would be obligated to eliminate. But that wasn't going to save Gareth…or Kennedy. That meant today wouldn't be the day dark magick's temptation seduced him from both his oath and his obligation.

Cailleach had worked her way back to Gareth's still form. Dylan moved in closer and fought to drive her away from the downed man, but she refused to give ground.

Shouts sounded behind him. The Arcanum had rounded the keep and headed toward them.

The goddess deflected his next blows with vigor, and it pissed him off.

"Cnámha boil fola, lasair craicinn, a dhó agus a defame comhlacht!" Blood boil, skin flame, bones burn and body defame! The killing curse arrowed toward its target, the darkest magick in his compendium. Rarely used, it never missed. His throat closed in horror. He wanted to scream to the heavens, command the blight to dissipate, to somehow stop it from reaching Kennedy. But magick such as that couldn't be undone. If it struck her true, she'd experience a slow, horrific death. Her blood would heat to boiling and her organs would gradually burn. Her brain would expand and she'd suffer indescribable horrors as the curse's heat internally seared her body. Cailleach would

undoubtedly abandon her. And Kennedy would know it was his hand that had killed her.

The curse cut through Cailleach's aura, and she flung an arm out to defend her core. Her right forearm turned an angry red and she screamed.

Dylan started forward without thinking.

Sweat rolled down her temples as she fought to cast the curse off. With a hefty grunt, she marshaled enough magick to dispel the worst of his efforts.

He stumbled to a stop as unmitigated relief washed through him. Kennedy was safe.

Cailleach rallied and hurled a hex at him, one he'd never encountered. It roared toward him, a bottomless black that sucked in light as if it were fuel.

He dropped his dirk and drove the broadsword into the ground in time to get both hands up and shield himself before the curse hit. It lifted him off his feet and tossed him with less consideration than the wind gave the clouds. He landed with a heavy thud. Fighting to draw a breath, he struggled to his feet and half ran, half stumbled to reclaim his broadsword.

The Arcanum was closing in.

Cailleach looked between him and his sword, emphatically backing up as he came forward, this time with support.

Air burned Dylan's lungs as if it had been laced with acetone. Still, he sucked it in with great gulps. He loosed a hoarse battle cry as he raised his sword in a two-handed grip and swung it in a vicious downward arc at the goddess.

She deflected the blow, but her arms trembled. Her movements slowed and became less tactically refined, her execution poor as she fought back. The confrontation's zenith had passed with no discernible victor. Yet.

"Block her retreat to the cliffs," he shouted at his men.

The warrior in him roared with the satisfaction of know-ing he could end this thing, end *her*, on his terms. An invisible fist squeezed his heart. His slight hesitation af-forded her an opportunity to strike and she did, rallying with strength born of desperation.

He met her blow for blow. Swords rang against each other, the sound of steel sliding against steel became a hissed promise of violence. Their broadswords clashed at an odd angle, forcing hers to the side and breaking her hold. She was left with an unbalanced, one-handed grasp on the hilt. Her gaze was wild as it darted between him and the cliff's edge.

He leveled his sword at her. "Think to throw yourself from the rim and I'll stop you before you get there."

"You'd not hurt this body. Your restraint in battle speaks volumes as to your desire." She licked her lips and pushed long, loose curls from her face with impatience.

His savage grin stopped her. "I'd think you'd realize I'll use killing curses without hesitation. Force my hand, and I'll sacrifice that body for the good of mankind."

She smiled, slow and knowing. "Your lie reeks of a misery that's as pungent as fresh pine."

Dylan was so prepared for her to sprint toward the cliff's edge that he failed to predict the other alternative at her disposal, one that would hurt him just as much.

Flipping the hilt of the sword up, she grabbed it and took a single large step forward. Then, eyes locked on his, she drove the blade through Gareth with a single down-ward thrust.

His body jerked, and his fingers clawed the turf. An involuntary sound of excruciating pain escaped him, both animalistic and raw.

Dylan stopped breathing.

Kennedy collapsed into a boneless heap.

And Gareth—Gareth lay dying under a cloudless sky.

* * *

Kennedy saw two—three?—of everything as the world came into focus. Dylan's face hovered inches from hers. She blinked hard and fast, moving to sit up. He tightened his grip on the nape of her neck, shaking her by the proverbial scruff with one hand while tapping her face with the other.

"Ease up." She croaked out the words. Once he'd stopped, she realized that every muscle she owned, and some she may have only had on loan, ached like she'd been in Zumba hell for a week—nonstop.

"Help him." Desperation and anger saturated Dylan's words.

Her skin prickled, and every hair on her body stood up. "Help who?"

Still on his knees, he hauled her around. A discarded coat lying ten paces away registered first, its prone pose macabre. No more than three feet from her right knee, the wind ruffled blond hair. When she tried to take in the hair in relation to the man, though, nothing made sense. A dark, almost black stain sullied the clifftop's raw grass. It seeped from below the man's torso. Another stain, this one a dark, familiar red, saturated his white shirt on the side nearest her. He was facedown and unmoving. The individual snapshots coalesced, and she realized he'd been run through with a substantial sword.

A sharp, keening wail broke from her as she scrambled out of Dylan's arms. "No, no, no." She fervently repeated the denial again and again.

Dylan grabbed her shoulder and hauled her to her feet. "You were in that body and let this happen, so you help him. Now," he roared.

Help him. Help him. "I'm only a nurse." Flat and broken, she stared up at Dylan. "He needs a hospital."

"Help him," he screamed, spittle flying. "Our surgeon's

in the city and the nearest hospital is more than an hour and a half away. If I pull that sword, he'll bleed to death before I can get him there. If I leave it and send for someone, he'll go further into shock and die. You're my only choice and his only chance, so help him."

She stumbled as she stood. "I'll need supplies."

"Give me a list." Muscles at the back of his jaw seized up.

"Gauze, sutures, needles, alcohol, iodine, saline, morphine, scalpels, blankets…" With every item she named, her clinical training and logical mind kicked in. "Gather everything as fast as possible. I'm not pulling anything out until you're back. Hurry."

Dylan turned and split his men up to gather the materials as quickly as possible. "And bring reinforcements."

They sprinted away.

Kennedy sank to her knees beside Gareth and laid a shaking hand on his shoulder. Nothing. Closing her eyes, she let the sounds of the sea wash over her and fought to keep calm as shock and grief threatened to throw her into an emotional abyss. If the goddess had done this, if *she* had done this, she'd never forgive herself. *Can't think about that right now.* Instead, she focused on things that needed immediate attention—triage, wound assessment, offering comfort—all of which she could control.

As she mentally ran down the list of things she'd need, as well as need to do, her self-confidence fell into a mental bog. "Stop it, Jefferson. You were a surgical nurse for more than three years and a trauma nurse for more than five. You worked ICU and SICU for three years after that. You've been through enough that you should be able to figure out the basics before handing him over to their surgeon."

Rubbing her hands together, she moved Gareth's hair aside. His moist, cool skin likely had nothing to do with the temperature out here but everything to do with shock. Gently taking off his watch, she crawled back up to his neck, found his carotid artery and laid her first two fingers over it. It hammered out a beat of 124. Kennedy took the pulse a second time with the same results. She stroked Gareth's hair, alternating between murmuring words of encouragement and creatively cursing him for being pinned to the earth like a giant bug. Tears flowed like lazy tributaries down her face to drip off her chin.

A hand on her shoulder made her gasp and strike out, but the man behind her was quick. "Easy, lass."

He beseeched the gods in prayer. Not that she had much use for the gods after the insanity that had been wreaked in her life by one of their own, but she wasn't above accepting help at the moment.

He stopped speaking a second before he curled a finger under her chin and tilted her head back until their gazes met. "Exercise your skill in this, but do not lose your faith over it."

Her brows winged upward. "How did you know what I was thinking?"

"I guessed. You only confirmed it." He let her go with a faint smile at the same time the sounds of men on the move reached her.

A small battalion rushed toward her; the Arcanum arriving first and spreading out. The next group of men to arrive were grouped by responsibility with the front-runners teamed four to each large trunk. She counted three trunks, which meant twelve men, but damn if they didn't seem larger in presence than a mere twelve. At least ten more men, larger in size and more seasoned, followed the first dozen. The closer they came, the more she realized that they glared at her with open contempt.

An older man stepped away from the group. "I'm Riordan."

The way he said it let Kennedy know this was supposed to mean something, but there wasn't time for niceties. She nodded once in acknowledgment. "Kennedy." Looking at the younger men carrying the chests, she said, "Bring those over here. Roll out a tarp because we're not going to do this on the ground if we can help it. You, curly blond guy, I'm going to need you to anchor the tarp, even if all you do is set chests on three corners and stand on the fourth. Brown-haired guy—no, you, right there—unfold two more tarps and work out who's going to hold them and create a wind-free zone. Whatever you do, make sure you leave enough room for me to operate."

Riordan moved into her field of view. "I'll be handling the healing from this point forward."

Kennedy's shoulders drooped. "You're a surgeon? Thank you, Lord."

"I'm a healer," he said with an air of self-importance bordering on disdain.

She slowly stood to her full height. "Yeah? Well, that means nothing to me. Gareth's *mine*. Mine," she shouted, drawing everyone's attention. "And you're wasting time he doesn't have. I've got the opportunity for one Hail Mary pass, and you're either offense or defense. Your choice."

His brow wrinkled. "You make no sense."

"Go figure."

"Leave her to work." Aylish laid a hand on Riordan's forearm. "Maybe you can learn something in the ways of new medicine."

Riordan shook off Aylish's hand. "I don't need modern medicine to know I'm superior to—"

Aylish grabbed the shorter man by the throat. "And I am The Elder. I tell you what the Order will embrace and what it won't. Do not ever forget it." Aylish relaxed his hand and Riordan hit the ground in a gasping heap. "Do what you must, Kennedy."

She turned her back on the healer. "I need anyone with

significant medical training to get over here and sanitize your hands." Several guys looked at each other. "Move it!"

Dylan, Riordan, Aylish—who had arrived on news of Gareth's attack—and four younger men came forward as a group. Dylan stepped closer, his body rigid. "I'll be your primary support, Riordan and Aylish will assist via magick, and the lads will fetch supplies as you call for them."

Kennedy grabbed the sanitizer gel, dousing her hands. "Generous handful. Run it up to your elbows. Use a clean toothbrush and get it under your nails. Then you get gloved up. Dylan, hurry." They snapped gloves on at the same time. "You're familiar with the names of surgical instruments and supplies?"

"Aye."

She swallowed around the lump in her throat and nodded. Moving to kneel beside Gareth, she called for IV supplies. She found a decent vein and stuck him. Flushing the line, she began injecting morphine until she reached the maximum dose she was comfortable with in an uncontrolled environment. With trembling fingers, she checked his pupils. Wide but not blown. She held a mirror under his nose and got short, sharp breaths. "I'm so sorry, baby. It's the best I can do for you."

"Kennedy?" Dylan watched her, his gaze shuttered, emotions locked down.

She positioned herself so her knees rested lightly on Gareth's back, one on either side of the sword. "Gauze and saline flush on my left. Manual suction on my right. Someone be ready with needle and thread. Aylish, do your thing."

Looking at Dylan, she shifted forward so her weight held Gareth's torso to the earth. Then she issued the hardest order she'd ever given in her life. "Pull the sword."

Chapter 11

It was quite some time later before Dylan silently made his way back to the keep. He held Kennedy close to his side, his arm wrapped around her protectively. Every now and again, a shiver would take her—or maybe it was he who shook. Regardless, he'd pull her closer. Finding the right words to thank her for what she'd done proved impossible. They were there, but damn if he could force them out. He'd experienced some horrific things in his life, and he'd witnessed some brave ones. Today topped them all.

The fiercest shaking yet nearly took Kennedy to her knees.

Dylan ignored her feeble protests as he scooped her up in his arms and carried her through the foyer. He was well aware the Assassin didn't offer aid, and it caught the men off guard when he seized on the opportunity. Very few men were bold enough to stare, though. Those who did quickly turned away as Dylan met their gazes one by one and held them, silently issuing a cold, calm challenge. Any who wanted to take issue with him were welcome to come, but they better bring their best game. Tired as he was, he could still take anyone in the Nest.

And if anyone had an issue with the woman? She was off-limits, and he'd make his point by fighting twice as dirty and leaving offenders thrice as bloody.

He glanced at Kennedy. Her presence was no longer a secret. Neither was Cailleach's. Several of the young men made the sign of evil behind her back. Dylan glared at them hard enough they began looking for other things to do—things that would take them far from the Assassin's reach.

She turned her face into his shoulder and curled her arms up over her breasts. "I'm sorry. I'm so sorry." Her heartfelt apology replayed over and over as he started up the stairs, her tears dampening his shirt.

"Not another word," he ordered. He didn't like this, didn't like the way guilt ate at her. And that he worried over her? Well, that was another disturbing development.

Entering his suite, he locked the door behind them. With a flick of his hand, fire roared to life in the hearth. He did the same when they entered his bedroom.

Kennedy lifted her head and looked around. "I'm imagining this. I'm not back here."

His spine stiffened. "And what the bluidy hell's wrong with *here*?"

Her head lolled to the side and rested against his shoulder again. "Nothing. Just that my most recent memories, both good and bad, are tied up with you and this place."

"As are mine." He lowered his lips to her forehead and ignored her sharp intake of breath. He had become nothing more than a passenger to driving instinct, and he was too tired to care.

"About Gareth…" She choked on his name, and Dylan's arms tightened around her.

"Enough. You did what you were able, as did our healers." The image of his father stooped and sweating as he worked with Kennedy over Gareth's massive injuries would haunt him forever.

She buried her face in his shoulder, wadding his shirt up in her fingers. He strode to the bed and flipped the covers back. Laying her down, he began removing her bloodied and filthy clothes.

Her protest was feeble.

"Hush." His harsh command made her drop her hands and turn away. "Just hush, Kennedy." Softer this time.

He reached for the laces on her pants. When she didn't object, he continued to undress her. Destroyed garments were flipped into the fire one by one. The smells of burning wool and leather billowed into the room, prompting him to open the nearest window. The wind whipped in and carried with it the sea's briny scent.

Returning to Kennedy, Dylan quickly disrobed and moved to the hearth, tossing his own clothes into the fire. Fresh waves of smoke billowed upward. He wanted no physical reminders of the day. Dreams would be bad enough, undoubtedly haunting him with high-definition clarity.

He turned to the woman in his bed. Cast in firelight, exhaustion's deep bruises couldn't hide beneath glazed blue eyes. The wind on the cliffs had whipped her hair into a frenzy of curls before one of the lads thought to pull it back and bind it as she worked. Her lower lip was plump and raw where she'd worried it with her teeth. A rosy flush decorated her cheeks, a by-product of the cold and, likely, a bit of embarrassment. She clutched the bedding to her chest, narrow shoulders shivering in the persistent breeze. Slender, capable fingers traced the sheet's hemline one stitch at a time as she watched him like an injured animal might—distrusting, hurt, knackered, wounded of spirit.

That last was too hard for Dylan to face head-on. Instead, he moved to the opposite side of the bed and slid under the covers. "Damn if these sheets aren't frigid." He rolled toward her, wrapping an arm about her waist and pulling her down and into him.

"What are you doing?" What was undoubtedly meant to be a demand for answers rode the airwaves on a deep yawn.

His hand found hers.

She didn't push him away. Instead, she laced their fingers together.

He froze, his own fingers suddenly stiff and unyielding.

She pulled her hand free before moving toward the edge of the bed.

He didn't know what to do. Confused and unsure of himself, yet unwilling to let her go the first time she voluntarily reached for him; he wrapped an arm around her waist and pulled her against him. "You're chilled, lass. Let me warm ye." He fumbled for her hand, trying to do what she'd done so effortlessly. His hands were both larger and rougher than hers. He'd never been more aware of their physical differences than now.

She shifted subtly, and their fingers wound together so easily it was if they'd performed the action a thousand times or more. Tension dissolved with the simple connection despite his heart's deceptive thundering pace. Holding her quietly, contentment stole up on him. He stilled. No one had ever held his hand. Not like this. For all he was debauched in body and black of spirit, he'd never allowed something so personal.

"Thank you." Her words carried back to him as she traced their joined fingers with her free hand, her touch soft, tentative.

"Ye're welcome." He stared at the tangle of curls still partially bound by the elastic band. One side of her neck was exposed, the long column displaying muscles knotted with tension. "Relax, *a stór*. We've earned a bit o' shared comfort after today." *And wasn't that the oddest thing of all, that he'd seek to take his ease from her after nearly losing so much?* He wanted her to find in him security, to sleep with the knowledge their hearts beat only inches apart and to find satisfaction in waking in his arms. The awkwardness of the realization made his next words gruff. "Lie back and let me hold you."

A jaw-cracking yawn shook her. "I should go."

"Aye, but only tae sleep. Here. With me." He situated her pliant body against his, ignoring his cock's interest while snugging the covers around them and creating a warm cocoon. Running an arm under her pillow, he was able to draw her even closer. His breath hitched when she tucked their joined hands under her cheek. He buried his nose in her hair. "Sweet dreams, *mo aingeal chothaímid.*" And then, behind the veil of his native tongue, he told her that which he couldn't translate. "*Thug tú dom le bronntanas lómhara. Tá mé faoi chomaoin agat agus geallaim a thabhairt ar ais ar an dtús báire. Tá do íobairt thar luachmhar dom, agus fós ní féidir liom a insint duit.*" You gave me a precious gift. I am indebted to you and promise to return the favor. Your sacrifice is beyond valuable to me, and yet I cannot tell you.

"You're language is so raw and beautiful."

The open sincerity of her words further unraveled him. All he wanted was her. It went against his code of honor, defied the depth of his commitment to the oath he'd taken as the Assassin. None of it mattered. Not now, maybe not tomorrow, maybe not ever. He leaned forward and laid a tender kiss at her hairline, the salty residue of sweat teasing his tongue when he licked his lips. Something urged him to do it again, and he followed the push without question. Without thinking, he tightened the arm around her waist and rolled her on top of him.

She gasped, staring wide-eyed at him as a faint smile tugged at his mouth. "What are you doing?"

He cupped her face and closed his eyes. "I need the affirmation of life. I need to block out the images seared into my mind and replace them with something…more." Then he looked at her, his eyes searching hers in an effort she'd see the truth of his declaration. "I need you, lass."

"Me or a warm body?" she asked quietly.

He opened his mouth to answer her and his eyes widened fractionally. He tried again, rubbing his chest as he coughed to clear his throat but he couldn't seem to get the words out. He shook his head and looked away. "It would be far easier for me if any warm body would suffice."

She cupped his face and nodded, the action more solemn than any words she might have offered. Then, breaths coming shallow, she moved to him and laid a tender kiss on his lips. "Make me forget, Dylan. Remind me that I'm alive. We're all alive."

He rolled them over swiftly, reversing their positions. Wrapping her hair around his fist, he began to kiss his way down her neck. Biting and nipping, he paused to lay tender kisses from the hollow of her throat, along her collarbone and out to the edge of her shoulder.

His heart thundered in his chest with a locomotive's fierce, ground-rattling force. Blood hummed under his skin. Nerves began firing faster, yet he didn't struggle to control the situation. No, with Kennedy's soft encouragements, he simply let go and followed where the moment led.

"You'll be the death of me, Kennedy Jefferson." He raised her hands over her head, his hands tracing down the soft undersides of her arms and down her sides, thumbs tracing the outer swells of her breasts.

"Dylan." His name was nothing more than a tender sigh.

He lowered his head and sought out the nearest of her nipples. The sensitive skin pearled under the heat of his breath, and she arched her back before weaving a hand through his hair and pulling him closer.

"Like that, is it?" He caught the tight bud gently between his teeth and sucked on it while flicking the tip with his tongue.

Kennedy gasped and arched harder, dipping her chin to find his gaze. Blue eyes saturated with passion met the yearning echo that no doubt lit his green ones.

Her skin was so cool beneath the heat of his hands. Unsteadily, she reached for him and encouraged him to cup her breasts. She curled her fingers around the edge of his palm with one hand as the other slid down his side and sought the heavy weight of his arousal. When she found him, she gripped his length and stroked, her touch tentative.

Dylan's hips jerked forward of their own volition. He gripped her as she slowly stroked him. "Harder."

She complied.

He worked a hand between their bodies and coaxed her legs farther open. Deft fingers stroked her slick sex, and her whole body shuddered. He watched her response, hungered for her mewls, learned from every shift of her body under his touch, each tender gasp, the way she shot him wide-eyed looks of surprise and the way the jerking of her finely muscled abdomen gave away both her surprise and her pleasure.

"Dylan." His name was an unsteady invocation on her lips. "Don't let me go."

He heard the words, knew there was more to them than the superficial meaning, but damn if he could get his mind to work. Hands full of hot woman, he couldn't get his common sense to withdraw to that clinical place he'd always been able to access, the place that let him think clearly. Kennedy broke that connection in him.

Thoughts he had no business entertaining crept in and whispered dark promises of what might be if he could beat the goddess, beat Fate's predetermined outcome, hold on to the woman in his arms. Fighting the temptation to fall into the possibilities, he drove Kennedy ruthlessly with his fingers, demanded her release on *his* terms, not hers.

Her back arched so hard only her feet, shoulders and head rested on the bed. She pushed herself toward his touch. A harsh sob ripped through her as desperation ruled her body.

Dylan draped a leg over one of hers, pulling her down and holding her in place. Shifting his touch, he pinched the small bundle of nerves at the apex of her cleft, thrumming it with his forefinger. Then it was a matter of holding her as she came apart in his arms with a keening cry, hips bucking wildly.

Her legs sawed back and forth. He lowered his lips to one nipple and tugged, earning desperate, wordless pleading.

Legs tangled, she rolled toward him, eyelids at half-mast, and reached blindly for his shaft. "I need you. Now."

His heart lurched, and he struggled against the urge to push away, to withdraw. She was everything he'd ever wanted in a woman and more, but her end came nearer with the second hand's every tick. Panting through the dense, emotional fog that made every breath a challenge and pulled her impossibly closer. The need to find that irrefutable truth between them, to make tangible this invisible need, drove him to move over her and spread her legs.

Wide blue eyes stared up at him, wild with unspoken demand.

"Aye, *anamchara*, yer soul calls to mine." He slid into her slick heat, those feminine walls stretching to accept his girth. The sensation briefly robbed him of speech. Then he began to move, a slow, rolling motion that tested his stamina even as it drove Kennedy to the edge of reason in moments. He gritted his teeth, vowing not to give her the words that would lay him at her feet, defenseless in the face of duty and impending loss. It didn't mean the thoughts weren't there, the words hovering with the desire for release. No, the demands of the gods were at the forefront of his mind. But parallel to those demands stood something fresh and new, something he didn't recognize.

All he knew was that she was destined to die by his hand, but she'd been gifted to him tonight. Kennedy Jefferson was right where she belonged.

The pace of their lovemaking became frantic with his realization, and he sought to push her to crazed heights of passion that she might never forget him. Her hips bucked against his every downstroke, and he wondered that he didn't hurt her. Yet when he tried to restrain himself, she demanded more, hooking her leg around him and drawing him deeper.

She pulled his face to hers for a blinding kiss, one that tasted of her—sunshine and spring water. Her scent descended like a veil across his senses until he was bound to her by invisible chains made equally of mandated duty and willing surrender.

Her fingers dug into his shoulder muscles as she pushed him harder, straining toward that elusive pinnacle.

He thrust harder, leaning into her mounting pleasure. Slipping a hand between them, he reached between them, placed his thumb on her clitoris, massaged it. Hard.

"Dylan!" Her hips moved of their own accord. She raked her nails down his arms before stopping above his elbows to use his strength as anchor points to ride out each overwhelmingly pleasurable wave of release.

He was more than lost as he fell into the abyss with a roar of unspeakable satisfaction and inarticulate terror. He saw in her all that might have been had his life taken a different course, and he grieved that truth even as his own release shattered him, body and soul.

Dylan groaned at the sharp knock on his door that pulled him from the depths of sleep. An answering sound of disgust echoed from somewhere under the heavy comforter. He dug around for Kennedy, finding her sprawled out only inches away. She didn't fight him when he drew her back against his chest and rested his hand on the slender swell of her hip.

A second knock sounded, this time on his bedroom door.

Propping himself up on an elbow, he shook his hair back. "Come." He bent to lay a kiss on Kennedy's bare shoulder at the same time the door opened.

Aylish stood frozen on the threshold, eyes wide with disbelief.

"You surely didn't come to ensure we had a good night's sleep." Dylan reached for a sardonic tone, well aware it was a matter of self-defense. He didn't want his father saying anything about the fact he had a woman in his bed.

The tenor of his words snapped Aylish out of the stupor that gripped him. "No. I... It's a relief to see you looking so well."

Dylan's brows rose. "Thanks. What's brought the Elder to my bedroom door?" Sudden images of Gareth, bleeding, dying, had him bounding out of bed and racing for his closet.

"Easy, Dylan."

Aylish's use of his given name caught his attention. He faced his father. "Gareth?"

"Sleeps, though it's restless. Angus stayed with him all night and has just taken to bed. I thought to let him sleep, instead I came to see your woman about a second dosage of penicillin for him as his fever's risen."

Dylan's gaze shot to the soft light of dawn. *They'd slept through the whole night?*

"How high?" Kennedy was sitting up now, searching the room for her clothes. Her attention stopped on him. He saw the moment she realized he was nude, that *they* were nude. She let out a distressed sound, her gaze darting back and forth between him and Aylish.

A furious blush climbed her neck and settled on her

cheeks. She waved a hand in his general direction. "Okay. I know how it looks… I mean, it obviously appears… we'll explain this later." Gathering the sheet about her, she tugged until it came free. Then she slid from the bed and, catching two corners, tied them at her side and flipped the remainder of the sheet around her then over one shoulder like a toga. It trailed behind her as she rushed from the room, hauling Aylish with her while firing questions at him with the speed of a semi-automatic weapon. They stopped at the outer door and she looked back at Dylan. "How long are you going to stand there butt-ass naked? Grab some pants and let's go."

He turned away quickly so neither she nor Aylish would catch him smiling at her audacity. She wouldn't have wondered at his response, but his father—his father would have known the expression was out of character. Grabbing the first pair of leathers he could reach, he hauled them on and jogged through the living area as he laced them up.

Chapter 12

Kennedy's false bravado faded with every step she took until she was unsure whether to move ahead or turn back. She slowed to a stop, her bare toes curling into the uneven runner. The father and son duo that comprised her escort carried on. Tuning out their conversation, she stepped to the stone banister and gripped it with the ferocity of a delusional woman struggling to hold on to reality. Her bare arms trembled with tension.

Sleep had provided a blessed respite from yesterday's unforgivable events. Now that she was awake? Personal culpability struck her emotional Achilles' heel with such lethal efficiency that she was left wondering just how large a target she actually presented. Facing Gareth, seeing him in pain she was responsible for, was going to kill some part of her. She'd willingly pay the price if it meant she could help heal the harm she'd caused, though. She deserved no less than what it would cost her emotionally. How they'd saved him she still didn't know. Treating Gareth in the field should have made things harder, but it hadn't. Every obstacle had been inexplicably overcome. She shook her head, reaching back to pull her tangled hair around and over her bare shoulder. While she'd forever be grateful that he lived, she still needed a minute to work up the nerve to walk through the doorway that loomed less than thirty feet away.

Somewhere below, a door slammed. The sound—a distinctive *whump*—ricocheted around the empty foyer. She waited for someone to move, but no one did. Her vision blurred until stone and shadow blended together to form a monochromatic carpet shaded with time's inevitable patina. Unrelieved cold crept through her again. She shivered, breaking her unfocused stare.

"Kennedy?" Aylish's warm hand closed over her upper arm. "You're chilled."

"Sheet. Drafty castle. Late fall in Ireland." She shrugged and, instead of moving into that fatherly warmth she'd spent a lifetime craving, she gently dislodged his hand. "Warmth is a little out of reach at the moment."

Dylan stepped around Aylish and dropped his arm around her shoulders, snugging her in close to his body. "Let's get this done so we can take care of you, too."

She rolled her shoulders gently first and then with more insistence. He wouldn't be dislodged, so she relented. The door he steered her toward loomed large. She rubbed her arms with brisk strokes and nodded in private acceptance of responsibility's astronomical costs.

Dylan looked down at her, dipping his chin once in acknowledgment. He tightened his hold.

She leaned into him and closed her eyes, certain he'd guide her true. That he supported her, that she trusted him to not let her fall, spoke to her. That he'd believed with absolute faith she'd save Gareth moved her. He'd never doubted her when she was in possession of herself. And then there was last night. What they'd shared had been raw and undiluted, passion in its basest form. Need without lengthy explanation. Desire without boundaries. She'd never known anything like it, had never thought to experience it. That she had, and so close to the end… A small sound of distress escaped her.

His gaze narrowed. "Are ye well, lass?"

Aylish turned back and looked at them, his eyes clear

and far too observant. "We should attend to Gareth before we address anything else."

With obvious deliberation, Dylan's gaze shifted to his father. "Clearly." He released Kennedy and turned to the heavy door to Gareth's quarters. A faint curl of magick emanated from his fingertips as he traced them down the door, drawing a complicated pattern. The iron lock clanked and the handle turned.

Dylan pulled her close again, tucked her into his side and stepped through the doorway.

Several assassins, a combination of the program's older graduates and younger trainees, stood on the other side. Hands on their weapons, they assessed her with cold, loosely controlled contempt.

One lifted his lip in a sneer and stepped forward. "You don't intend to see Gareth, surely. You're the reason he stood at Death's door and knocked. Be grateful no one answered, woman."

The sudden absence of Dylan's arm around her shoulders surprised her, though not as much as seeing his hand close around the man's throat. He lifted the other man up so he stood on tiptoe. When Dylan spoke, his subarctic tone was nothing compared to the cold fury in his stare. "You don't disrespect her, Logan. Not now. Not ever. Do it again, and you'll get kicked out of the program *after* I kick your arse so thoroughly your own mother won't be able to put the pieces back together. Spread the word." He let the man go.

Logan lurched backward, one hand on his throat and the other on a dagger. He struggled to get enough air, blowing like a racehorse at the end of a hard loss. "Sir."

"Drop your dagger hand, lad." Dylan turned his attention to Kennedy, dismissing the young man without further consideration.

She couldn't stop glancing from one man to the other.

Logan arched a brow at her, tracing the handle of his dagger. The unspoken threat was all the more effective for its silence following Dylan's anger.

Aylish laid a hand on her bare shoulder as he stepped up beside her. "You'll do well to heed the Assassin, Logan. You have promise, but your judgment is clouded on this issue."

"Sir."

She reached for Dylan's hand without thinking. Their fingers met and twined together with familiarity. Glancing up, she met his gaze. It wasn't clear who was more surprised or confused. She tried to take her hand back, but his grip tightened.

A soft groan came from behind the next door. The noise grabbed her attention, slicing her guilt open so it bled like a fresh wound. She yanked her hand from Dylan's and moved toward the door with purpose. Gareth deserved no less than the best of her skills. She could sort out the argument between head and heart after he was seen to.

Pain, ragged and blinding, ripped through the bones of her hand and arm when she grabbed the handle. She yanked her hand away and cradled it to her chest. "What the hell?"

Dylan's guarded face told her nothing. His eyes, though— they burned. Small whisps of aether licked at his fingertips, blurring them.

She stumbled back a step, putting distance between them.

He shook his hands out. Magick faded. His balled-up fists were equally as dangerous, and muscles at the back of his jaw bunched up hard. Dylan's scent, colored with peat smoke and frustration, wrapped around her with intimate familiarity.

Kennedy couldn't deny that, despite the threat he posed, she wanted him. Things she'd never thought to feel stirred in her when he was near. And when he touched her? Muscles on her back twitched at the thought of those capable, dangerous hands on her bare skin. He mirrored the sea he so loved, unpredictable with tendencies toward violence followed by unexplained benedictions. It would be crazy to try and harness that wildness, to think she had even an infinitesimal chance of successfully navigating the very surface of who he was. Turning her back on him was an act of faith. She dug fingertips into her quivering belly. "Enough." One word, low and harsh. She looked for Aylish and found him moving toward her. "Will you open the door?"

He stepped up and laid a palm against it. Bright eyes turned to her even as the lock clicked open.

She stepped through the door. "You know this isn't your fault."

"It's all my fault," he said.

She ignored the beginning of his denial and, keeping out of reach, stepped through the door.

Gareth's room had been done in beautiful shades of blue and gray. Decorated with large antique furniture and rich silks, it gave off the same warmth his living area did. It was something she hadn't appreciated when she'd woken here so hungover. Ignoring the stares of the Assassin's Arcanum, who stood watch in his inner sanctum, she moved closer to the man in the bed. His multicolored blond hair spread around him, the dark blue pillow emphasizing bruises shadowed beneath closed eyes. Gauze pads and surgical tape marked each wound as though his body was a living crime scene. The IV line in his thick arm further denounced his apparent physical health, and the infusion pump's electronic censure sounded with every tick and click.

Kennedy reached out and brushed a stray hair from his forehead. "Gareth." And just like that, by speaking his name, the guilt she'd been fending off breached her defenses. It wound the dark tentacles of responsibility around her, tightening and choking until every punishing heartbeat was its own damning accusation.

His eyelids fluttered open, and he looked at every face in the room before settling on hers. The haze of narcotics clouded his vision but he smiled, winsome and sincere.

She laid a hand on his forehead. A bit warm but dry. A good sign. Her hand rested there, fingers gently stroking. "I'm so sorry, Gareth. I never meant to—"

"Doona." The single word cut her off. "Ye are no' 'sponsible." He blinked slowly enough she wondered if he'd dozed off, but his eyes opened and refocused. "You saved me." He lifted an unsteady hand and reached for her.

She grasped it and lifted it to her lips. "I saved you from damage I inflicted, you darling man. I'm so sorry." Unexpected tears welled, and she shook her head, looking away. One broke free and ran down her cheek, leaving in its wake a trail of regret so astringent that it should have blistered her skin. She'd give anything to turn back the clock and change even this one thing.

He tightened his hand around hers and jerked it toward him, forcing her attention back. "Kenny. No tears. I'm gonna be okay."

A small sob escaped and she pulled her hand from his forehead, covering her mouth. She blinked furiously and tilted her head back, trying to stymie the emotions threatening to pull her under and drown her on dry land.

The small refrigerator seal sucked open and then closed with a soft *thunk*. She looked back and found Aylish holding out the penicillin and a syringe. Laying Gareth's hand down, she turned and accepted Aylish's offering. Clinical training clicked in as she loaded the hypodermic, dumping the penicillin vial in the trash and grabbing an alcohol pad from the box atop the temporary fridge.

She looked at him, considering. "I've got to get you rolled over, honey. This has to go in the muscle, so you're going to have to bare that bum."

"I get to show you my ass?" He grinned beatifically.

Kennedy managed a weak smile this time. "Me and everyone else in the room."

"I've wanted to show you my ass since I met you, Kenny."

Somewhere nearby, Dylan snorted. "Trust me, man. You're doing a fine job of it."

The exchange loosened guilt's hold on her so she could draw a full breath. She looked back and found Dylan had moved in close. Her gaze locked with his. "I need a couple of you to roll him over so I can administer the drug. This is a slower-acting antibiotic. I can push the second dose, a fast-acting type of penicillin, through his IV. Combined, they'll be enough to fight off any infection that threatens."

Dylan looked over her shoulder. "Aylish?"

"Aye." The older man moved to her side and folded the covers back.

Dylan leaned over the bed. Taking his friend by the shoulder and hip, he gently pulled while Aylish pushed from a near identical position beside her.

It didn't matter that Gareth didn't blame her. Kennedy bore enough self-recrimination for the two of them—hell, for all of them, all the people involved in this screwed-up mess her life had become. And because of what? The fact she was the last in her line so no one would miss her when she was gone? *Get over yourself already. Think.*

Mentally shaking herself, she ripped the alcohol pad open, swabbed a spot high on Gareth's ass cheek and stuck him. He grunted as the thick serum worked its way into his muscle. She knew it burned like hell. Around three-quarters of the way through, he tried to flex away from her. She slapped a hand on his hip next to Dylan's, never looking away from the syringe. "Hold him still, please."

Aylish handed her a tiny metal pail that had several needles in it to discard her shot.

Kennedy stepped over to the fridge, withdrew both the second antibiotic and the morphine, and turned back in time to see them rearrange Gareth. She looked down at him—a patient by necessity, a burgeoning friend by choice—and stroked his hair. "Second antibiotic and the morphine go into the IV, handsome, so no more discomfort. You want the pain meds first?"

"I'll hold. Antibiotic first." His eyes had taken on that lazy, half-lidded look she'd seen for years as a nurse—that look that said his private thoughts were about to become public and to hell with the consequences. Narcotics had that effect on people. He rolled his head to the side and looked for Dylan, who still stood vigil on the far side of the bed. "You better do this right, brother. I'm a little more than half in love with your woman. Wanna grab her and run away. But I'd kiss her first. Those lips," he said on a sigh.

She couldn't stop the involuntary twitch in her fingers. The plunger depressed too fast, dumping a concentrated dose through the IV. Gareth grunted and closed his eyes again. It had to hurt. Afraid of Dylan's reaction to the man's unexpected declaration, she focused on holding the depression rate slow and steady.

It took two hands.

Assassins, including *the* Assassin, ceased their small movements that let her know where they were in the room. Silence grew heavy, even the sounds of their breathing fading. Of course, it could be the rushing noise in her ears. Withdrawing the needle, she managed to disassemble it without meeting anyone's gaze. Grabbing a new sterile pack, she dug out the nearest vial of morphine from the fridge before anyone offered help.

Gareth's hair slithered across the pillow, the sound like silk sliding over silk. "Kenny?"

Under the shadow of heavy silence, a riot of conflicting emotions battled for top billing. Disappointment at Dylan's silence won, demanding acknowledgment, but the hurt simply cut too deep. He had not only failed to defend his relationship with her, he'd also failed to acknowledge even the most rudimentary of feelings that would tell Gareth and the other men to cut a wide berth—at least while they sorted this out. But it was obviously pointless to him. He would always put duty before her. That meant she would forever live her life, regardless of how long it turned out to be, no more than second on his list of priorities. The truth hurt. Bad.

Shoving her hair back, she checked Gareth's pulse while keeping her eyes on him. Only him. "Right here, Gareth."

His brows drew together, a deep V forming between them. "Doona be sad. He's a right gobshite."

She stopped, her fingers on the sharp edge of his jaw-line. With a world of words available to her, she couldn't find the right combination to adequately respond. The silence grew heavy, and still no one moved. Eyes locked with Gareth's, she opened her mouth to say something. Anything. But nothing came out.

Still refusing to look up, she started to draw the morphine.

White noise drowned out the dull thud of her pulse. Her mouth went dry at the same time her limbs grew heavy. Something moved under her skin. Muscles chilled so fast she knew they cramped. She felt nothing. Awareness of self was secondary to the voice that chanted, whisper-soft, in her ear. She looked down. Her hands weren't shaking. Fear clawed at her consciousness and screamed through her head as she watched herself overdraw the maximum safe dose. Fingers kept on pulling despite the fact she fought the compulsion. Vial emptied, she dropped it to the floor and, swabbing the IV port, injected the needle.

Thumb on the plunger, she started pressing.

Chapter 13

Dylan rubbed the back of his neck and wished like hell Kennedy would step it up with the morphine. If she heard half of what his damnable mate rambled on about, she'd think the man a fecking romantic. The man had hit on her. *Wanker.*

Gareth thumped a loose fist against Dylan's abs.

"Ye care fer the lass and ye're too feckin' thick tae do anything aboot it." Gareth took a wild swing and missed hitting anything, let alone any*one*, by a fair distance. He rolled onto his back, throwing an arm over his eyes while cupping his hand over his abdomen. "Be a *bonnie cailín* an' slip me the droogs, Kenny."

"Gods preserve us all, mates," Dylan said, arching a brow as he looked back at the three assassins who stood with carefully neutral faces as they watched the argument. "He's reverted to the Irish. It's all bound to go downhill." Directing the room's mood toward the humor of Gareth's drunkenness drew smiles from the men. Dylan relaxed a bit.

"Feck off, would ye?"

Dylan crossed his arms and, shaking his head in mock severity, moved to the foot of the bed. "Any time ye want tae knock this *bowsie* oot, have at him." He didn't look at Kennedy, instead focusing on Gareth's face.

"Thas the stuff," Gareth slurred, his lids drooping and lips going slack.

Dropping his arms, Dylan rolled his shoulders, then stuck his hands in his pockets. Kennedy's heavy grunt snapped his head up.

She'd paled, a sickly gray wash making her appear corpselike. Muscles strained, and tendons in her neck stood out. Sweat both trailed down her temple and dotted her upper lip. She gritted her teeth. Lips were nothing more than a severe slash in a face gone taut. With apparent herculean effort, she yanked her hand off the syringe and jerked her chin up. She turned toward him with choppy, unnatural movements. Wide eyes stared at him, pupils blown. "Help. Me."

"Grab that syringe," Dylan bellowed, starting for her as the assassins drew their swords. Somewhere in his hind brain he heard someone chamber a round.

Aylish shoved her toward Dylan and went for the syringe hanging in the IV port.

Dylan caught her around the waist with one arm while wrapping the other under her arm and up her back. His fingers skid across sweat-slicked skin and into her hair as he bent her backward. Fear warred with fury in her eyes. He couldn't know who controlled which emotion. It didn't matter.

She arched under his touch, squeezing her eyes closed. "Please," she begged. "Bring me back."

He hauled her up and slammed the front of their bodies together. Her chilled skin gave him goose flesh. It didn't matter. He crushed his mouth to hers and struggled to ignore the way her lips moved—rubbery, like a bad impersonation of kisses remembered. Supporting her by the back of the head, he pulled his arm free and grasped her jaw. He dug his fingers into her skin and forced her mouth open. His tongue delved inside.

Ash. She tasted like ash. It was wrong. Infuriated, he traced her tongue then withdrew to nibble on her lips.

Breathing her in, he fought to coax the woman in his arms back to life. He wound his hand through her hair and gripped hard enough he knew it pulled. Then he yanked.

No response.

He stared her down. "Ye doona leave me, Kennedy." He shook her, but she didn't blink. "Respond, damn you!"

"Again," she breathed.

His lips met hers in an onslaught of desperation and rage. A whiff of vanilla tickled his nose, and he let go of her jaw. Reaching down, he clutched the back of one knee and hauled her leg up the outside of his thigh. The sheet fell away and he worked the frigid limb higher. Propping his thigh under her leg, he grabbed her near arm and hooked it around his neck. Never did he stop plundering her mouth, silently daring her to deny him.

Her tongue touched his, and he wanted to roar with satisfaction. Tightening his grip, he canted her head to better accommodate his mouth as he worked at hers—passion flavored with a fear chaser.

Her lips moved against his, unsure.

The movement, so minute at first, grew more insistent as he drove her. The more heat he poured into her, the more animated her responses became. And he drove her hard. His heartbeat pounded around deep-seated uneasiness. Fingernails dug into his neck, raking bare skin with agonizing slowness. Grabbing her leg again, he hauled it higher and shoved his thigh between hers. Blood flooded his groin. The head of his erection scraped across the leather's smooth waistband.

Oh, hell. He'd forgotten. He'd gone commando.

Her exhales were cold across his cheek, but her lips were warming. Then her leg twitched beneath his hand. Her foot dragged up the outside of his calf as she moved the leg higher and out of his grasp. She controlled the descent, reaching his hand and starting back up. When her knee reached his waist, she curled the leg around him and ground her sex against his thigh. A short mewl escaped her, the sound one of pure, unadulterated need, and he swallowed it down.

Greed made Dylan crave more, left him completely unwilling to settle for anything less.

Cupping her ass, he slid his thigh back and forth against her core. The heat seeping through that intimate connection made his shoulders bunch.

She fed the fingers of her hand into his hair. Her other arm she hooked around his neck to aid in hauling herself up his body.

He let go of her hair and cupped her other butt cheek, speeding her climb.

She fed from his mouth as if he was the only connection to life she had.

It thrilled him. He squeezed her ass and she wrapped her loose leg around his waist, locking her heels behind him.

Dylan got his feet under him and turned for the door, waving a hand absently in its direction. It opened with a thunderous bang.

If Kennedy noticed, she didn't give any indication.

He moved through the outer room, careening off furniture and repeating what should have been minor magick with the next door. Aether licked down his fingertips. It slipped from his control, twining around his legs before slithering away. A young voice yelled, "Snakes!" Somewhere in his consciousness he knew he'd let his magick go, that it had manifested as he'd thought of the fear slithering through his belly. His magick had created the snakes as a result. It came down to a choice between keeping Kennedy grounded or helping the blokes contain the reptiles.

Consider it crisis training, lads.

He didn't stop.

For all the years he'd lived next door to Gareth, he'd

never counted exactly how many steps lay between their rooms. He hadn't thought there'd be a need. Instead, he focused on keeping the worn carpet under his bare feet and not tripping over the sheet that trailed from Kennedy's shoulder.

Forced to seek out his door, he broke the kiss.

She tightened her legs around his waist, gripped handfuls of hair tight enough there was a razor's edge of pain to it. "Don't stop."

"I need to find—" That was all he got out before she squeezed her thighs; pushing up at the same time, she pulled his head back with a vicious yank. Then she dropped her lips to his.

Dylan stumbled to a stop, his fingers digging into her ass hard enough he knew she'd bruise. Damn if he could stop himself. She made love to his mouth, thrusting in and out with her tongue. He struggled to stay in control of the kiss. Then he found himself fighting to keep from undoing his laces and sliding into her wet heat in the unguarded hallway. His hips bucked forward at the thought. She slid slowly down his rock-hard abs to position herself over the ridge of his erection.

"Sweet gods." He spoke the words into her mouth when she began to gently ride him.

She'd gone from cold and almost catatonic to an inferno in his arms. Never had he imagined anyone capable of rousing such unquenchable desire in him. He shivered when she traced his bottom lip with the tip of her tongue.

Lurching forward, he flicked a hand in the general direction of his door and staggered toward the booming echo of its opening. They bounced off the door frame. Dylan slid a hand under the sheet, desperate to touch her.

Skin like silk. His rough hands moved over her, hungry, needing.

Wrapping an arm around Kennedy's waist, he tugged

at the sheet with the other. The knot let go with an almost inaudible whisper, the fabric slithering to the floor to pool at his feet. He kicked it away. Double doors to the bedroom beckoned, one left open from his rushed exit earlier. The promise of her lay on the other side of those doors and sparked memories of loving her—the tickle of her hair on the sensitive inside of his arm as she lay with him, waking to find wide blue eyes watching him, the smell of lavender and vanilla on his pillow, the taste of whiskey on her tongue. Backing that direction, his spine hit the closed door. It held. He rolled around it and stepped into his room. The smell of rain washed in through the open window. Thunder rolled in the distance. Unpredictable as his magick was, fueled by high emotion, he had the presence of mind to close the door and command the fire to light.

Thank the goddess I didn't get them backward.

The bed, still rumpled from their night together, beckoned—a willing host to their desire. Memory fed his need for her. Reality, though… That left him starved for her. She continued to burn in his arms, her body heat restored, her own passion burning him alive. He, whose element was aether, he, who'd always maintained control of his magicks, his people, his environment. But not her. Never her. The wild blaze inside her, both impulsive and unpredictable, called to him as strong as his element ever had.

They tumbled onto the bed. With a curse, he was forced to break the kiss in order to get his leathers undone. He pushed off the bed to shed them, and she followed him up, trailing kisses up his torso.

Her hand found him when his pants were only halfway down.

He sucked in a breath as she stroked his erection.

Using the tip of her tongue, she traced the cut of one pec and found his nipple.

The same breath hissed out in a rush, his hand winding

through her soft tangle of curls and encouraged her forward, pressed her harder into him. And when her free hand stroked feather-light across his hip, he groaned her name.

She moved deeper onto the bed, drawing him down with her.

Dylan paused. "Kennedy." Her name was both an invocation and a guarded plea. He needed to know the woman he was with in that moment was her and only her.

She cupped his jaw and traced his kiss-swollen bottom lip with the soft pad of her thumb. "Just Kennedy."

Closing his eyes, he issued the shortest gratitude ever before working his way up the front of her body with teasing nips and strategic caresses. He dominated her, ruling her mouth with a kiss that branded her, claimed her.

The metallic, copper tang said someone's lip had been nicked.

It gave neither of them pause.

A rumble of need rolled up from deep inside him. She lifted her hips and he eased into her, working back and forth with slow, controlled thrusts until he slid as far into her hot core as he could go. Hard-won control turned to dust when she began increasing the rhythm, driving their lovemaking with the same frenetic tenor she had the kiss. Fierce determination to see her through to her own release was the only thing that helped him hold out. The effort paid off when she fractured, coming apart in his arms.

With her body pulsing around him, he followed her into the depths of ultimate pleasure.

Time meant nothing to him as Dylan held her. Outside he could hear thunder crack, and through the window, sheets of rain obscured the cliffs as the storm's fury lashed out. Kennedy shivered in his arms, and he stroked her hair from her forehead before leaning down to kiss her softly. He worked the heavy comforter up and tucked

it around them. Turning toward her, he stretched his arm
out and encouraged her to lay her head on the pillow of
his biceps so he could better see her. Maybe not the most
comfortable thing but—

Sudden understanding dealt him a phantom blow that
stole his breath. What a fool he was to have ever thought
he was saving her when, from the very beginning, it had
been the other way around. She'd broken through his defenses in days, filled up a life he'd long ago stopped living, breathed life into the walking shadow he'd become.
There would be no slaking his lust and moving on. Not
from her. Never from her.

The rise and fall of her chest grew slower. She buried
her face in the hollow of his shoulder, and his arms slid
around her as he shifted to his side, holding her close. A
fleeting thought whispered through his mind and left him
staring out the window in abject horror. *In her, I'm home.*

Since Danu had first come to him nearly three hundred
years earlier and told him to find his truth, he'd denied
the possibility. No longer. Kennedy *was* his truth. She
was what he was supposed to find. What the goddess had
never told him, though, was how to hold on to the truth
once found.

Because in less than a week, he had to kill her.

Beneath her cheek, Dylan's arm stiffened. Kennedy
snuggled closer, unwilling to let go of the quiet moment.
He'd just have to deal.

She traced a fingertip across the ridges, planes and valleys of his chest. *Such a hard man in so many ways.* Life
hadn't been kind to him, casting him as moldable clay only
to require he become immovable as granite. His nipples
peaked under the teasing of her finger. Leaning forward,
her lips gravitated to the hollow of his throat. A soft kiss.

His skin radiated heat and sweat and musk with undertones of smoke and linen.

He moved away, gently removing the arm from under her head before sitting up. Knees bent, he propped his arms across them, his back curved forward. Firelight danced across his bare skin, casting deep lines and hollows in shadow.

Kennedy sat up and reached out, tucking the waterfall of his thick hair behind one ear.

He laid a cheek against his forearms and looked at her, face impassive.

She chanced a small smile. When he only continued to stare, the small gesture quickly faded. "What's wrong?"

Dark brows drew down in a scowl. He looked away.

Oh shit oh shit oh shit. "I'm sorry." She scooted toward the edge of the bed. "I didn't mean to…" The words vibrated with emotion. "Gareth." His name was squeezed from her throat by the tight fingers of remorse. "I didn't hurt him. I stopped." She looked back when he didn't answer. "Tell me I didn't hurt him, that you forgive me for using you."

He glanced at her sharply. "Pardon?"

Limbs shaking, she started to turn away from him. "If you'll let me borrow a robe, I'll find your father and ask him to, I don't know, chain me somewhere safe until…" The words wouldn't come.

An arm whipped around her and bore her back to the mattress.

He loomed over her, trapped her with his body and lowered his face until their noses were inches apart. Anger and sorrow flashed across his face like a strobe. "I'll be damned if I'll allow anyone else to finish this." Surprise entered the strobe sequence. He'd clearly not meant to say it, likely didn't mean it the way it sounded.

Understanding delivered the proverbial kill shot to her

heart. She was a job he'd see through to the end. Any emotional connection would be overruled by obligation. It wasn't the same for her, though. When she'd turned to him in that room, when she'd known she was about to go under, she'd sought him out. Only him. He'd been all she could see, all she could hear, all she had wanted. His strong arms promised a safe haven if she could just get to them. And she had. In his embrace, she'd found her way back. He had anchored her.

Not once had she considered how he felt about that. When they ended up in bed, she'd followed ageless instinct and taken him into her, defied the cold dark with the heat of life in its most vital and irrefutable form. She'd simply done what felt right at the time.

Face it. All *of him feels right.*

She looked away and closed her eyes. Rage-tinged sorrow made some part of her want to lash out, to cause him pain. She'd bleed emotionally while he bled literally. But no matter how satisfying it sounded, she couldn't intentionally hurt him.

His warm hand closed around her jaw before she worked up the nerve to act out. Turning her face back to him, he said, "Open yer eyes."

She hesitated. *Does he really think you need the visual to go with this conversation?*

He squeezed her jaw lightly. "Kennedy." The warning in his voice was clear.

She didn't give a shit. He let go of her chin, and her inner self sagged. Relief? No. More like shallow grief. If losing his touch was hard, how was she going to deal with losing him? Her chest ached all the way through to her spine. It was as if someone had wrapped a six-inch-wide band of steel around her and was slowly tightening it, cranking down on the fastener with brutal glee. Breathing changed to soft panting as she focused on getting that band to relax.

"Open yer eyes." Dylan sighed, his breath a hot wash across her face. "Please."

She'd wait him out. All she had to do was lie there. He'd either lose interest and move away or she'd get irritated enough to make him move. An invisible fingertip traced across her brow, down her temple and down the side of her neck. Instinct screamed at her to move into his touch, to reciprocate. A well-developed sense of self-preservation demanded she lie still.

The bed shifted a bit. Warm lips brushed her eyelids, the tip of her nose, each corner of her mouth. She rested her palm against her stomach and pressed. Hard. That evil bastard "hope" reared its damnable head, and she tried like hell to suppress it.

"Look at me." His words caressed her with intimate familiarity.

Hope escaped her, flaring brightly as if to mock her best efforts. "I will not be denied," its light said.

Biting her bottom lip, Kennedy opened her eyes and blinked a couple of times. Her gaze roamed over his face, searching for any hint of deception, but there was none. He watched her assessment, carefully neutral in every aspect. Except his touch. That would leave an indelible mark.

Dylan shifted to lie on his side, head propped in one hand. Skimming his fingertips across her shoulder and down her arm, he followed the outline of her hand before lazily moving up and down her forearm. "Yer no' a burden," he said softly.

The longing to believe him drilled through her, pressing and twisting and creating friction between the logical and illogical thoughts crowding her mind. "How can I not be? I mean, look, I'm not stupid. This is the second time I nearly cost Gareth his life because I couldn't stop what I've become. And you? You've been ordered to stick close to me, but you shouldn't have to—" she waggled a hand "—give up your body to keep my personal Doomsday parasite at bay." She cleared her throat and looked away. "It's not fair to you."

His fingers stilled. His brogue disappeared under the slow precision of each word when he spoke. "You're not suggesting I'm playing whore, surely."

She rubbed at her breastbone. "I don't know what I'm suggesting."

"Let me be very clear seeing as this is the second time you've made the allegation. I don't whore for anyone—not elevated gods, not damned goddesses and not the Order. The only reason you're in my bed is because I want you here and you, I assume, want to be here. If either of those two factors change, we'll make other arrangements."

"I have only seven days left, Dylan. There isn't enough time to burn through even a short affair." She licked her lips and rubbed a damp palm against her bare hip. *There needed to be a cosmic rule—hard conversations should never be held naked.*

His jaw tightened as he stared at her.

She reached out, scraping a nail along scruffy stubble, then let her attention drift back to eyes that burned with intelligence.

"We'll deal with the time frame."

"Deal?" She couldn't stop the short, bitter laugh that escaped. "There's nothing to deal *with*. I've played out the hand I was handed, and it looks like the house wins."

"You haven't played all your cards until your last breath's drawn. And clearly you don't know shit about poker, because for what it's worth—" he stared at her, eyes narrowing slightly "—I haven't played *my* cards. Considering I'm the house, it's a little early to be calling the hand."

"Don't do this," she whispered, looking up and blinking furiously.

"Do what?"

"Feed the little bit of hope I've managed to cling to. It's not fair."

"I don't have the time or inclination for niceties. If I tell you something, Kennedy, it's truth. Hard or not."

"Yeah, well, I don't have time. Seems luck always favors the house." A face flashed through her mind, ripping at her like a dull knife against thick skin. "I have a request. A favor, actually." When he didn't say anything, she forged ahead. "I'd like to bring Ethan over."

"Ethan." He sneered. "And why would ye want tae see that *bastún*?" And just like that, the brogue was back.

She pushed at his shoulder, and he let himself fall to the mattress. Sitting up made the covers shift. Cold air brushed against what had been shared warmth. The tumbled mass of her hair hung past the middle of her back and tickled bare skin. Sweeping the hair around her shoulder, she tried to coax it into submission, separating tangled curls with nimble fingers. "I want to see Ethan one last time before this is over." Her voice had gone thick and low. "Please."

The mattress shifted. Dylan's arm wrapped around her shoulders and pulled her against his chest.

She went, turning toward him and accepting the comfort of his arms. Her mind screamed at her to keep her distance, to protect herself from reality's looming inevitability. It didn't matter. None of this mattered except the moment at hand because she had no guarantee that the next tic of the second hand wouldn't be the one to see her pulled under, unable to return. She gave in to the questioning pressure he'd settled beneath her chin and tilted her face up. Dylan kissed her with a tenderness that made her toes curl.

Leaning back, he gave a curt nod. "I'll send for him."

"How soon?"

"I can go now." He started to move away.

She threw herself at him and knocked him back to the bed.

He lay there, dark hair spread across the pillowcase. A faint sheen of sweat in the valley between his pecs shimmered in the variable light. Above impossibly green eyes, one brow rose with lazy insolence. "What's this about? I thought you wanted Ethan."

"I want…" *I want you, you fool.* "I do. I just… In a minute. You don't need to go right this second."

"No? If you want him here in the morning then I do, in fact, have to go right this second."

Her eyes were so wide they watered in the dry air. "Don't leave me."

He cocked his head to the side. Then that jaunty brow fell and seriousness overtook the sardonic look he'd affected. "You think Caillea—"

"Don't!" The shouted command stopped him before he'd said the goddess's name. Kennedy knew Cailleach listened, knew she waited for the opportunity to rise. "Don't say her name."

"She's close, then." A statement, not a question.

He didn't even ask how she knew, what had changed that she *would* know now and not before. It was a good thing, because she didn't have any answers. So she nodded and said the only thing she could. "Yeah. Closer than she's ever been, I think." Simple truth. Somehow Kennedy knew the bitch had crossed another barrier with that last rising, had drawn one step closer to getting what she wanted.

They had to come up with a plan. Kennedy couldn't be alone. Not anymore. Without Dylan, she'd have killed Gareth earlier. Possessed or not, the responsibility would have ridden her to her grave, been the last thought she'd ever had. A boom of thunder punctuated the sentiment.

Without comment or acknowledgment, Dylan rolled out from under the hand she'd held him down with and headed for the living area.

"Dylan?" She slid out of bed and moved toward him when he turned. "Don't leave me." Desperation-tinged pleas, paired with her fighting not to look at his exposed junk, constituted a new low for her.

"I'm no leaving you, *a stór*." He spoke softly. "I'll get the phone and bring it in here."

She glanced at his discarded pants. "You don't have a cell?"

"I do." He shrugged one shoulder. "I intended to page the Elder's secretary. He'd hear the call if not in his office and call me back. He'll make the arrangements to fetch Ethan. The internal system is more likely to work in this weather than a cell. Service is a bit spotty along the coast as is. The storm likely took the local tower out."

"Oh." The one-word answer seemed small. Her gaze fell to the floor, and she chewed her bottom lip.

Dylan's feet moved into her line of sight. "I'll be right back."

She nodded quickly. "Sure."

"Look at me, Kennedy."

Her eyes met his, and an understanding settled into the space between them. He'd be back. She'd be here. And the bitch working to hijack her body would be waiting.

Chapter 14

Dylan absently swiped a thumb across his smartphone's screen and disconnected the call before tossing the phone onto his nightstand. His mind returned to the woman at his side before the phone stopped spinning where it had landed. Ethan didn't know it yet, but arrangements were in the works to get him on the next available flight out of Atlanta, escorted by one of Dylan's men. The Order's jet would fly the duo from wherever they landed in Ireland to the local airport. A driver would see them safely arrived and Ethan delivered to Kennedy no later than noon tomorrow.

Knowing she'd asked for the man curdled the contents of Dylan's stomach. He wanted her to need *him* with that same desperation. She didn't, though. Chances were she still saw him as untrustworthy, and didn't that just gall the shit out of him? The one woman he'd brought into his personal space, been as vulnerable as he'd ever allowed himself to be, and she didn't trust him. Not only that, he'd made arrangements to deliver up to her the one man she *did* trust.

Dylan knew he didn't deserve her and had been lying to himself to think he did. His life wasn't conducive to a relationship, and he wasn't capable of love. No doubt he wanted her, but want and love were ages apart.

History marched over him. Mental images of the worst assignments he'd carried out dropped in his lap like high-definition reminders of the remorseless violence he was capable of carrying out. To expose her to the darkness in him, to have her unblemished skin forever caressed with hands drenched in the blood of his obligation, was blasphemy. Gods preserve him, he'd been a fool to ever think otherwise.

Dylan glanced over to find her watching him with wide eyes. "Ethan should be here in time for lunch tomorrow."

The tremulous smile she rewarded him with didn't do much to reassure him or affirm his decision in bringing the warlock to the Nest. Ethan knew enough about the assassins to pose a threat of sorts, and would have to be dealt with after... Tension flooded him, locking his muscles up with a suddenness that made his bones feel too large for his frame. The soft weight of Kennedy's hand on his arm made him force himself to face her. He watched her through narrowed eyes, unsure what might come next.

"Thank you." She moved to her knees and leaned forward, pressing her lips against his.

The touch was so soft he would have believed he was imagining it if he hadn't continued to watch her.

Dylan grasped the back of her head, angling her mouth to deepen the kiss. Her pliant lips followed without hesitation. Lowering her to the bed, he palmed her bare breast and thrilled at the way the nipple beaded under his touch. Her response to him was so organic. There was no denying they were good together in bed, but there was no way to give her more than that. The want she had for him wasn't deep enough, and he didn't know how to make it more, knew it wouldn't be honorable to try.

Dylan rolled onto his back and dropped an arm over his face. There had to be a way out of this, a way to change their fates. How, he didn't know, but he'd start searching immediately. Maybe the Elders knew something more about the goddess's binding to the Shadow Realm. He would look for an avenue no one had explored. Whatever the answer, wherever it hid, he'd find it because Kennedy's end fate was unjust. He couldn't see it through. The consequences would be so severe there'd be no surviving them.

A soft knock on the door made her gasp and scramble for the bulky comforter, hauling it up by the fistful.

"Come," Dylan called out as he propped pillows behind his head and shoulders and leaned against the headboard.

Aylish stepped into the room.

Dylan knew he needed his father's help to get into the Elders' private library. There was no way to get into that veritable vault of information without Aylish's blessing… or without using his magick against the Order and its covenants. But nowhere else could he hope to find a history of the goddess's strengths and weaknesses as well as the Order's role in her banishment to the Shadow Realm.

His eye twitched.

Aylish's gaze locked on Kennedy. "I wanted to let you know Gareth is quite well." He closed the door behind him. "We roused Angus and he stood watch for the first hour. Seems you stopped Caill—"

"No!" Dylan and Kennedy shouted at the same time.

Aylish stepped back, leaned against the wall and crossed his arms over his chest. "I see. She will become more powerful the closer we get to the full moon. The harder she is to contain, the more dangerous the situation becomes." He darted a knowing glance at Dylan before returning his attention to Kennedy. "Are you experiencing any other changes? Visions perhaps?"

"Visions?" Kennedy seemed to think that over, then paled.

Dylan grabbed her arm. "What is it, *mo síorghrá*?" And just like that, with nothing more than those two Gaelic words, he found himself laid bare in front of the one man who could see right through him.

"Fuck." Dylan threw the covers back and stalked around the bed. Grabbing his leathers, he yanked them on before retrieving Kennedy's clothes from the closet. She gasped when he tossed them on the bed and said, "Get dressed."

Hurt warred with anger in eyes as dark blue as new denim. She snatched her shirt from atop the small pile of clothes.

"Wait outside." Dylan issued the sharp command without looking at Aylish.

The click of the door had hardly sounded before he hauled Kennedy up to face him.

She barely kept from shouting when she said, "I don't appreciate you treating me like an inconvenient bed partner just because you've got an audience. You promised to help, yet the first time you encounter the man I likely most need help from, you go all Neanderthal on me. You're nothing more than pretty words and empty promises, Dylan. Let me go." She spoke through gritted teeth, her eyes flashing in the firelight.

"I doona think so."

Kennedy struggled.

Better this way. Prove you're the man her beloved Ethan accused you of being. He pinned her wrists behind her back and held them there with one hand. Cupping the back of her head, he crushed his mouth to hers. Biting nips and scorching kisses that should have been her undoing failed to move her, and he struggled to stay in control of the moment. Elemental magick burned beneath his skin. It spread out from his torso to lick down his arms and legs, up his neck and across his skull. No doubt he would have lit up the room had he allowed himself to blaze unchecked. Outside the wind howled and the squalor of the storm deteriorated. It had been ages since he'd been so on edge.

The idea of striding away from her after that fatal slip in his native tongue—with his pride placated and balance restored—disappeared under an onslaught of unfamiliar emotions. He wrenched his head to the side, breathing hard. "Doona do this tae me." His quiet words were nearly lost in the wind's screams outside the window.

"Do what to you?"

Coming back to her, he lowered his face and rubbed his nose along her neck. Vanilla and lavender, ever faint, never far, called him home. He kissed her reddened lips softly in wordless atonement. "Ye need tae mind me, Kennedy."

"Let me go. I don't like bullies and I don't take orders."

"Aye, in this ye'll obey me." He nipped her earlobe and she tried to pull away. His fingers flexed in her hair, and her sharp inhale whistled past his ear. "Ye're no' tae go anywhere without me. Understand?"

"And where, exactly, would I go?"

Each word she snapped out was a lick to his groin. His cock stirred. "Anywhere."

"Why?" she demanded.

Good question. "If she rises again, I'll no' have any other near ye. I can keep ye safe. Ye've use o' me body, but no others, aye?" He waited as she undoubtedly sorted through her possible responses. What she finally settled on made him nearly choke on surprised laughter.

"You're *not* keeping me company in the bathroom." Heat radiated from her cheeks and warmed his ear.

"The loo's ye're one privacy, though I'll wait outside the door. But the bathroom itself?" He leaned back and waited for her to meet his gaze. "No' off-limits. If ye want tae shower, ye'll wait for me." Leaning forward, he spoke against her lips. "Someone's got tae wash that lush backside."

She shivered. "Damn you, Dylan."

"Even if ye meant it, *a stór*, ye're centuries too late. I was damned long ago." He closed the paper-thin distance between them and kissed her slowly, teasing the seam of her lips with his tongue.

Gradually, she opened to him and, between heartbeats, came alive in his arms.

Their tongues danced over each other, touching, tasting, savoring. He kept the pace slow despite her frustrated mewls. She tried to push him higher, nibbling his bottom lip and working to get her hands free. The hard peaks of her nipples dragged across his chest every time he forgot himself and relaxed into her. As a reminder, they were effective. He'd tighten his grip and regain control and receive another sound of protest for his efforts.

He smiled against her, earning a huff of frustration. "I've tae go tae the Elder. No doubt he's here for more than a status update." It likely had something to do with Cailleach rising. Of course, it could just as well be about Dylan's established timetable—the very one the Council had set for Kennedy's execution. Should that be the case, the Elder and his bloody Council could feck off. He'd buy whatever time he could with Kennedy and use whatever currency the Council would accept or understand, be it logic or violence.

She leaned back. "Why don't you call Aylish *Dad*, Dylan?"

"He's never been a da. Only a father in that he impregnated my ma, but that's as far as it's ever gone between us." When she would have pressed, he quickly kissed her. "Enough. Get dressed so we can see why he's here."

"You were quick to leave a minute ago," she muttered.

"And more the fool was I."

She sat on the bed when he let her go. After pulling her shirt over her head, she grabbed her underwear and grinned. "Never thought I'd be so glad to see these."

"Never thought I'd be so remiss to return them to you." A smile tugged at the corner of his lips.

"Funny guy." Tossing them aside, she pulled her sweats

on. At his raised brows, she shrugged. "Seems fair that if you have underwear but go without, I can do the same."

The smile that had threatened broke free. "Tickles your fancy, does it?"

"Hey. Just because I'm a woman doesn't mean I spend my free time knitting and thinking pure thoughts."

"And thank the gods for that." Reaching out, he took her hand and fumbled again with lacing their fingers together.

With that same subtle shift, she fit their hands together as he led her out of the room.

Aylish stood in the living room watching the storm. He didn't turn when they entered, irritating Dylan. No doubt that's why his father did it. And though the behavior wasn't out of the ordinary between them, the snub still pissed him off.

"Show a little courtesy, if not for me then for the woman." Keeping Kennedy's hand in his, he sank to the sofa. A gentle tug encouraged her to follow him down, though she sat too far away. No need for propriety after his father had seen them in bed—twice—and heard Dylan refer to her as *mo síorghrá*, his eternal love. Privacy on the matter would never be regained.

Aylish tossed another brick of peat on the fire before taking his seat on the opposite sofa. His gaze was far too shrewd for comfort.

When Dylan gave a finite shake of his head, he was relieved to see Aylish dip his chin a fraction. No doubt the old man would demand a conversation regarding Dylan's epic failure in getting personal with his target, but this was neither the time nor place. Let the Elder censure him. Fuck, let the entire Elder Council take disciplinary action after the full moon. Until that time, he needed Aylish's help, which meant Dylan would have to behave civilly.

Contrary to general consensus, he did in fact know the definition of that word—civil.

Settling back, he drew Kennedy close to his side and draped an arm over her shoulders. "Thanks for staying while we sorted out a minor issue. I assume you're here to discuss the, ah, time factor." Beneath his arm, Kennedy stiffened. Never looking away from his father, Dylan ran a hand under her hair and gently massaged her neck. "Easy. We'll sort this out."

"Okay," she whispered.

He realized that, in that moment, she'd placed her faith in him—the same blind faith she seemed to have in Ethan and the one thing he'd been craving less than thirty minutes ago.

He prayed her faith wasn't misplaced.

Kennedy tried to relax under Dylan's touch. It was impossible. Each man's body language sang with tension, but the tunes were entirely different. Aylish watched them like he'd discovered a new species of animal under his roof while a fine vibration ran through Dylan, primal and violent. She laid her hand on his thigh, and the muscles twitched in protest. Yet when she tried to move back, he covered her hand with his and pressed down.

Fighting to slow her heartbeat and put her crisis training to use, she focused on Aylish. What she meant to say and what came out of her mouth were two different things. "I don't want to die."

Dylan went preternaturally still. It was like he stopped living for the count of five and then came back to himself. "Ye'll no' be dyin'."

"Brogue's awfully thick," she observed. "Is that because you're convinced you're going to stop this and change my fate, or is it because you're scared to tell me you can't?"

He finally looked at her. She kind of wished he hadn't.

A fine muscle under his eye took up a sporadic tic, and the green of his eyes glowed. "You doubt me?"

No. Yes. No. "I'm scared." She clutched his hand tighter and looked back to Aylish. "Is there anything I can do? Anything that stands a chance, even remotely, of stopping this?"

His chin lifted a fraction and, though she'd addressed him, he never took his eyes off his son. He was quiet for so long, she was pretty sure she wouldn't get an answer.

If he wouldn't help her, if Dylan couldn't deliver, she'd have to find a way to end this before she could hurt anyone else. Ethan was coming in tomorrow. Maybe he'd suggest the best way for her to choose her own time to bow out instead of waiting around to meet an excruciating end by Dylan's blessed sword. She couldn't stand there and let him do it. The emotional costs were too high with so much between them now. If he had to take her out, she didn't want her death to be the last thing he remembered of her. There was also the very real probability she'd run or, if the Cowlick took the controls, she'd end up killing someone.

Aylish's low, ageless voice cut through her building panic. "We need to meet with the Elder Council. It will be best to apprise them of my intentions." He stood.

She shot to her feet, as well. "That doesn't tell me anything. Am I following you like a sheep to slaughter, or are you speaking Druidic code for 'I'll help you'?"

A soft smile brought out deep lines around his mouth. "Come."

"Not an answer." No doubt her chin jutted out. Whatever. She'd never look back, whether in a few days or a few years, and accuse herself of having been too stupid to live during a crisis.

"We'll go to the Observatory," Aylish told Dylan. I intend to call the Council together. Beyond that, I don't care to disclose my intentions. You have an eavesdropper who would benefit far too much from the information she'd potentially overhear. As it seems she's close to the surface of your consciousness, I must take precautions for those under my protection." He looked at Dylan. "Know that I would spare you this."

Kennedy cocked her head to the side, considering the Elder. "So why try now and not before?"

"You matter." Aylish's answer was fast and decisive. He glanced at Dylan, and she watched as private understanding passed between them.

"And I didn't matter before?" She looked between the two men, moving to regain Aylish's attention. "I had a life, friends, a future, hope. The Elder Council thought to steal that from me without any more consideration than a hungry snake might offer a mouse. I don't care if the reasons were considered just. You profess to respect life, to be observers of the natural order, but you sure as hell didn't respect mine when you chose to intervene." A stretching sensation deep inside made her step back, and she hugged herself tight. Anger was definitely something the goddess thrived on.

"No one could have predicted the impact you'd have on—" Aylish glanced at Dylan and then back to her "—aspects of the Order. You matter, Kennedy."

She closed her eyes for a moment as a sharp pain pulsed at the base of her skull. When it passed, she squinted at Aylish. "Thank you."

Aylish nodded. "You're welcome. I'd like you both to come with me for this meeting. Kennedy, you'll have to step out for the details, but the Council will do well to see that you and our Assassin are united in this."

She worried her bottom lip for a moment. "You're not concerned she'll rise? Because if she does—"

"We'll handle it." Dylan's firm answer pulled her

around to face him, the draw as strong as Earth's gravitational pull on the moon.

She stared into grave green eyes. "Are you okay with the Council seeing us? I mean, I'm pretty sure it's not a secret that we, uh…"

He opened and closed his mouth in a couple of false starts before he simply said, "It's fine."

"Okay, then." Not the rousing answer she'd hoped for, but it would have to do. Kennedy rolled her head back and forth and focused on slowing her heartbeat. The pressure in her belly ebbed. There wasn't some overwhelming sense of relief but rather this gut-wrenching knowledge the goddess had simply settled back to wait. For what, she didn't know, but one thing was certain.

If Cailleach wanted it, it couldn't be good.

Kennedy moved down the hall with the men. They were all silent save for the creak of leather. Every now and again a faint clink of metal would remind her they were armed to the teeth. Somehow, that made the surreal processional terrifyingly credible.

Dylan had insisted on getting her another pair of boots. This pair fit a little better than those Gareth had lifted for her, though they were still large enough they flopped on her feet. Dylan also had the same delivery guy drop off a pair of socks and a heavy sweater.

He'd also taken the opportunity to change clothes and weapon up. Dressed in black leather pants and boots, he wore a black linen shirt with obsidian buttons and had pulled his hair back in a low, formal queue. A black leather belt served as a holster for two short daggers on his left side and a 9 mm handgun with two spare clips on his right. Across his back was a dark scabbard that held a sword with a decorative cross-guard and leather-wrapped hilt. Unable to stop herself, she'd gaped at him. His answer had been a one-shouldered shrug.

Dylan's hand now rested on her lower back, a constant and reassuring connection. He seemed to know every time she considered turning around because he would exert a little more pressure and keep her from making a break for it. Not once did he say anything that would have given her away as a coward, though.

Her mind wandered as they started down the stairs. The entire Council would meet them at whatever the Observatory was. She had no idea who, what or how many comprised the Council. *What if they voted against the idea of looking for an alternative to my death? What if they rebelled and ousted Aylish from power? Could someone shout "Off with her head!" and force Dylan to see this matter put to an end tonight?* Every muffled step forward found her dreaming up more catastrophic possibilities until nausea made her mouth water profusely. She started to speak and had to clear her throat, the sound swallowed by the vast open space of the foyer. "Dylan?"

His hand snaked around her waist and pulled her to his side, slowing their pace and letting Aylish gain some distance. Dylan kept them moving but dipped his head toward her. "Never admit to fear until you've first identified the reason for it and, second, mastered it."

Kennedy shot him a quick glance. "How did you know?"

"You started twisting your fingers together, and the muscles of your lower back tensed enough for me to notice despite the sweater's bulk." He spared her a quick glance. "Now isn't the time to show weakness, *a stór*. Understand?"

As far as warnings went, it was subtle but clear. She nodded. "What does *a stór* mean?"

"Term of endearment," Dylan said, gaze straight ahead.

Applying more pressure to her back, he urged her forward. "We need to round that next corner with him."

She lengthened her stride, barely registering the impact of each step as her mind raced over possibilities. It took a mental slap to knock her thoughts off the proverbial hamster wheel. *Get it together, Jefferson. You worked with trauma surgeons. Those guys had egos large enough they had to buy companion tickets for solo air travel. None of them respected you at your first meeting. Not one of them could say that when you left trauma medicine, though. You* survived *long before you* thrived. *Time to do it again.*

Catching up to Aylish, Dylan moved to his father's right side and placed her between them. She stayed in step with both men as they rounded the corner in a move so smooth it could have been choreographed. The three of them matched strides as they approached a pair of enormous arched wooden doors. Kayden and Niall, both fully armed, stood at rest. Their eyes fixed on Dylan, unwavering.

Had she not been so hyperaware of her escorts, she would have missed the slight movement of Dylan's left hand. The double doors swung open without protest.

Magick. How long would it be before that wasn't strange anymore?

Here was hoping she lived long enough to find out.

The doors closed behind them with a muffled *whump*. Kennedy jumped. A quick look around the room revealed only one other point of exit—a smaller wood-and-iron door with an elaborate design carved into its scarred face. Dylan's final assassin, Rowan, stood in front of it. His hands rested one over the other atop the pommel of the largest sword she'd ever seen, its tip balanced on the stone floor. Rowan's dark brown hair had been pulled back, and eyes of palest arctic blue were all the more surreal for their bold exposure. His attention became hyper-focused on Dylan and stayed there, just as both Kayden's and Niall's had.

The Council looked her over with undisguised derision and open accusations in their eyes. Kennedy looked away, taking the room in as she gathered her wits. Bookcases had been built to follow the wall's wide curve. Matching worktables and shelves separated each case. They held various assortments of jars and boxes of miscellany she couldn't identify, but the smell of both fresh and dried herbs was pungent. A stained-glass window dominated the wall across from the main doors and emphasized the size of the room. The glasswork depicted a large stone circle beneath a full moon and starlit sky, the dark glass at the top fading to a faint blue before abruptly switching to green where the ground began. Runes had been worked into the window's stone casing.

Above the windows was a platform with railing that circled the entire room. Four professional-looking telescopes peered through windows with sashes that would slide down to provide an uninterrupted view of the night sky. It felt as if the windows were situated to align with the four points of the compass, but she was so turned around she couldn't be sure.

A flash of lightning lit the room. Kennedy looked up and couldn't stifle her gasp. An enormous stained-glass dome created the majority of the roof. Dragons soared through the light blue background, each one done in jewel tones that made her want to run her fingers over their skin—scales?—and trace the fine detail of their wings. Lightning streaked across the sky again and the glass-work shimmered, creating the illusion the dragons moved.

Someone cleared his throat, a deep bass rumble in a room gone quiet. Kennedy squared her shoulders and turned her attention to the Elder Council. Dressed in everything from tunics and pants to linen shirts and fine trousers, seven men assessed her with varying degrees of hostility. She'd never met a single one of them, so their undisguised aggression galled. They sat around a circular table in chairs right out of the Middle Ages. Three chairs were unoccupied. The one farthest from the door that faced her had arms and a higher back while the other two were made of a wood so dark it was almost black, their seats a dark red velvet.

Candles of varying heights filled a shallow metal tray inset in the table's center. None burned, save one. A thick black candle, somewhere around four feet tall, towered over the others. Symbols had been carved into its exterior. The wick burned below the rim, and the internal glow illuminated the carvings in dark gray. Without warning, the flame would shoot well above the candle's upper edge. Those random flares gave the candle a sentient, malicious air.

If someone calls for the sacrificial goat, I'm so out of here.

The power sputtered. Lights flickered and cast the room in shadow before flaring back to life.

Faced with the reality of the Council's open animosity, Kennedy wanted nothing more than to go back to the comparative safety of Dylan's room. Aylish chose that moment to move toward the table. Dylan followed a few steps behind. She wasn't sure who to stay close to or if she should just stand there. Dylan pulled out one of the dark chairs. Looking at the seat and back to her, he gave a small jerk of his chin.

Her feet moved forward of their own volition, her gaze never leaving his. He looked so out of place standing there in leather pants that fit like a second skin, a variety of weapons at his fingertips—weapons that labeled him a mobile executioner—all while those seven Councilmen affected an air of personal refinement and superiority. Dylan, and probably Aylish, were the only honest men among them. They didn't pretend to be anything other than what they were.

That hard truth turned out to be the single most powerful reason why she trusted Dylan. Why it had taken so long, why she'd withheld the core of her faith in him until now, she couldn't remember—not with him watching her with that heavy-lidded stare. She knew that look. It said he was imagining her without her underwear...and other things.

Kennedy looked away and started to lower herself to the chair he had pulled out. As she began to sit down, the truth struck her. Her legs gave out, and she dropped onto her seat. Her stomach didn't acknowledge the abrupt stop but continued the free fall even as he scooted her forward to the table's edge.

She'd been trying to keep from looking too closely at what Dylan was coming to mean to her. Not in such a fundamental way in such a public forum. But rarely did a heart get to choose when and where its revelations occurred. For her? The revelations were apparently here and now.

Kennedy simply hadn't wanted to acknowledge the truth because to truly care for her assigned executioner smacked of genuine insanity. But the truth couldn't be denied. He meant so much to her, somehow represented both the beginning and the end, the worst of who she was as well as the best. It was so confusing, so difficult and so amazing, the way he made her feel. She wasn't entirely ready to put it all together, though, and look at the pieces as a whole.

What good could come of it?

Chapter 15

Dylan wasn't sure what had happened, but something had knocked Kennedy for a loop. She'd dropped into her chair like a stone, her typical grace abandoning her, limbs flopping loosely, eyes wide but glazed. It had concerned him enough he'd drawn on the aether to silently check her over for magicks, dark *or* light. It wouldn't have surprised him to discover that one of the Elders had struck out at her, but he'd found nothing.

He took his seat beside her, his gaze on his father. Dylan nodded and settled back to wait. If he'd interpreted his father's earlier cryptic conversation, this was going to get interesting. Fast.

Aylish stood and looked over the group.

Dylan pulled his hands from the tabletop and slid them along his thighs. His palms were slick. Anxiety crept up his spine with tiny, biting steps, sweat blossoming in its wake. His shirt stuck to his back. The scabbard he wore irritated him, and he tugged at the strap in an effort to move it enough so he could breathe easier. It didn't help.

Aylish pinned him with a hard stare and he stilled. Gods preserve him, he'd been *fidgeting*. He, who was known for being able to sit for hours on end while bugs and snakes and such moved all around and over him without so much as twitching, couldn't sit still. Digging his fingers into his thighs, he forced himself to settle.

Not once did Kennedy look his way.

His father finally spoke, his voice low and fierce as it swept through the room. "I will warn you once that you are not to use the parasitic goddess's name within this woman's hearing." He glanced around the table. When no one balked, he continued. "I called you here tonight in order to introduce you to Kennedy Jefferson. She's the host we sought. She is also the Assassin's *céile sa todhchaí*."

Every Councilman sucked in a breath.

Dylan had been staring at the tallest candle and contemplating Kennedy's strange behavior when his father's announcement penetrated his thoughts. His eyes widened and slowly lifted to meet the Elder's stare. Shock made Dylan's thoughts dull and slow. He was peripherally aware that everyone stared at him with similar looks of surprise. Even stoic Rowan was unable to keep his expression neutral.

Kennedy looked at Dylan, her brows drawn together and a small frown pulling at her lips. "What did Aylish just call me?"

Dylan swallowed hard. *What the hell am I supposed to say to her? Not to worry. My father just declared you my chosen bride for the Council's approval as is customary when the Assassin chooses to marry. Oh, by the way, do you want to get married?* The last thought stole his ability to speak. Married. Him. But he couldn't deny it in front of the Council in case this was part of Aylish's plan. Nor could he answer her honestly. She'd likely slap him, and that wouldn't win her any admirers at this table. He'd also be obligated to discipline her.

Pleading that the gods might intervene and spare him having to answer her, Dylan took his time as he swiveled to face her. "The Elder invoked Old World custom. We'll discuss it later." He pressed his foot against hers.

Kennedy's eyes widened before she nodded, folded her hands in her lap and shifted back to face Aylish.

"We'll ask that you step outside the room and stay with

the guards until this meeting is concluded. Instruct Kayden and Niall to retrieve the Assassin should his presence be required." Aylish smiled at her mischievously, and Dylan fought his own grin when she blushed.

Dylan rose, pulled her chair back and offered Kennedy his hand. She hesitated but took it, rising with the grace that had abandoned her minutes before. Clearly, whatever had troubled her as she took her seat was past. He'd still have to remember to ask her about it, though. At this point, the smallest things could prove relevant.

Dylan waved the doors open and she passed through them without a backward glance. Damn but her confidence, even if fabricated, was sexy. He shut the doors with a little more force than necessary and reclaimed his seat. A subtle creaking and shifting had him looking from one face to another, finally stopping on Aylish. "No well-wishes for the groom? Or are you already playing a dirge for the bonnie bride?"

His father's lips thinned. "We'll leave the toasts for another time. The purpose of this meeting was to make the announcement and to advise you that we will begin this afternoon to look for an alternative solution to Dagda's command that we kill the host."

The room erupted in denials and arguments, voices rising one over another until the seven Elders were out of their chairs and shouting at Aylish. The Elder didn't respond, but stared at Dylan with a look of open expectation.

Apparently, he was supposed to do something. Rising, he braced his knuckles on the table and leaned forward. The move would have looked intimidating, he was sure, if anyone had been paying him any mind. He hadn't done it for appearances but to help support legs gone leaden and weak. *Marriage.* He focused on a spot between his knuckles and drew a deep breath. "Enough!"

All seven Elders fell silent save for their harsh breathing.

He sank back into his chair, his thighs trembling.

"Thank you." Aylish took his seat and leaned back, crossing his hands over his stomach. "You seem to forget that you're each members of the Elder's Council, but I'm *the* Elder." He raised a hand casually over his head.

Every council member cringed. He had to admit the act was a gentle but effective reminder of the control Aylish had over his magick. He could strike any or all of them at will. When his father continued, he kept his attention focused on Dylan, and Dylan found himself unable to look away.

"When the wards began to break down in the Shadow Realm, we recognized the signs from our oral histories. We came together and did nothing more than a cursory reading of the Scrolls of Lewillwen to determine what had been recorded and what was required of us to keep the world whole and the Shadow Realm's inhabitants imprisoned. We reached Dagda's word on the matter. He said that, should the five banished gods attempt to rise, we were directed to find and destroy each of their chosen hosts. We researched no further."

Aylish pushed himself from his chair again and started around the table with measured steps, pausing at each Elder and laying a hand on his shoulder before moving on. "When the Assassin showed up with the host, I railed at him, called him a fool for putting us at risk."

"As he did," Elder Fergus snapped. "He's let her wander the castle, left her unattended, allowed her to grievously injure his second-in-command *twice* and without consequence. And now we're called together to hear that he intends to make her his wife? When? The marriage will end, and violently, before the honeymoon's over. It's bullshit. She needs to be shackled and caged until the full moon. One of the other assassins can wield his sword to

strike the deathblow. The Assassin has clearly lost his per-
spective on this."

Dylan shoved out of his chair, a sneer curling his lip.
The air wavered and thinned as his magick unfurled, the
aether seeking to break each element down into its most
basic form. The Councilmen stilled, staring at him wide-
eyed. He often harnessed one of the elements in their presence, but rarely did he allow the full force of his element
reign. Unchecked, the aether could rip apart everything,
and everyone, in this room.

Leaning more heavily on his fists, he glared at this piss
ant who dared call him out. "You think I've left her unattended? You think there's been a single time that she hasn't
been watched? Even when she was in the hallway that first
night and believed herself alone, Rowan stood mere feet
from her." He shoved off the table and stalked toward the
other man. The air moved fluidly around Dylan's skin,
leaving a trail that marked his passing. He stopped in front
of Fergus and yanked his chair out, turning the coward to
face him. "She wounded Gareth because he was unwilling to hurt her. The second time—"

"Was my fault," Aylish interjected. "I should have insisted we call Angus to deal with Gareth's fever."

Dylan turned back to Fergus. "I have stopped that bitch
every time she's risen in Kennedy. Did you consider that?
That I've essentially laid myself bare to the host, all in
the name of what's best for the Order? And you think to
suggest she be locked up." Voice dropping so low he was
sure the others strained to hear, he leaned into the wide-
eyed Councilman's space. "I'll manage her, and the goddess, and honor my oath. Until you can do my job better
than I, until you're strong enough to challenge and kill me,
you'll have to settle for the manner in which I choose, or
am forced, to carry out my assignments. All of you." He

shoved the Councilman's chair back and stood, fighting the urge to punctuate his impromptu speech with his fists.

Aylish caught Dylan's attention and shook his head sharply in silent rebuke.

Dylan wheeled around and stormed back to his seat, fighting the magick that called to him with seductive promises of power and destruction.

His father waited until Dylan was seated before he made his way back to Fergus. Stopping behind the Councilman's chair, Aylish rested his hands on the man's shoulders and said something under his breath. Fergus's skin twitched and his eyes grew wide. His face reddened. Guttural sounds erupted from his throat. Sweat beaded, transparent pearls that dotted his hairline. His eyes rolled back and forth, silently beseeching those around him for help. No one acknowledged him.

"I'll return Fergus the use of his major muscles when I feel he's been reminded of the deference with which he should treat the Elder, as well as the Assassin." Aylish resumed his slow walk around the table. "The Assassin was right to bring Kennedy here. We, who profess to hold life dear, to revere the natural order of things, did nothing to protect the life of an innocent woman. Hubris ruled our decision-making, not intelligence or heart. I have come to know Kennedy Jefferson, and I am ashamed at my rash decision to rob her of her future." Having made it to his chair, he pushed it under the table and leaned on the back. He let his gaze travel over each Councilman, pausing just long enough to let them experience the weight of his full attention. "We have acted irresponsibly. It is even possible we've abused our power as the final word for the Order. Knowing this, I must wonder how many others we have sentenced to death unjustly? Their blood is on our hands, my brothers."

Dylan had been focused on keeping his mind blank and

his arms loose, ready to meet any challenge. His father's last words plowed into him with the force of a runaway truck. He'd killed on their orders. Had he executed innocents in the name of Dagda and Danu? Had he invoked their blessings for acts of violence that would have forced them to turn away from him? Worse, had he taken a child's parent the same way his had been taken? How many had he orphaned?

Bile rushed up the back of his throat and burned his nose, acrid and foul. Focused on a spot two feet in front of him, he tuned out the murmurs of what he hoped were contrition and tried to drown out the low buzzing in his ears. The bloodstained guilt he'd carried with him for years, the weight of each death that had burdened the last shreds of his conscience, bore down on him and curled his shoulders forward with slow but persistent force.

He wanted to fall to his knees and beseech the gods for absolution. Fear snaked through his belly, a twisting, insidious viper that threatened to poison him every time it bared its fangs. Had the gods forsaken him for the merciless acts he'd blindly carried out himself or ordered carried out by his men? His head snapped up and he found Rowan staring straight ahead. Had his blind acceptance of the Council's orders damned his men, good men who'd done nothing but serve the Druidic Order? They had trusted him to validate any order before dispatching an assassin to eliminate the threat. The precarious slopes of trust and his duty to see to the Order's safety were intimately interwoven, but those realities didn't change the truth. He'd failed them, and Dylan didn't suffer failure well. Aylish's next words yanked him free of his dark thoughts.

"Beginning immediately and for the next seven days, the Elder's Library will be open. I will assign each of you extensive readings from the Scrolls of Lewillwen and will assist in translations and research." The Elder's voice resonated above the storm with the strength of his convictions and an authority that dared those in the room to challenge him. He looked at Dylan. "They will seek options, Assassin. In the meantime, you must agree to keep Kennedy with you at all times, preferably in your quarters. None of the five gods imprisoned in the Shadow Realm must ever obtain information from the Scrolls."

Unblinking, Dylan met his father's intense stare. "Why?"

Aylish straightened and lifted his face to the dome above, one finger tapping absently against his chair. No one counted the seconds that turned into minutes as silence overruled time and the Elder studied the ceiling. "Most relevant to this discussion is the fact that our forefathers, the first Druid Elder and his Council, recorded the variety of magicks used to imprison the gods." He lowered his chin and glanced toward the door to the Elder's Library.

Dylan followed his father's gaze and found Rowan standing preternaturally still, his stoic stare pinned on something across the room. He didn't acknowledge their attention or flinch under the scrutiny. In fact, the man hadn't reacted to anything since the announcement his boss would take a wife. The truth became transparent, and Dylan couldn't deny he envied Rowan his position as one of the body instead of its head. The lack of supreme responsibility appealed in that moment.

Aylish turned back to Dylan and cleared his throat.

Dylan took his time returning his full attention to his father. Too much warred for his immediate consideration. The last time he'd been this overloaded was…never.

Aylish's eyes glittered almost dangerously when the black candle shot a flame well above its wax rim. "In addition to the magicks used to imprison the gods, those first Druids recorded the countermagicks required to release them." He waited, his focus never leaving the sporadic flame that spit and hissed every time it surged upward.

"With all due respect, Elder, my question was actually a request for clarification. Why keep the woman locked in my quarters? She could sit in the Observatory while I translate scrolls. I could keep an eye on her as I assist in the search for the alternative to…to her…" *Death.* The last word wouldn't come, no matter how much he tried to force it through lips gone numb with the stark realization that these men represented Kennedy's last chance. To lock him up would be to shut him out of their efforts.

Ignoring everything but the candle that hissed and spit in the middle of the room, Aylish absently toyed with a loose button on his shirt cuff. "She cannot be allowed access to the Elder's Library any more than she can be left to wait in the Observatory. Both pose potentially unmanageable risks. If Kennedy fell to the goddess's influence while in the Elder's Library, the parasitic bitch she carries could obtain information we've been ordained to guard at any cost. The results could be catastrophic." He shifted his focus from the candle, his stare drilling into Dylan. "If you were thinking clearly, son, you'd see this yourself."

Son. Thick emotions wadded up in his throat, petrifying his vocal cords and forcing him to fight for air. Heat skated across his shoulders and down his arms. His fingers trembled. The air around his hands began to shimmer like a desert mirage as aether leaked out his fingertips in invisible threads and hovered around his hands. They became hazy and misshapen. Dylan reined it in, calling the fickle element home. The magick returned without a fight, moving through him like a lazy river, slow and winding, as it made its way back to the center of his body and settled in to await his call.

Speaking and breathing were individually impossible, and he was glad. Had he been able to respond, he couldn't have hidden the impact that one word had carried. Of course, they could have simply assumed he was emotionally wrecked because of Kennedy. They wouldn't have been wrong on either count.

Bah, emotion! It made him dim-witted and soft, fouled his logic and challenged his notorious control. The woman, his declared woman, had begun unraveling him from the first, pushing him to think beyond physical desire, forcing him to see her as something more than the most expeditious means to an end. Centuries of ruthlessly squashing his emotion into an imaginary black box and, in days, one woman had undone it all. He barked out a humorless laugh, his mouth curling up on one side as he considered how effectively she'd dismantled his defenses.

Dylan leaned back and crossed his arms over his chest, concentrating on Aylish. "You're absolutely right. I'm clearly addle-brained at the moment. I'll see to it that she's under my control at all times." The idea of controlling Kennedy led to images of her, hands bound and blindfolded, kneeling before him so her breasts were displayed. Fire licked through his groin, and his body hastened at the thought. *What the ever-loving hell?* He slid a bit lower in his chair, trying to get his erection straightened out without having to draw attention to it.

Aylish inclined his head. "Under the circumstances, it's understandable and immediately forgiven." He pushed off the back of his chair and strode around the table with purpose.

Dylan watched him approach, his stomach tightening when his father stopped behind his chair. A large, warm hand rested on his shoulder, and Dylan did his best not to give in to the urge to shrug it off. Dylan stood and faced Aylish, effectively dislodging his hand.

Undeterred, the Elder brought both hands down on Dylan's shoulders. "If there is knowledge that will allow us to circumvent what we originally believed inevitable, we'll find it. I give you my word."

Dylan wanted to cling to that promise, but truth was truth. He wondered briefly if that was what Danu wanted him to take from this—that words had power. As a Druid, he bloody well knew that. What his father had offered weren't words of power, though. They were just words. Still, he couldn't deny the actions that preceded them. Aylish had put the entire Council to work finding a way to exorcise Cailleach. By virtue of having slipped and called Kennedy his eternal love in front of his father, there was now a chance they'd save her. He wasn't a fool. The chance they'd find a way to destroy Cailleach was, at best, slim. Hell, he'd take "slim" over "none" any day. There wasn't time to master his emotions before the grin escaped.

The room went silent as everyone stilled, their surprise clear.

Apparently, he didn't smile much. Fair enough. No way was he apologizing—not any more than he was thanking them for doing what they should have done to start with.

Offering his father his hand, they shook and Dylan wordlessly spun on his heel. He was anxious to get to Kennedy. The sooner he got her back to his rooms, the sooner the Elder's Library would be opened and the Council could get to work.

He'd only taken three steps when his assassins began pounding on the door.

Kennedy's feet had started to hurt, the borrowed boots with their leather soles offering no padding against the stone floor. Of course, if she hadn't taken up pacing as soon as she'd been asked to leave the Observatory, it wouldn't have been so bad. But she had. Now the men behind those huge double doors were discussing her future without her input. More than once she'd started for the doors only to find her self-righteous approach coolly intercepted by one of Dylan's assassins. *Irritating Irishmen, both of them.*

She froze mid-step and swung out as hard as she could when a heavy hand closed over her upper arm. Her fist met something with the equivalent density of plutonium. The impact sent a reverberation up her arm and through her shoulder. Squinting through the resolute darkness, she cradled her injured hand and tried to figure out who had grabbed her. The mystery man yanked his hand back and, at the same time, his Gaelic curse ripped through the veil of darkness.

Lightning flashed outside the nearest window and seared Kennedy's eyes, but not before illuminating the man. Thunder shattered the air. The floor vibrated beneath her feet. Ozone tickled her nose, the smell not unlike burning dust. Her toes curled, wadding the rough wool socks up in the toe box of the too-large boots. She hated storms that stalled out. Their destruction seemed premeditated, as if they'd blown and raged until they hit their final stop where they determinedly shed their vengeance before yielding to blue skies. Another bright flash made her eyes water. She slammed her eyelids closed against the storm's blinding assault, intent on preserving her vision against Mother Nature's attacks.

Deep, appreciative laughter made her shiver. She made a quarter-turn toward the voice. "Niall?"

"Here, lass. It sounds as if you just knocked Kayden in the head. He may be soft of heart, but the bloke is thick as morning fog in the fields." A strangled cough that might have been masked laughter came from behind her. "You didn't hurt yourself, did you?"

Seeking hands—*warm* hands—found her face when the owner's fingers stabbed her chilled cheeks. Instinct had her jerking back and fumbling to grab the phantom hands before they did unintentional damage. Habit made her open her eyes.

"Holy. Shit." Kennedy's voice spun a tapestry from those two words—silvery filaments of fear woven between silken strands of disbelief anchored with the coarser threads of confusion. Shadows moved through her vision. The hunched and misshapen figures might have resembled human bodies had they not been so impossibly twisted and their faces not locked in silent screams.

Familiar stone walls faded to an enormous obsidian cavern that looked as if it had been carved out with dynamite. Darkness loomed above her, an inverted abyss.

Something moved in the corner of one eye, circling wide to come at her from the front. *Less threatening if you see me*, the apparition seemed to say. Twisted shadows scattered like pollen on the wind the closer the specter moved, only to coalesce behind her, but never within reach. Never.

What she'd taken as a ghost was actually a woman. Petite and ethereal, she moved with unerring grace over the keep's hall floor. When Kennedy noticed that concrete detail, the hand-laid stones sank, and wave upon wave of broken, jagged shale rose up to form the uneven, punishing landscape. It should have tripped the woman up— particularly since she never looked down. Mahogany hair fell to her hips, swaying gently as she moved closer. Dark eyes glittered far too brightly for a room with no discernible light source. Tiny feet with vermillion-painted toenails peeked out from the hem of her long silver gown with every confident step she took. Fainter silver embroidery flashed as it caught the light.

"Barefoot?" Kennedy took a short step back. "You can't cross that—" she pointed at the sharp and unforgiving terrain "—without tearing your feet to hell."

The woman tilted her head back and laughed, the genteel sound swallowed by the cavernous space. "But Kennedy, I'm already *in* hell."

It took Kennedy a moment to realize that the cavern hadn't sent back an echo, not of the laugh or the words. The base of her skull tingled. Her concentration softened, and she let her gaze drift to the walls. She should do something, but she couldn't remember what. The answer was there, just out of reach. Stepping toward the woman, Kennedy slipped and fell. Her hand struck something sharp, and she hissed in pain. Lifting the heel of her hand to her mouth, the coppery tang of blood curled around her tongue.

The stranger moved closer.

A single thought speared Kennedy's brain. *If those freaky-ass shadows didn't want this woman touching them, I sure as hell don't.* Scrambling backward, she ignored the pain in her hand.

"I'd tend your wound with your consent." The woman reached out, eyes suddenly fathoms deep. Worlds were held in them, galaxy stacked upon galaxy until Kennedy knew she'd glimpsed the beginning and the end.

She screamed.

Fingers slid around her throat, back to front. Nearby, metal hissed against metal as a blade was drawn from its scabbard. Furious pounding thundered in her ears. A large, hot body moved in tight behind her.

Kayden's breath washed over her ear, his large hand tightening fractionally around her throat. "Talk to me, Kennedy. Tell me what's happening."

"Can't," she croaked out.

"Ah, shit."

A dark figure sliced across Kennedy's field of view. It grabbed her by the arms and yanked her up so hard and fast that Kayden's fingers caught on her sweater and ripped it down her shoulders. Her arms ended up pinned behind her. Firm lips wrestled with her mouth, trying to force her to give herself up. She wouldn't. The only one who had a right to her was, "Dylan?"

"Don't make me come after you, Kennedy. You won't be pleased if you force my hand."

Warm breath snuffled against her neck, and she relaxed into the sensation. He wove his hand through her hair and cupped her skull. Then he bit her. She arched her back, pressing her breasts into his chest. He snaked an arm around her waist and pulled her flush against him. His deep rumble of satisfaction vibrated against her skin, but he didn't let go. Instead, he bent her backward, looming over her.

"Get your ass back here, Jefferson." He laid a tender kiss under her chin, pulling her up an inch at a time, reeling her in with strength of body, iron will and tender kisses. "I'm going to count to five. If you're not back, you're going to be chained in the dungeon."

Kennedy dragged herself up, pulling away from invisible shackles that sought to bind her in an undeniable hell.

Cailleach watched her go with a sensuous grin, her tongue darting out to trace her upper lip. "Soon."

That one word cleared Kennedy's mind, and her fury rode her fear as she catapulted toward consciousness. The smell of the storm, clean and pure, filled her lungs. A fine tremor in the hands that held her silently translated to a language her own private fears recognized and interpreted. It was a language that neither had nor needed words. Her eyes fluttered open.

Dylan leaned in, his lips hovering so close to hers that, when she spoke, they brushed.

"You don't really have a dungeon, do you?"

He grinned. "I'll take you on a tour tomorrow."

She narrowed her eyes. "If I'd known whips and chains did it for yo—oompf!"

Dylan crushed his lips against hers at the same time

masculine laughter mixed with back slaps and shouts of congratulations.

Shit. Leave it to her to forget they had an audience.

She shifted, and Dylan mirrored her movement, pressing up against her. His erection was unmistakable. "So... whips and chains, huh?"

He grinned and shook his head. "Shut up, Kennedy."

"You kinky, ancient Druid, you." Even though she'd spoken so low no one could have heard her, twin bright spots of color settled high on his cheeks.

She'd deal with the lingering horror in a bit.

For now? She laughed.

Chapter 16

Dylan wasn't exactly proud he clung to Kennedy as they headed upstairs, but holding her tight gave his trembling arms something to do. Otherwise he'd have appeared shaken. Shaken didn't begin to describe the uncontrolled terror he had experienced as he called Kennedy's soul back to her body. The moment she'd opened her eyes, when she'd stared at him in bewilderment, had sent him into a tailspin of confusion as he'd fought the urge to shake her, hug her, kiss her. Even love her. Damn Aylish and his suggestion she was his intended bride. Now Dylan couldn't look at her without thinking about her in terms of lifetimes. Thank the gods she didn't know what Aylish had said. She'd kill them both. It was irrelevant, though, because he couldn't marry her. No way could he marry and still serve as the Assassin, and six full days with Kennedy didn't change a 256-year-old oath. She could never be first in his life. And a woman like Kennedy would never settle for being second to anything. Nor should she have to.

Dylan's fingers dug into her side and she flinched. Relaxing his grip, he moved her up the stairs and down the hall with long strides that forced her to work to keep up.

"Where are we going?"

Her voice cut through his dismal thoughts. He dropped his gaze to her and smiled, slow and suggestive. "I promised you the dungeon, did I not?"

She shook her head and laughed. "Dungeons are in the basement."

"An American film notion. Punishments can occur anywhere." He stroked his thumb up and down her ribs, unwilling and unable to master his hunger for her. Six full days left them. He'd spend them worshipping her body before facing whatever was demanded of him.

"Punishments? What have I done to warrant punishments?" she challenged.

Lust ignited, an inferno of need that made him close his eyes and lock his jaw until the initial flash passed. All he needed now was to take her against a wall where anyone might see. He let her go. That she continued to hold him tight encouraged him to wrap his arm around her again. She snuggled into his side.

"You don't think you've earned punishment?"

"Earned it? No." She looked up slyly. "But, like I said, if the Druid's got a thing for being tied up, I'd oblige him." Heat stained her cheeks with a pretty blush.

"We've got to make a stop before I can get you back to my room and…" His words died. How could he articulate what he wanted? How could he tell her that one more night, one whole month, even one full lifetime would never be enough? How could he explain that this, what they had right now, was all she—*they*—could ever hope for? That stubborn ache in his chest was back, and he rubbed his free hand absently over the area.

"And what?" Her breathy response didn't appease the pain.

Dylan stared at her, the quiet between them comfortable, and let himself simply be. His fingertips traced the smooth skin of her cheek, along her jaw and down her neck before resting at her collarbone. He bent forward and laid an open-mouthed kiss there. "The sooner we get through this, the sooner we can finish that thought."

He steered her toward Gareth's door, secretly amused that the hammering of her pulse matched his. Pausing, he unwound the protective spell that had been wrapped around the door like twine. The magick tasted of exotic spices paired with the bitter undertones of dandelion and the peppery bite of watercress. No doubt their surgeon, Angus, had been the caster. Reaching for the door handle, Dylan was surprised when Kennedy let go of his waist. He glanced back at her, raising his brows in silent question.

"I can't go in there." She shook her head slowly, eyes wide, the pretty blush bleached out.

"You won't hurt him. I'll have you by my side at all times." Dylan reached for her and she stepped farther back.

"How can you be sure you can stop her? I don't know what she's capable of or where she's at right now." Her hand went to her belly button and pressed. "I don't feel her, Dylan, and I've felt her for so long. Now? She's totally silent."

He grabbed her wrist and pulled her unyielding body into his arms. Running his hands up and down her back, he bent and placed his lips next to her ear. "I promise to stop things if she rises."

Kennedy's chin jerked up, and he narrowly escaped a hard shot to the jaw. Her pupils swallowed the dark blue of her irises. "Promise you won't hesitate again. Promise me that, if she threatens Gareth, you'll kill me."

Dylan's head snapped back and bounced off the door with a solid *crack*. "What the hell are ye talking about?"

She laid her hand over his heart, and he had only a moment to consider what she'd think of its galloping beat before she rose to her tiptoes and reached for his head. He followed the gentle pull of her hand, closing his eyes and losing himself in the scents of vanilla and lavender—smells he knew with certainty he'd never be able to separate again. Where one was, so should the other be. Her lips were tender, moving with slow deliberation as she coaxed him away from the anger that had swamped him at her request.

His hands slid down her ribs to rest on the slight swell of her hips.

Kennedy's fingers traced his jaw, and she nipped at his lower lip before pulling away. "I need to know you won't hold back, Dylan. You have to promise me you'll stop this, no matter what."

To tell her that even now the Council hunted for a way to stay her execution but still bind the goddess was an impossibility, though it was the one thing she most needed to know. The way she stared up at him, fear warring with faith, left him grasping for handholds on anxiety's slippery terrain. "We'll deal with what comes moment to moment. No promises beyond that."

She traced one of the Celtic designs he'd tooled into his weapon harness. "Don't let her use me to hurt him again, Dylan—to hurt *anyone*. I can't live with myself if she does."

Guileless blue eyes stared up at him and silently elicited his nod of agreement. No matter what, he'd ensure that Kennedy got through this without any more pain than she'd already suffered. He'd willingly pay whatever price the gods deemed adequate a thousand times over to ensure she lived without suffering.

No matter how long her life might be.

Dylan heard Gareth the moment he opened the door.

"I'm telling ye, Angus, I'm wasting away on nothing but this bluidy broth an' toast. A man needs *meat*. He needs *carbs* tae feed his muscles. He needs coffee instead o' weak tea and by the gods, he needs a bracing nip o' the *whiskey* tae keep him sane!" Silk and cotton rustled. The bed frame clacked against the wall. A very disgruntled huff punctuated the temper tantrum when it didn't garner the surgeon's sympathy. Dylan looked down to find her eyes watering and nostrils flaring.

"He's fine, *mo chroí*."

She nodded quickly, tears breaking the lower dam of her lashes. Blinking rapidly, she sucked in a lungful of air and choked.

Dylan grabbed her hand away from her mouth and was nearly struck dumb.

Uncontrollable laughter racked her body. She wrapped her arms around herself and bent forward, gasping for air. Bracing a hand on one knee, she pushed up and shoved her hair out of her face. Cheeks that had appeared waxen only moments before were now tear-stained and reddened with mirth. A lone hiccup escaped, and she clapped a hand over her mouth again.

His own grin was wide enough his cheeks hurt. Reaching for her, he pulled her hand away to find her still fighting her laughter. "No need to rob the world of that smile, *mo chroí*. Besides, I believe he knows we're here." She'd stilled as he spoke. His own smile faltered. "What?"

"You're unbelievably gorgeous." She fisted his shirt in one hand when he opened his mouth, the denial ripe on his tongue. "Stop it. I've never been anything but honest with you. I don't intend to ruin my track record, particularly over something like this. You're gorgeous, Dylan, but when you smile?" She shook her head and looked toward the open doorway to Gareth's bedroom. No doubt both men across that threshold listened carefully.

Dylan didn't care. Laying his hand over hers where it still gripped his shirt, he squeezed lightly and regained her attention. "Finish the thought." When she hesitated, one corner of his mouth tipped up. "Humor me."

She caught him completely off guard when she threw her arms around him and buried her face in his chest. She spoke so low and rapidly that he doubted he would have understood her even if she hadn't been intimately addressing his pecs. Wrapping his hand through her hair, he tugged gently, pleased when she looked up. "I didn't understand a word of what you just said. Again, please. And this time I'd ask that you look at me when you answer."

She worried her bottom lip with her teeth, seeming to consider her options before resigning herself to his request. "I said that, when you smile, you lose the haunted look that's always there, in your eyes. It's like your walls come down and there's just you, Dylan, and you're the most beautiful human being I've ever seen."

She wrecked him with her words, building him up and tearing him down with the truth as she saw it.

"Kennedy—"

"Get yer arse in here, mate…and Kennedy," Gareth called. "I thought ye'd given me up, thrown me over for a new pretty face."

Dylan shook his head, half entertained, half annoyed. "We'll finish this later, you and I."

They stepped into Gareth's room, and Kennedy sagged against Dylan's side, shaking.

"I see ye did just that." Gareth winked at Dylan and turned to Kennedy, mouth open to undoubtedly jest with her about running him through. He stopped whatever he'd been about to say. "Kennedy?"

She stumbled out from under Dylan's arm and sank to her knees beside Gareth's bed. "I'm so sorry," she whispered.

Gareth rolled to his side and swung his feet to the floor. Bending forward, he pulled Kennedy to her feet despite the healing wound. "Shhh, Kennedy." He wrapped her in his arms and let her shake. It took a few minutes, but her arms finally snaked around his neck and held on tight.

Dylan had no doubt the movements cost Gareth, his

payment a stout measure of pain, but the man's concern was clearly comforting Kennedy. Dense emotion rose for the second time in mere minutes. Seeing Kennedy so broken and prostrate in front of one of Dylan's Arcanum did something to him, brought unnamed emotions higher, closer to the surface of consciousness. And the closer they came, the more compelled he was to name them. That couldn't end well. For anyone.

The urge to put his fist through something made him tighten his hands until they ached. If he had to carry through with the execution order, he couldn't afford to be left with this deluge of raw emotions. None of the gods would be so cruel. He snorted. *Right. Because they've been so good to me so far.*

Stepping forward, he pulled Kennedy into his arms. She resisted at first, firing up a latent sense of jealousy he'd never known existed in him. *First bluidy emotion named, and a fine one it is at that.*

Kennedy turned to him and buried her tear-stained face in his shirt, hiccupping and slowly calming. She mumbled something, shaking her head gently.

Dylan leaned back and lifted her chin. "What's that, *grá mo chroí*?"

A strange sense of satisfaction settled over Gareth's face, a soft smile tugging at his lips.

Dylan glared at him. "Shut it, *tú asal ar.*" Shifting his attention, Dylan focused solely on Kennedy, not acknowledging Angus when he slipped from the room. "I'll ask again, what is it, *grá mo chroí*?"

Reddened eyes found his and she sniffed. "It would help if I knew whether that was a term of endearment or if you were calling me a ripe goat's ass."

Dylan couldn't hide his surprise.

Gareth burst out laughing.

A smile tugged at Kennedy's lips, and she reached up

to smooth the hair from his forehead. "Though I suppose if you *are* calling me a ripe goat's ass, it would seriously hamper your love life."

Dylan spun her around and, ignoring her surprised gasp, wrapped his arms around her and tucked her up against him. Lips whispering over her ear, he said, "Ye're no' a goat's ass, lass. Yer ass is much too fine for tha' comparison." The heat of her body bled through his linen shirt. Nothing would have made him happier than to have her backed up to him like this as they stared out their bedroom window.

Their bedroom... He stilled, lips lingering.

"There's a room next door or, if that would take you two too long, I can hop out o' bed and shut the doors behind me." Gareth's mischievous grin said he assumed sex was what had given Dylan pause.

How wrong you are, my friend.

Dylan stood and chuffed out a forced laugh. "You're a fine one to bicker about needing to get a room."

The blush that stole over Gareth started at his chest and raced into his hairline. "Let's not go there, mate."

"Right. Let's get you settled, then."

"Settled?" Skepticism marked his expression as he watched Dylan and waited.

Dylan's lip curled on one side. "Settled—in my suite." When Gareth started to protest, Dylan waved him off. "No arguments. We need you in the event she rises again, man."

Gareth crossed his arms over his chest. His jaw tightened and his whole face shut down. "And why can't Kayden or Niall, even Rowan, take these duties?"

Kennedy's shoulders slumped so much that she sagged against Dylan, her chin dipping. He jerked her upright so hard her head bounced off his chest. "You'll be there and we'll discuss the best ways to manage Kennedy should, uh, *Maxine* rise."

"Aye." Dylan slid one arm up and pinned Kennedy's shoulders against his chest. "So either pack a bag or have Angus do it for you, but you're moving in with us."

Kennedy rubbed her forehead. "If he doesn't want to come, don't make him." She wiggled out of Dylan's arms and went to the window, looking out over the sea. "I don't blame him."

"Kennedy," Gareth started, shifting his feet to the other side of the bed and standing, albeit ungracefully. Dylan watched him rest his hand on the worst of his wounds, instinctively protecting it. "It's not you, love. It's…well, it *is* you, but it's not what you think." He turned her around. "I don't want to hurt you should she rise again. It's why I didn't strike you on the cliffs."

She glanced his way, her face blank. "You didn't want to hurt me."

"You're too important."

Baring her teeth, she all but snapped at him. "*You* didn't want to hurt *me*."

Jaw working and lips thinning, Gareth's eyes blazed a furious blue. "Aye. That's what I said. At least *Maxine* hasn't affected your hearing."

Kennedy hauled a fist back and punched Gareth in the shoulder.

"Ow! What was that for?"

Dylan started for her when she snarled at Gareth.

Then she spoke, and her words nearly dropped him where he stood, gutting him more effectively than a sword. "How dare you? How *dare* you let her almost kill you? And for what? Honor? That's a beautiful notion, but the end of the world as we know it is staring us all in the face if she actually releases Chaos. Do you not *get* that?" Her hands fisted again, vibrating at her sides.

Gareth took a couple of steps backward, a dumbfounded

look on his face. Then his bright blue eyes focused on her and narrowed.

Dylan made to intervene, but Gareth swiped a hand at him. The Assassin's second looked down at Kennedy, temper clearly brewing. "You think I didn't consider that? You think I let you live because of what, Kennedy? A misguided sense of chivalry? It's not just you who would lose out if you died. Did you consider that?"

Dylan's stomach plummeted at the idea Gareth might reveal what he so clearly believed—that Dylan had fallen in... *Not going there.* "Enough," he said, nearly snarling.

Neither of them listened.

Kennedy stepped into Gareth's space and looked up at him, jaw set. "Misguided chivalry? That's not even close to the truth, is it? How about you were too cowardly to deal the deathblow? I was there," she screamed. "I saw... I saw..." She shook her head and stumbled backward, hands out as if to ward off a blow.

Dylan moved in behind her to keep her from running.

Gareth looked at him in total bewilderment.

"She's been able to see Maxine's actions of late."

Gareth reached out and grabbed Kennedy's wrist, pulling her into his embrace. Stroking her hair, he stared at Dylan, a look of absolute horror on his face. "Oh, gods, *a stóirín*, I had no idea."

Dylan stepped in close and took Kennedy back.

She slumped in his embrace. "It's fine." Her voice seemed small when moments before it had been so sure of itself.

"No, it's not." Gareth reached out and lifted her chin. Bending forward, he laid a gentle kiss on Kennedy's lips. "I'm sorry."

"You want to keep your lips?" Dylan jerked Kennedy to the side and set her well away from the other man. "Then keep them to yourself." Glaring at Gareth, he spoke to

Kennedy. "You've been a braw lass. That jaunt you took
to the Shadow Realm—"

Gareth grabbed Dylan's arm. "She went *where*?"

"Unwilling spiritual trip to the Shadow Realm. Leave
it alone, mate. I'm not toying with you on this one." Dylan
turned to Kennedy, even as he spoke to Gareth. "Let's get
you settled in front of the fire, yeah? You can rest there
while I get her taken care of." He glanced at the other man.
"Who's next on your guard rotation?"

"Rowan."

"Have him brief you before you pack a few things and
move into my suite."

"Aye, I'll, uh, do that." Gareth looked at Kennedy mo-
rosely. "I'm sorry to have made a balls of the conversation, Kennedy."

She smiled. "I think you're apologizing."

He nodded, a single dip of the chin.

"It's okay." She stepped up to him and went up on tiptoe to lay a gentle kiss on his cheek. "I suppose I should
apologize for nearly overdosing you with morphine—you
know, since it was my second attempt on your life and
all." Reaching up, she tucked a hank of hair behind his
ear, smoothing it down with gentle strokes.

Dylan's heart tightened, as did his fists.

When Gareth's brows drew together, Dylan braced himself for an argument. Instead, the man surprised him. "If
you feel the need, then apology accepted."

Kennedy turned back to Dylan, and he slipped his hand
into hers. Fingers slid into place as if they'd held each other
for years, not calculable hours.

Kennedy followed Dylan back to his suite, her mind
awash in memories of the fight with Gareth on the cliffs
and Cailleach's spiritual summoning outside the Observatory. It had been odd, with something stranger than normal about the "visit," but she couldn't put a finger on it.

The door to the suite shut, and she shivered.

Dylan moved to the fire and tossed another turf brick into the hearth. Sparks danced and crackled, the rejuvenated blaze releasing an earthy, smoky scent. He dusted his hands off and placed them on the mantel, pressing against it so hard his shoulders bunched and his biceps flexed. "Let me look at that hand, *a muirnín*."

Kennedy looked down at the cut. "How was I able to cut my hand if she was pulling on my spirit, not my body?"

The mantel creaked as Dylan pushed off and turned toward her. His eyes were guarded. "I'm not sure. I've a guess, though."

She had her own guesses, as well, but they were so far-fetched as to be laughable. "Go ahead. Wow me with that brilliant Assassin's mind."

A smile teased the corners of his mouth, and suddenly she was less interested in guesswork and more interested in touching that soft pillow of his lower lip with her tongue.

"Keep looking at me like that, Kennedy, and you'll end up back in my bed."

His words rolled around her with soft yet persistent intent. *Sensual. He could make any statement sensual.* One step, then two and they were suddenly moving toward each other. She craved him like the savannah craved monsoon season. He was a downpour, an emotional onslaught that flooded her senses. Trickles of once slow-moving feelings were suddenly raging rivers, and she knew just enough to know she stood a good chance of drowning.

They met at the end of the sofa, coming together in a tangle of hot breath and searching hands. The kiss was tinged with a franticness she was relieved he shared. Her sweater came off seconds before his shirt did. Her nipples rasped against his smooth chest; the hot, hard skin raising them to furious peaks. Toeing her boots off, she tried to kick them free. Apparently, she wasn't fast enough because Dylan grasped her by the armpits and picked her straight up and out of the shoes. She wrapped her legs around his waist.

He turned and strode toward the bedroom.

"Too far." A fist in his hair forced him to turn.

Dylan took three large steps to the narrow space between bookshelves.

Kennedy's back slammed against the smooth stone wall. The laces of her borrowed pants were ripped free, and he set her down to peel them off. Pant legs were tangled in her socks, and it quickly became a wadded mess that had her stumbling to stay upright.

She couldn't stop the laugh that escaped as she struggled to stand and still work her feet free with Dylan's "help."

He shot her a quick glance. "Laugh, will ye?"

Hot hands gripped her hips and spun her around so she faced the wall.

"Hands out." When she braced herself, he pulled her hips backward. Bending over her and spreading her arms wider, he encouraged her to grab on to the bookshelves on either side. "Spread your legs."

"I need my feet free." She started to stand and gasped when he grabbed her wrists and put her hands back where he'd initially placed them. Then he kicked her tangled feet as far apart as they would go. There was no choice left for her but to hang on to the shelves.

"I told ye there'd be the wee matter o' punishment, did I no'?" His voice had devolved to a deep burr that rumbled against her spine.

"Dylan." His name was little more than a moan. She arched her back and pushed back at him, anxious, needing.

"Sweet heavens," he rasped.

Kennedy rubbed against him. A huge hand grabbed her hip and held her as he ground his leather-clad groin against her. From her peripheral vision, she saw him fling a hand at the door. Metal and wood melded together, breaking apart with a grinding noise. Where the door had hung, a stone wall now stood.

"Doona want tae be interrupted."

Movement. Then the broad head of his arousal breached her outer folds. She couldn't stop the surprised gasp.

"Sae wet for me, lass." Bending over her again, he wrapped an arm around her hips and fed his length into her one slow, controlled inch at a time.

She shuddered, the sensation of being stretched so exquisitely more than she could take without crying out.

"Did I hurt ye?" He started to stand.

Kennedy gripped the bookcases and shoved back, seating herself so hard and fast they both shouted. But when she tried to ride him, he rose up and gripped her hips, effectively stilling her.

"Nay, *mo síorghrá*, ye'll take it as I'm willing tae give it this time."

And then he took up the most exquisite, torturous and controlled rhythm she'd ever experienced. She wanted to weep and scream. Every time she tried to force him to move faster, he'd slow down. She'd finally relent and arch her back to take him deeper, and he'd move more shallow than before. When he wrapped his hand around her hair and pulled her upright, gripping her throat with his free hand, she wanted to curse him. Seeming to sense her frustration at being on the brink of what she needed most, he upped the pace. His thrusts lifted her to her toes. His grip on her hair and throat refusing to let her brace herself. The hand around her throat tightened.

His voice was hot against the shell of her ear. "Come for me, Kennedy."

Her body took that as its cue. Release ripped through her, tearing a brutal scream from her throat. He rode her hard, giving no quarter and pushed her into a second crest before the first orgasm faded. She shuddered and shook under the onslaught, her body completely bending to his will.

With a shout, his hips pistoned harder before slowing to long, languorous strokes.

Kennedy's knees gave out. Dylan stumbled in his efforts to help her to the floor without hurting her. Chances were she never would have known she was in pain.

Too many endorphins. Happy, happy endorphins.

Kennedy let Dylan shower with her before pushing him out of the bathroom. "Go put the door back in the wall or Gareth will never get in."

"Chances are he'd just blow a bloody hole in the wall and be done with it. Call it a 'remodel' or some such shite." Towel slung around his hips and wet hair pushed back from his face, he was the picture of every desire she'd ever had. He wiped at the mirror and caught her staring. "Kennedy?"

She sighed. "You need to get out of here before I do something neither of us will regret."

He turned slowly, the front of the towel revealing a significant bulge. "And just what would it be we'd not regret?"

"Use your imagination. Now go." She wrapped a towel around her hair and stood, tightening the towel around her torso.

"Trust me, my imagination's in overdrive." He rolled his shoulders. "I'm going to regret having him here as my backup, aren't I?"

"Can't imagine it'll be easy on either of us, but we'll manage." She started out of the room and he grabbed her around the waist, hauling her in for a deep kiss that left her shaking.

"Use your imagination, *mo duine dorcha*, as ye've instructed I do, and ye'll be joost fine." He nipped her bottom lip and stepped back when she growled. "Put some clothes on before I leave the new wall as it is."

"Silly magician." The towel snapped across her ass, and she yelped. Spinning, she watched him saunter out of the bathroom half hard and entirely naked. "Cute," she called after him.

"Och, no. I'm bluidy *gorgeous*, an' ye said so yerself." He laid the brogue on thick, teasing her as he disappeared into the closet.

"I'm going to regret that, aren't I?" she said, imitating him and grinning as she fought the urge to laugh. None of this was funny—the timeline, the fact he was still her executioner, the realization she didn't know what the Council had decided on. "Hey," she called, hurrying from the room. "What did Aylish say to the Council?"

Dylan stepped out of the closet, nearly colliding with her. "Nothing you need to worry about."

"I think I *do* need to worry about it." The towel began to slip off her head. She yanked it away, ignoring the stinging pull of hair.

"No, ye don't."

Brogue's back, serious this time. Too bad. "You're effectively making end-of-life decisions for me, and I don't appreciate it. I should have final say in how I..." She ran a hand down her throat, encouraging that word that hung up to break free. "In how I die." *There. I said it.*

Dylan grabbed her by the shoulders. "Ye're not tae die. I'll—" he spun and punched the wall, splitting his knuckles wide open "—ye'll trust me tae make the best choices I can."

Kennedy stepped back and shook her head. "No."

"Ye trust me with yer body, but no' this?"

"I..." He had no idea how much she trusted him with. *So much more than my body.*

Dylan sucked at his knuckles while they stood there,

facing off. Finally, after interminable minutes, he let his hand fall away from his lips. "I canna tell ye," he said softly. "I canna risk Maxine knowin'."

Kennedy closed her eyes and took a calming breath. It made so much sense that she couldn't know, that he couldn't tell her and still ensure the safety of those working to unseat the goddess. *The goddess*... "Dylan?"

Nostrils flaring, he jerked his chin to go ahead.

"If...if Maxine is upset, unseated, what happens to the connection between us? What happens to me?" The tremor in her voice couldn't be disguised as anything other than fear. She'd never considered what might happen should she survive. "Will she always be there?"

Fists resting on his hips, his chin dipped low and his hair hung in a protective curtain around his face. "I doona know."

"Okay."

His gaze roved over her body, from feet to face. He stopped then, looking at her with such intensity she wanted to squirm, to deny, to confess, to drop the towel and force him to soften the scrutiny. "Just okay, then."

She lifted her chin a notch. "Yes, just *okay*. You expected what? Irrational behavior? Demands for empty promises maybe? When have I ever been that woman, Dylan? When have I ever pushed when there was nothing to gain?"

The stunned realization on his face should have been an emotional win for her. She'd held her ground, proved her point. Yet the triumph left her so hollow that any internal shout of conquest would have echoed throughout the void. All she wanted was the truth. Even if it was hard to accept, it was irrefutable. "Am I so difficult that you can't accept that the truth satisfies me?"

"No." He moved forward, stopping mere inches from

her. Warm hands cupped her face. "It's that I've never dealt with someone so rational about…things."

"What will screaming get me, Dylan?" Lids slipping closed and shoulders sagging, she felt his hands tighten on her jaw.

"Not a thing, but it's what I expected." Warm lips met hers, searching for absolution. The kiss was tender, intimate in a way she'd never experienced with him. He pulled away. "Look at me, Kennedy."

Her eyes fluttered open.

"You've surprised me from the beginning, so I shouldn't expect anything less now."

Pounding sounded against the outer wall, the noise so loud it was as if someone had taken a jackhammer to the castle.

She pivoted, assuming an attack stance in one move, her old military training combining with circumstance to put her on edge. A broad hand settled on her back. She glanced over her shoulder to find Dylan fighting a smile.

"I told you Gareth would likely tear down the wall to get in."

"For the love of all that's holy, just fix the damn door," she shouted over the din.

Her favorite grin escaped as she stood. "As my lady wills it." A look of surprise darted across his face before he tamped it down and jogged from the room. Seconds later, the door crashed in and the shouting commenced, Gareth's voice significantly louder than Dylan's.

Kennedy yanked on her leather pants and grabbed one of Dylan's T-shirts, shoving her arms through as she hustled to the door. The sight that met her as she entered the living room made her stumble to a stop—part shock, part self-preservation. Had she walked through the shattered lamps and destroyed wooden sofa table she'd have torn her feet all to hell.

"What *happened*?" She glanced from man to man and found their sheepish yet sullen features ridiculously endearing. No one answered her so she crossed her arms, glaring when Gareth's pleading gaze met hers.

"I thought you were having trouble with Maxine, so I was, hmm, *emphatic* about getting into the room."

"An' I hid the door so that ye wouldna disturb me 'til I was good an' ready," Dylan said, his voice rising with each word.

"Get this cleaned up," she snapped in her best commander's voice. When they both gawked at her, she let her arms fall to her sides, shook them out and then parked her fists on her hips.

"I'll stay right outside the door." She started through the mess, deftly sidestepping the worst of it—and Dylan's reach—to make it through the doorway. Once outside, she collapsed against the wall, laughing. Those two were the most volatile men she knew.

"You always laugh so often?"

The dark voice, vaguely familiar and entirely frightening, rocketed her heart to her throat as she whirled to face its owner. "Rowan."

He inclined his head, at the same time shifting so she saw he leaned on his huge sword.

Swallowing hard and cursing herself for not paying better attention, she backed away from him slowly. When he began matching her step for step, she fought the urge to call for Dylan. Forcing herself to stop, she squared up to the immense man. "Can I help you with something, Rowan?"

"Depends." He pulled his sword up and swung it around in a sweeping circle at his side, his wrist loose, the movement fluid. "You want to let her out?"

"Who do you—oh. Maxine."

His brows drew down. "I don't care what you call her.

She stole from me more than two centuries ago, and I'd have back what she took."

Deep inside, a shift occurred—a realignment that promised grief for him, terror for her. "Don't," she whispered, shaking her head and backing away.

Rowan took larger steps, moving closer to her. Grief ripped across his visage, raw and unencumbered by time. Stumbling to a stop, he dropped his sword to his side. The tip sliced the archaic runner and buried itself in a stone seam. He shook his head and looked up.

Kennedy gasped.

His eyes had lost all color, leaving the irises a brilliant white ringed in cobalt blue. The pupil of one eye was blown, the other a pinprick. "No," he said, his voice little more than a growl. Raising his free hand, he clutched the side of his head and shook it. "Can you bring her forward?"

"You're calling her up." Kennedy was ready to plead, grovel, scream or even threaten—anything to keep Cailleach subdued.

"Let her come." Fury resonated through him, drawing the tendons in his neck into sharp relief.

"Rowan." Dylan's voice was a lifeline, a safe harbor in the face of Rowan's emotional storm. "Enough. She's the Assassin's *céile sa todhchaí* and will be afforded all the rights therein."

The giant assassin stared at her, that consuming grief echoing in his eyes so loudly Kennedy thought she heard something. Shaking her head, she looked up to find Dylan barreling down on them, sword in hand. "*Go leor.*" Enough.

Rowan nodded once, sharp. "Apologies, Ms. Jefferson."

Unsure what compelled her, she reached out to touch his arm, to ask what the parasitic bitch had stolen from him.

He recoiled, whipping his arm out of reach. "Just... don't."

Kennedy swallowed hard. "Okay." Forcing that one word out left her throat miserably tight.

Rowan retreated, responding to Dylan's unintelligible words with a grunt. He didn't go far, though. Instead, he resumed his post outside Dylan's door, his sword resting on its tip, his hands crossed over the peen and pommel.

Dylan turned back to her, swinging his sword in a familiar wide arc at his side, wrist as loose as Rowan's had been. Closing in, he twisted the blade and slapped the flat of the fuller down on his shoulder with a *whap*. "You okay?"

She stepped into the arms he held out to her. "Fine. What did you tell him I was? It sounded similar to what Aylish called me in the Observatory." He hesitated, and she knew she was right. The words had been the same. "C'mon, Assassin. Whatever he said got the Council's attention then and Rowan's attention now. I want to know if your dad's calling me your concubine or some such horrid title."

"Far from it," came Aylish's voice.

"Just fecking perfect." Dylan spun them around in a move so fluid they could have been dancing. "We're not doing this in the hallway." He cocked his head to the side. "No, we're not doing this *ever*. Understand, Elder?"

Aylish inclined his head. Turning, he spoke softly to Rowan. The man's shoulders sagged under the weight of the Elder's words. Then Aylish laid a hand on the side of Rowan's head and pressed their foreheads together in intimate camaraderie. Rowan responded softly and Aylish stepped back, giving the assassin enough room to square his shoulders and resume his guard post.

"What did you call me, Aylish?" Kennedy struggled to get out of Dylan's hold, glaring at him until he finally let her go. He cursed every step she took toward the Elder.

"Nothing sinister, Kennedy." Aylish looked over her

head toward his son. "I assure you, it was a title of utmost respect, second only to—"

"Stop." Dylan's command slammed into Aylish and shoved him back a step.

The Elder's eyes narrowed. He passed a hand down the front of his neck and cleared his throat. "Striking out against the Elder yet again, Assassin?"

Kennedy looked back, surprised to the see the faint tightening of lines around Dylan's eyes. *Always Assassin, so rarely Dylan and never son.* "Look, whatever you called me isn't important. Forget I asked," she said, holding her hand out to Dylan. He moved to her side but refused to take her offering. Fine. If he wanted to act like an ass, she could play that way.

"I'm going to help Gareth clean up." She started toward Dylan's suite. The urge to look back, to see his face and know that he watched her, screamed through her.

She ignored it and kept on walking.

Chapter 17

Eyes narrowed, Dylan watched Kennedy saunter toward his rooms. The moment she turned through the doorway, he shifted his attention back to his father. "You're not to tell her that you've identified her as my bride. Understand?"

Aylish examined his nails before settling his hands in his pockets. "If you don't tell her how you feel, how's she to know what she's willing to risk?"

"Risk? For what?" The sneer in his voice smeared the air between them.

His father considered him carefully before answering. "For you."

Had the man struck him dumb, left him permanently mute or stolen the air from his lungs, Dylan couldn't have been more surprised. His mouth opened and closed several times before he wheezed out, "*Me*? Are ye thick?"

"Not that anyone's been brave enough to try and prove it, but I'll answer you anyway. No." Aylish narrowed his stare. "She's a right to know how you feel, Dylan."

"Och, aye? And ye know that on me behalf, do ye? For sure as I can tell, I've no' told a soul seein' as how I'm no' sure meself!" Every word saw his brogue thickening until he slipped into the Irish. "*Conas is féidir liom a insint di cad fiú níl a fhios agam*?" How can I tell her what even I don't know?

Aylish got in his face. "Because ye *do* know, shite for

brains." He started to storm away, only to turn, rush back and shove his finger in Dylan's face. "Ye do!"

Grinding teeth echoed through his head and forced Dylan to stop. *Gods, the man makes me insane.* When Aylish didn't return, Dylan could only hope he stayed gone for a good, long while. The last thing he needed was the complication of having his father looming as Dylan tried to figure out what the hell he was to do about the woman. That she called to his very soul was irrefutable, but so too was the fact her death was his responsibility. "Maybe that's Danu's blessed truth, that no Assassin is meant to be happy. I should resign myself to my fate by killing her and getting it over—"

A sharp crash behind him was followed by a heavy blow to his shoulder. Stumbling forward, he was nearly driven to his knees by the sharp wind that rushed through the corridor. He spun, sword at the ready. The long hallway was empty. "What was *that*?" he shouted, looking around. "Now we've got bleedin' *ghosts*?"

Rowan rushed to take up his post at Dylan's back, and Gareth emerged from the room carrying a short sword. Seeing the doorway unguarded, he took up a combative stance. No one would get through him to Kennedy. This was exactly what they would have done if... *Oh,* hell *no.* They were treating her as if she was his gods-given bride. History supported the fact that the Assassin rarely, rarely married. Druids didn't even have a title for the Assassin's wife, because it was the rarest of couples who serve the Order's demands first and a family's second. It had always been so simple for Dylan—no life equaled no wife. Besides, if he was going to be forced to give her up as proof of his dedication to the Order, he couldn't think about her in longer terms than the moment at hand.

Slashing at the air that bandied about him, he started down the hallway to assess the damage to the stained-glass window. That glass had survived the rise and fall of kingdoms. It had seen the changing of seasons a thousand times over. Yet whatever had slammed into him had thoroughly dismantled it. He growled, the low sound vibrating through his chest. Spinning on his heel, he moved by Rowan. "Send for one of the lads to clean this up and seal off the window. We'll commission a replacement from one of the Order's artists."

"Sir." Rowan bent over the railing and hailed a lad below. "Send up McCork and O'Doherty with brooms and bins."

Dylan closed in on Gareth. "Stand down. She's my mark, Gareth, nothing more."

"Uh-huh." Gareth gave a slow blink. "Keep telling yourself that and I'll know for sure you're not the full shilling, mate."

"I'm not mad. I'm just not willing to let things between me and Kennedy get any further out of hand." He leaned on his sword, irritated at his sweat-slicked palms. "There's a job to be done. It seems we've all forgotten why we're here." He scrubbed his free hand over his face, dropping it just in time to see Gareth jerk straighter.

His assassin stepped out of the doorway.

Eyes huge in a face gone pale as fresh milk, Kennedy stood perfectly still. Bloodless lips barely moved when she said, "I thought… I mean, I'd really believed…" She opened her mouth once, twice, then closed it. "I suppose I should thank you for not letting it get any more out of hand than it did." She nodded, the movement quick and jerky, as she stepped into the hallway. "Right. Thanks, then."

"You've been ordered to stay in my suite." When he reached for her, she shied away so sharply she tripped and nearly went to her knees.

Catching herself on Gareth's arm, she spared a glance over her shoulder. "I'll go to Aylish. He can manage this until you're…needed." Her bare feet were silent as she raced down the stairs.

Gareth didn't even try to stop her from leaving.

Dylan made to go around him and was stunned to find a sword point piercing the hollow of his throat.

"You know, she dashed into your suite thinking to surprise you with a game of poker with the Arcanum. Kind gesture, that." Gareth rubbed his chin. "I think, brother, you'd be wise to let her go and find her peace either some-*where* else or with some*one* else. Handy that the warlock arrives at sunrise." With a look of utter disgust, he dropped the blade and chucked it into Dylan's suite. "It's good for her to have someone she can trust outright."

How on Earth he could possibly fix everything that had gone wrong in the space of less than ten minutes? He wasn't even sure where to start.

Aylish's door was closed. That alone wasn't enough to stop Dylan from barging in. Magick coursed through wood and iron, catapulting him back when he grabbed the latch. He landed sprawled out across the hallway and was forced to prop himself up against the wall before reclaiming the breath that had been knocked out of him.

"Playing like that, are you?" Dylan struggled to his feet and studied the door, thinking about the Elder's rooms. Approaching the hall wall with caution, he tested a small area left of the door. Finding nothing but residual magicks, he laid his fingertips against the wall.

Aether's power coursed through him, a low-level electrical current between the layers of skin and muscle. His fingers began to hum with an insistent, low-level buzz that only he could hear. The air around him began to swirl and distort, morphing into a heavy, viscous material he dragged himself through. Breathing hurt. He flattened his palm on the wall, curling his fingertips against the stone and mentally pushing. Magick flooded into the stone and overrode any of the Elder's residual magicks.

Dylan pushed harder, thrilling when the stone broke down into its fundamental components. Using both hands, he twisted and shaped the components, whispering suggestions, coaxing the magick to reach farther, become *more*. The swirling gray snapped back together. The piney scent of fresh lumber washed over him even as the smell of hot metal charring the wood stung the back of his nose. A new door stood where the wall had been. Dylan considered knocking before he walked in but changed his mind. They knew he was here.

Stepping into the lavish living area, he was surprised to find it silent. He wandered room to room, listening with every silent step, hoping to hear something. Anything. What he met was a whole lot of nothing.

He made it back to the living room before he sensed the change. His father was coming through the door and he was supremely pissed off.

"Dylan O'Shea," he said, the accusation heavy in his voice.

"Warranted use of both my names? Huh. Been centuries since you've taken it that far." Dylan looked around and didn't see Kennedy. "Where's the woman?"

"*The woman* is resting." Aylish stomped over to the sideboard where he poured a solid two fingers of whiskey, neat. He tossed it back and poured again, three fingers this time.

"If you're drinking, I'll have one, too."

Aylish faced him with calculated movements. "Pour it yourself." He hurled the decanter at Dylan. The stopper crashed against a bookshelf, shattering when it bounced to the floor. Whiskey sloshed all over Dylan's upper body as he fumbled the heavy crystal.

"What's your damage, auld man?" Gripping the slippery neck, he tilted the decanter back and took a long pull straight from the crystal bottle. His breath exploded from his lungs, the whiskey burning through him. Guilt over the words he'd thrown at Kennedy had him taking a second hit from the bottle.

Aylish dropped into the nearest chair, face in his hands. The fireplace blazed to life without a single word or incantation. He looked up, and Dylan couldn't help but think his father had aged. "You've sent the woman into an emotional hell she's not willing to climb out of at this point."

Decanter hanging between two fingers, Dylan crossed his arms and stared down his nose at his father. "You sent me to kill her. You and the Order. Seems she's been falling into that particular hell for more than just an afternoon or because of a few ill-timed words."

Aylish's head fell back, resting on the upper swell of the sofa cushion. "You think to hide behind semantics?"

Dylan blinked slowly. "Where's the woman, Aylish?"

A wicked grin revealed perfect white teeth. "Two can play by your rules. She's *sleeping*, Assassin."

Molars grinding, he forced himself to still. *I'll be reduced to drinking milkshakes and gumming mush if I wear the chompers out.* He drew another dram of whiskey straight from the bottleneck and blew the fumes out his nose. "Where is she sleeping?"

"The *where* would be semantics, good man. Semantics. And since you're not interested in dealing in specifics, as in specific truths, you're out of luck."

Dylan dropped the decanter, the sound of crystal shattering against stone diffused by his hammering pulse. He pitched forward and grabbed Aylish's arm. "Say that again."

"What the bloody hell, Dylan?" Aylish shoved him down onto the sofa, pressing his head between his knees.

Struggling, Dylan forced his way up and grabbed the

back of Aylish's neck, forcing the man to look at him. "Say that." His teeth chattered. "Again."

"I…what? Say what again?" Aylish grasped Dylan's wrist and held on. "Son?"

Dylan yanked his hand out of his father's hold. "Forget it, Elder O'Shea."

Shoving to his feet, Dylan lurched toward the doorway. "I'll fix this…later." Sweat dotted his upper lip. His hands shook. Gravity rooted his boots to the floor and made every step forward a fight. By the time he reached the top of the stairs, Dylan had sweated through his shirt, and his hair was drenched. The cool breeze that blew down the hallway comforted him.

It wasn't until he'd shut his door that he realized the lads had already patched the window.

Perhaps Danu's temper and mothering nature weren't as far away as he thought.

The night was a fit of starts and stops for Dylan. He'd start to fall asleep and stop. He'd start to go look for Kennedy and stop. He'd start to order the warlock returned to the US and stop. He'd start to reach for her in the darkness and stop.

Her smell wound around him, a bittersweet reminder that she was under his skin. The urge to draw her into his arms saw him clutching her pillow like a lovesick lad, but even that realization couldn't force him to let it go. If anything, he held it closer. Eventually he gave up on trying to sleep and pulled on a pair of leathers, boots, a long-sleeved Henley and his watch cap, and headed for the Elder's Library.

The keep was eerily silent. Even the wind seemed to have given up its perpetual struggle to carve runnels in the walls. He moved quietly through the bright night, the waxing gibbous moon illuminating hallways and lightening shadows enough it would make it hard for a man to hide without magick. The doors to the Observatory were closed, and Niall and Kayden stood quietly chatting outside them. As he approached, they took up their formal positions and quieted, waiting.

He had no interest in disciplining them for such a small slight. "All's well?"

They glanced at each other.

"What?" When neither answered, he stopped. Hands on his hips, he let his chin fall forward. "What is it?"

"We're under orders to not allow you to pass." Niall tugged at the neck of his T-shirt.

"Whose orders?" Not that he really had to ask.

"The Elder's orders." Kayden stepped forward a bit, drawing Dylan's gaze. "He said we were to tell you to replace his whiskey if you needed something to do." The man cleared his throat, brows winging down. "We're not to go against the Elder, Dylan…sir. If you made it an order, though, we'd have to choose."

"And which side would you come down on?" The cold disconnect in his voice should have made the men shiver. Instead, it drew a grin from both of them.

"You're both dangerous, sir."

Turning, he strode away and stepped out onto the foggy moor. Pounding surf called to him. He broke into a jog, then a run and finally a wide-open sprint.

Wide, blue eyes, eyes that had stared at him first in passion and then in disbelief, haunted him, the words he'd shouted at his father echoing in his head.

How can I tell her what even I don't know?

Kennedy rolled over in bed. The sheets were cold. In fact, the whole bed was cold without Dylan, damn his black soul. She should have known, should have at the very least *suspected*, that he was using her. Men like him were nothing more than a fantasy. Reality? Well, it sucked. Royally.

She rolled over again, punching her pillow into a new shape. Not better, just different. Truth was, she couldn't seem to get Dylan out of her head. *Ethan'll help. He'll get me refocused.* She glanced at the clock. Roughly two more hours and he'd be here.

What would he think of this pretty little predicament? No doubt he'd have some choice words for Dylan. If she had understood the one-sided conversation earlier, Dylan had sent someone to retrieve Ethan and escort him all the way to the Nest. He'd likely be royally pissed he'd been "retrieved" like some dog toy. That wasn't what was eating at her, though. Not once had his wishes been taken into consideration. Guilt punched through her middle, its invisible trajectory passing through her front and out her back.

Shoving her hands through her hair, Kennedy sat up and swung her legs over the side of the bed. Aylish had left her in this room with strongly worded instructions that she wasn't to try to leave. The warning had turned the room into a gilded prison. Below the surface, there was no velvet or silk but rather sharp barbs and cutting blades. Dylan had been part of that below-the-surface view. She'd thought him honest. Then he'd opened his mouth and destroyed her, ripping her to shreds and in front of an audience, no less. He couldn't even allow her to experience the humiliating truth privately. She rose and went to the window. A heavy rime coated the glass, crystals of frost fracturing the smooth surface with a thousand tiny spines. The frozen window combined with the cold and damp to create a little biosphere behind the heavy curtain. Touching her finger to the surface, the initial shock of cold shot goose bumps up her arm. Instinct told her to pull away. She ignored it. *Just like I did with Dylan.*

He'd told her he was dangerous, that he'd go to any

length to finish this, and he'd never offered her more than the moment at hand.

She hadn't listened.

Lifting her finger, she peered through the tiny, melted portal she'd made. She'd had a similar window into Dylan, but when she'd tried to look, he'd drawn the emotional shades.

"Now I'm getting maudlin." Pulling her hair up into a loose topknot, she wrapped the ever-present hairband on her wrist around the mess. "I need to get—"

The word "dressed" was a hard exhale.

Her pulse thudded heavily against her eardrums. Shoved aside, Kennedy became a passenger in her body. Power built, a low-level hum that graduated to a buzz and morphed into biting stings at every nerve ending. Her body wasn't meant to channel the elements. She wasn't conditioned to harness this kind of power. It ate at her, small bites that created horrific pain.

Humming a soft tune, Cailleach moved to the warded door and passed a hand over it.

The skin on Kennedy's palm grew so hot she was sure it bubbled. Her scream was no more than a squeak. But...
I managed a noise?

Cailleach stepped back and, tapping a forefinger against her lips, considered the silvery lines that filtered up through a pale gray haze. "He thinks to keep me here with a scolding and an incantation?" She reached out and touched the end of one line. Magick coursed through her and sent her tripping backward. "Oh, no. This won't do at all, to have the Druids believe I'm containable. It's time to instruct these men in respect." She placed a hand over her stomach. "Lessons come with a cost, Kennedy. You may only have six days left, but you might find a chance to use the knowledge."

Kennedy started at the direct address. Never had Cailleach spoken to her like this. She opened her mouth and mind, intent on asking what the *lesson* might constitute, but her words were consumed in a blazing rush of power. Kennedy was lost to the inferno, the goddess's internal void sucking the life from the flames. But before Kennedy could claim relief, another wave of magick rushed in and began the torture all over again. Kennedy screamed, clawing at herself.

Cailleach grunted and clasped her flailing hands together. "Enough, woman!" Lips curled in a snarl, the goddess plunged her hands into Aylish's magick, methodically unraveling the knots and braids that made up the ward.

Raw, undiluted pain made Kennedy crazed. She struck out at Cailleach, not considering the how of it, only certain she had to make the goddess stop. Cailleach was killing Kennedy, and there was no way—mortal or not—she was willing to go down. Not now. Not when—

The brutalizing pain stopped so suddenly that Cailleach lurched away from the door as Kennedy stumbled. "You'll stop this nonsense, woman, or I'll see you finished before the full moon. I need your body. Your mind means nothing to me." Straightening, she adjusted her camisole and sweats. Her gaze swept the room, lighting on the hearth. She crossed the room and swept up the shovel, hefting its weight in her palm. Dissatisfied, that was tossed aside and the poker chosen next. She choked up on it, taking a couple of practice swipes as she turned back for the door. "Far from perfect but better than nothing."

Kennedy knew she was shaking but that out-of-body thing was going on. *Shock. I'm fighting shock. Can't let her wield that weapon, threat or no threat.*

Cailleach opened the door. The moment the hinges squeaked, she yanked the door inward and leaped into the hall, swinging with all her might.

Rowan started to turn, sword in hand. The pointed

hook on the poker smashed into his head with a sickening crunch. He crumpled to the floor, the poker's log hook lodged in his temple.

Cailleach left him there in a widening pool of blood. Toeing his shoulder, she smiled when he didn't move. "Can't afford to waste the energy to turn your heart to ash, assassin. The full moon's much too close for me to toy with inconsequential use of power. And trust me, pet. You're as inconsequential now as you were two centuries ago." In a sweeping move, she grabbed his sword and started off down the hall at a significant clip. "You see, Kennedy? You keep quiet, I spare their lives. Cause me grief?" She huffed. "For every inconvenience, I'll take a life. The choice is yours."

Kennedy wanted to rake her nails against Cailleach's eyes, but they were, in reality, her own eyes. She wanted to find a way to wrap her fist around the goddess's heart and squeeze, but the vital organ was, in reality, also Kennedy's. She wanted to scream and cause a scene, make enough noise to guarantee someone came running. Yet Cailleach only promised to strike them down as they came. So none of that would happen. No, Kennedy didn't see an alternative at the moment that allowed her to fight back. *But give me an inch, bitch, and I'm taking more than a mile.*

Cailleach stretched as she made her way through the keep, preparing to fight. The halls were as quiet as a chapel on a Tuesday morning. Slipping shadow to shadow, the early-morning light proved challenging to use to any advantage. The sword hung heavy in her hand, much larger than what she was used to wielding. She switched hands before propping the flat of the blade against her shoulder.

Kennedy watched and waited.

Voices, faint but deep, carried down the next corridor. Pausing at the hallway intersections, the goddess peeked around the corner. The doorway to the Observatory and, thus, the Elder's Library were closed. "Damn it all. I need the Scrolls of Lewillwen." A cold smile pulled at her mouth. "I'm too close to let something as inconsequential as myth stop me."

Kennedy listened, rapt. *What the hell is this squirrel going on about?*

Palms sweating, Cailleach was forced to rub them against her thighs before drying the damp sword pommel with her shirt hem. One deep breath, two, then she began to chant. Black smoke swirled around her ankles, twining through her legs intimately, climbing higher and higher. Her eyes closed in bliss. The magick felt good, liberating, even sexually stimulating. Power was the strongest aphrodisiac. Smoke encased her, swirling up and up, catching a faint draft from farther down the hall and trailing around the corner. In the false darkness, she smiled. "Perfect."

Without a doubt, Kennedy preferred being drunk—off her ass, in public, with strangers, without cab fare—to this spinning and bobbing sensation.

Cailleach apparently experienced some of Kennedy's trepidation at her ability to walk, tripping forward and slamming into the suit of armor. It crashed to the floor. Disorientation, and the confusion that came along with it, made her raise a hand to her head.

Preternatural silence immediately disguised all sound. Still, Kennedy had the overwhelming sense of impending destruction. But she couldn't be sure if she'd be the one swinging the blade or being deconstructed. Neither appealed.

Cailleach, cloaked in darkness, levitated. That tipsy feeling worsened, and Kennedy silently wished for Dramamine.

Niall rounded the corner with slow, measured steps, his gaze darting back and forth. Not once did he look up.

Cailleach shot over the assassin's head toward the Observatory. Swinging her blade as she passed, she aimed for the soft spot between neck and shoulder. She wobbled. Gravity intervened and hauled her ass to the ground.

Kennedy knew hitting the stone floor was going to hurt, but she was so focused on twisting her hand and forcing Cailleach's blade away that she didn't have time to duck and roll. Instead, she had the wind knocked out of her with brutal force. She was still reeling when Cailleach lurched to her feet.

Jaw tightened, the goddess refused to let Kennedy shout a warning to Dylan's men. Backing toward the wall, she kept her sword pointed at Niall. Her free hand, the one cupping that furiously coiling smoke, was aimed at Kayden. Both men hesitated, glancing from her to the other and back, and all the while, Cailleach inched toward the Observatory doors.

Niall shouted something unintelligible and flung out his hand. Wind swirled around her so viciously Kennedy's clothes were stretched, seams unraveling. Eyes watering, Cailleach pressed on.

Kayden knelt, eyes always on her, and touched the stones. Whispered words were lost to the abusive winds. Water seeped up through the floor and the bruising wind became bitterly cold. Ice formed and the goddess slipped, landing hard on one hip. The advantage that had taken her down, though, was the same disadvantage that kept the assassins at bay. They could no more cross the ice than she could.

Cupping her hand, she whispered into the smoke and blew. Black fire raced across the floor, leaving a charred, ice-free path in its wake. Kayden dove out of the way, and the flames hit the doors. The fire burned as if it had been laced with accelerant.

"Bull's-eye," she whispered.

Her joy made Kennedy sick.

"Black magick!" Niall shouted, taking a running slide across the ice. He dove to his belly as Cailleach screeched, sending a wave of blackened arrows in his direction. Most missed. A few found flesh and bone, embedding in Niall's vulnerable back and neck. He bellowed in pain and flailed about, trying desperately to get the points out before they began burrowing into his skin.

The doors boomed open and Aylish stepped out. Wind whipped around him, a product of his fury. Flame rolled through the fingers of one hand, an ever-lengthening vine through the others. In a commanding voice, he called out, "*Scáthanna an am atá caite Ordú, heed mo ghlao!*" Shadows of the Order past, heed my call! Hollow, clanking footsteps rounded the corner.

Kennedy gasped hard enough that she forced the same sound from Cailleach.

Empty suits of armor charged into the fray, weapons raised.

"*Cosain an Réadlann.*" Defend the Observatory.

Kayden moved in between the metal men and grabbed Niall's arm, dragging him toward Aylish. The Elder opened the door and sent the two assassins inside. "Order everyone to lock down the Library. They're to kill Kennedy if she makes it past me." He took Niall's sword and swung it in a tight figure eight as he moved forward.

Kennedy braced herself. There was one chance to make this happen. If she failed, Cailleach would have all the time in the world to shred Kennedy's mind and use her body to complete the reincarnation. *One shot.* Her drill sergeant's voice was the one she heard. *Any regrets, Jefferson?* The regret, her *only* regret, was one she'd never seen coming. *I never told Dylan I loved him.* Her heart stuttered before taking up a fierce, miserably joyous pounding. Loving him had simply happened. He'd worked his way under her skin and then into her heart. And now she'd never be able to tell him. She hoped beyond all hope he'd see her sacrifice for what it was—an attempt to put an end to this and save him from the obligation.

Blades clanged and crashed together. A glancing blow nearly felled Cailleach, but she rallied at the last moment and kept to the offensive. Black magicks sullied the air, tainting every breath.

Aylish moved forward. "Come to me, Kennedy." His voice boomed through the hall and whispered through her consciousness, such a wild opposite it made her dizzy.

Kayden fought viciously, driving the goddess back even as Aylish called Kennedy forward again. His voice encouraged her to fill in the small voids of space Cailleach had missed.

"Call her out and I shred her mind," Cailleach rasped.

Aylish's brows drew down over eyes gone furiously cold and tight. His mouth hardened into little more than a thin line.

Kayden pushed her back another step, and Cailleach hit the edge of the ice. She tried to keep her sword arm straight to block Kayden's blows, but instinct had her flailing just to keep her feet. She went down hard again, sprawled out on the ice like a sacrifice.

This is it. One chance. Kennedy's heart pounded, every beat a vicious ache. She pushed forward with all she had, shoving the goddess aside. There was a moment of disconnect, a pulse of time where she felt Cailleach's surprise, and then Kennedy found herself reseated and in control of her body.

Rolling over, she scrambled to her hands and knees, pulling her hair to the side to expose her neck. "End this, Kayden!" Kennedy took an internal blow to the base of her skull that nearly flattened her. Nose running, jaw chattering from the cold, she rolled her eyes toward the assassin.

He stood, poised to strike.

"Please." She knew stopping the goddess would become more and more difficult closer to the full moon. "Please." *Never thought I'd beg to have my head lopped off.*

"Stand aside!" The ear-shattering order came from behind the assassin. She looked past him and found Aylish moving toward her so rapidly he was hard to track.

Kayden dropped his sword and Aylish yanked her up and into his arms, holding her while she shook.

"What the hell is going on? You Irishmen do this for *fun*?" Ethan's voice shattered the tension.

She turned to him, relief washing through her. He was here.

Ethan held out his arms and she rushed into them. "Thank the gods there aren't sheep involved. That's all I'm sayin'."

Chapter 18

The last thing Dylan wanted to see when he came back to the keep was evidence that Cailleach had risen, but the general sense of prevailing chaos said he'd walked into the aftereffects of just that. Scattered suits of armor, a wet hallway, burned Observatory doors and the disjointed recovery efforts spoke loudly. Aylish was in the thick of it, working to create order.

Movement from a darkened corner drew his attention. Kennedy sagged in Ethan's embrace, wrapped up safe and secure. The warlock's clothes were rumpled, but not nearly as much as Kennedy's were. She looked as if she'd hastily redressed after—

Dylan had a near out-of-body experience as he charged across the floor. He consciously knew he shouldn't jump to conclusions while his emotions had already taken the terminal leap. Deadly and swift, he raised a fist and plowed it into Ethan's relaxed face. The man seemed to fold to the floor limp and boneless.

Kennedy started down with him, but Dylan grabbed her by the upper arms and hauled her back into him. Chest heaving, lungs burning, he held her there despite her struggles. When she stomped his foot, he wrapped one leg around hers and forced her to still. "He's down, but no' out. See? The bluidy Yank's already getting up."

"What's. Your. *Damage!*" Ethan bellowed, shoving himself more upright. "You kidnap me, haul my ass over the river and through the woods, take me on a three-hour tour to destination 'Middle of Fucking Nowhere,' then punch me when I get here?" He spat blood before standing and glaring pointedly at Dylan. "If she hadn't so nearly been beheaded, didn't so clearly need help—" he jerked his chin toward Kennedy "—I'd settle this *my* way."

The entire room went still. Waiting. "Beheaded." Steel-edged, the word cut all in earshot.

The warlock drew a shaky breath but only stared at Dylan.

He found himself running his hands over Kennedy, silently assuring himself she was whole. "Later, then." Curious, Dylan nodded once. "Tell me, then, how would you settle this? You know I'll tear you apart."

Ethan laughed, the sound bitter and vengeful. "Not by magick, you damned idiot. I'd take you down in a Call of Duty challenge. Winner takes all."

"I've my own duty, but you aren't taking Kennedy, no matter who wins."

Kennedy began to shake.

Dylan slipped an arm around her shoulders and hauled her even tighter to him. "Doona worry yourself, lass. It's going to be fine."

Ethan's hard stare had migrated from Dylan's face to Kennedy's. His lips twitched. "Don't do it, Jefferson."

She shook her head and sniffed.

"Have you made her cry?" Dylan glared at Ethan in open challenge, gently turning her around. His face went lax with confusion. "Not tears, then."

The sound of her laughter rang through the hallway. Peal after peal, she backed away and doubled over, arms over her stomach as she fought for air. Ethan stood behind her, grinning like an idiot. When he wiggled his thumbs, her laughter rang even louder. Tears streamed down her face.

"Enough." Aylish cut through the group of men who

stood staring, equally as confused as Dylan. He drew Kennedy into his embrace and she went, not fighting him as she had Dylan himself.

His da laid a kiss on her head, speaking softly into her hair. She jerked as if shocked then slowly lifted her face to his. An intimate, wordless understanding passed between them.

Dylan ran a hand behind his neck and pulled so hard his skin burned. She could frustrate him so damn much… His hand fell away. It wasn't frustration he was experiencing. No, the bile burning the back of his throat, the tightness in his chest—he was *scared*. He lifted his chin sharply and found his da staring at him. Whatever had passed between Kennedy and Aylish failed to translate between father and son. Time ground to a halt, fluid yet stagnant, as Dylan tried like mad to infer what it was his father wanted from him. Nothing happened.

Chuffing out his frustration, he shook his head. "I'll keep her in my suite. We'll need to—"

"Finish this upstairs," Aylish finished for him.

"Right." Dylan reached for Kennedy only to have her turn to Ethan.

"Come with us." She'd finally dried her face on Aylish's robes, but the merriment hung on in the flush of her cheeks.

"Like I'd let you go anywhere alone with him, baby girl." Ethan glared at Dylan and stepped closer to Kennedy. "We need to talk, anyway."

"Later," she said quickly, interrupting anything else he might have said.

Dylan closed his eyes and fought to center himself. "Fine. The warlock comes with us. We'll meet in my suite and sort this out." He looked at Aylish. "Send the Arcanum after us."

Aylish laid a hand on his arm; Ethan reached for Kennedy, and they started down the hall. "I'll follow in a moment, Dylan." He seemed to struggle to find his next words. "Be cautious with her, son."

Son. The term was nearly affectionate, never used between them. "Anything I should know... Da?"

Aylish went so still he could have been one of the patrons carved from stone and placed throughout the keep. His face relaxed enough for him to smile gently. His eyes were warm as they searched Dylan's face. "That's not for me to tell, though you should see the truth of it soon." He touched Dylan's arm. "Go. I'll see the Arcanum cared for and research resumed. We need to make the most out of our last few days. I'll join you upstairs as soon as I'm able."

Dylan turned away, confused yet energized.

For better or worse, the final countdown to the full moon had kicked into gear.

"You did what?" Dylan shouted. They'd all gathered in his suite, crowding the living room. He'd heard the entire rundown, a harmonious retelling of the wickedly fecked up earlier events, ending with Kennedy baring her neck to Kayden's blade.

Kennedy rubbed her neck exactly where Kayden would have struck the blow to behead her. "She wanted the Scrolls of Lewillwen, Dylan. I couldn't let her get that far. If taking her...*my*...head would end this, I thought—"

"You *didn't* think," he said, lip lifted in a snarl. "You reacted."

"She was clear of mind, Assassin." Kayden had filled in both his and Niall's involvement. "The goddess wasn't riding her when she made the call."

"Yet it was the wrong call for all that." His words were harsh enough his assassin winced.

Aylish shifted in his seat. "We need to know what's in

those Scrolls that's so important to her. Dylan, Kennedy did what she thought she had to do for the good of all."

"No, she didn't." *She clearly hadn't considered me at all.* He shoved out of the club chair and started for the windows. He whirled at the soft touch on his shoulder.

Kennedy looked up at him, guileless blue eyes locked on his own. "Dylan, if it would have saved you the obligation of delivering the killing blow…I'd spare you that." She sighed. "I don't want you remembering me that way."

He went deadly still. The sound of the surf was punctuated by the crackling fire and the subtle shifting of his men as they prepared to intervene on her behalf. "That's what this is about? You made the choice to have one of the Arcanum act in my stead to spare me what? My *duty*?"

"I—yes."

"No one assumes that responsibility, Kennedy. I was chosen as the Assassin. I. Was. *Chosen*," he said, pounding his chest. "You don't presume to end this before all our options are exhausted. Understand me?" He loomed over her, forcing her to step back.

The hunter in him wanted her to run, wanted to turn the clock back to Atlanta and take control of the situation from day one. He would have taken her immediately. He'd have used those extra days to get to know her better, learning the nuances that made her so unique. There would have been more time, more opportunity to stop this. He'd wasted what he could have had with her, what might have been. That she might have loved him in return—

Dylan stumbled back from her, crashing into a bookcase. He clutched a shelf with wood-creaking force as books rained around him, the smell of old paper and ink disturbed in the melee. The literary storm passed, leaving him up to his ankles in old tomes and recent bestsellers. Minutes ran into hours, which turned into days, which all blurred together, giving him a high-speed replay of their most intimate moments, from the smallest things to their greatest pleasures. He'd known. Oh yeah, he'd known he was in over his head. *But love?* "Oh, gods."

A broad hand settled on his shoulder. "Deep breaths, son."

And then there was this, this new development with Aylish. *Son.* Too much emotion flooded through him, breaching well-defended personal levies—levies he'd erected to keep him removed from who he'd been and what he was, from child to son to Assassin. Never enough. Never enough for anyone I've loved. She'll die and I canna stop it anymore than I can stop the fecking moon from rising.

Wheeling away, he grabbed Kennedy and hoisted her over his shoulder. "Everyone out." Ignoring her squeak of surprise and Ethan's belligerent objection, he headed to the bedroom. There would be one more night before he separated himself from her, re-centered himself and, come Samhain, was forced to honor his duty. Tonight, though, through his actions, he'd show her what he couldn't find the words to say. He'd have one more night.

They would have one more night.

Whatever had been between them, whatever had stood guard between two stalwart hearts, had crumbled for Kennedy the moment he'd pulled her out of Ethan's embrace and into his own. That he'd been moved to take her into the protection of his arms despite the way they'd parted the night before... His actions spoke to her in ways his words didn't, wouldn't, couldn't.

She knew what he was after as he hauled her away, and she couldn't bring herself to object. After all, she wanted the same. A night to get lost in him. One night where she could pretend that he loved her as much as she loved him.

Bracing a hand on his hip, she pushed up and shoved her hair out of her face. Finding Ethan poised to chase them down, she met his glinty-eyed stare. "It's okay."

"Like hell it is, Jefferson." He took that first step toward her. Of all the men in the room, it was Aylish who stopped him. A whispered incantation and Ethan's legs froze. "You and your magick," he shouted. "All you 'blokes' are missing are the wands, white owls and one creepy-ass professor. Oh. Wait. You've got Rowan. Yep, you're the whole package."

"Rich, coming from you and all," Gareth drawled in a bad Southern accent.

"He'll be good to her." Aylish looked back at Kennedy. She nodded. "See you tomorrow, Ethan."

"Why don't you come with me to the Library." Aylish released the binding on Ethan's legs once he had a firm grip on his arm and steered him from the room.

Dylan kicked the bedroom doors shut. Locks turned and latched under his direction.

Her world tilted and she bounced on the bed. Propping herself up on her elbows, she started to tease him a bit until she caught the look on his face. Hair undone, eyes wide, lips parted and a high flush riding his cheeks, he looked wild, untamed even.

He watched her, chest heaving as he rubbed his left pec. "I want..." He ran an unsteady hand through his hair. He moved away, bracing an arm on the stone window casing and letting his head fall forward.

Slow and quiet, Kennedy moved from the bed to stand behind him. Heat radiated off his back and caressed her exposed skin. Tenderness swamped her. She wanted nothing more than to hold him, to let him find his comfort in her. Her hands went to the knotted muscles of his shoulders and slowly swept down the corded muscles on either side of his spine, coming to rest on the sway of his back. A gentle squeeze earned her a shiver.

Stepping in closer, she went up on tiptoe and laid a kiss between his shoulders. Her hands moved to his front and pulled his shirt free of his waistband.

He began to turn toward her. "Kennedy, I—"

She stepped into him hard, stopping him as she plastered her body to his. "Shh. Be still." Blindly unbuttoning his shirt, she peeled it from his shoulders and let it puddle at their feet. She ran her hands over him, trying to memorize every dip and swell of his topography. Tracing her fingertip around his belly button, he sucked his stomach in, and she smiled against his skin.

Her hands dipped to his belt and she managed to undo it and his pants. She cupped his heavy sac with one hand and worked his erection free with the other. Gripping his swollen shaft, she stroked him leisurely, as if they had all the time in the world.

A shuddering sigh escaped him, and he leaned back into her, leaned *on* her, let himself go into her care without a fight.

She wanted to rage at the heavens, to weep, to rail at any gods or goddesses who would see fit to take her from him for any reason. Instead, she closed her eyes and breathed him in—the scent of the sea, the smell of his soap, the wildness of the moors on his skin—and vowed to never forget him.

He turned to her then, and this time she didn't stop him. Instead, she let her hands trail over his bared skin. Beautiful, damnable moonlight shone bright over his dark hair and broad shoulders.

I love you. Despite her best efforts, a sob escaped. She bit her lip. Hard.

Dylan curled a finger under her chin and forced her to look up. Green eyes glowed, impossibly lit from inside.

She gasped.

He shook his head. "It's nothing, *mo shearc*."

"Take me to bed, Dylan."

Tucking his hair behind one ear, his face became a study of angles, illumination and shadow. "Aye."

That one word, so soft and simple, pulled her into him as effectively as did his arms. In that singular moment, she knew he'd been looking for this, this communion with her. It was more than two bodies joining in the dark. It was two souls meeting for the first time.

His arms tightened as she stepped back. Reaching behind, she took his hand. He let her go, and she led him to the bed, never looking back. Shyness overwhelmed her. There would be a certain amount of vulnerability about their joining, and she didn't know if she was prepared.

Warm hands rested at her waist, sliding up and pulling her shirt along. Once free, he let it fall away. She stood facing the fireplace, fighting the urge to cover herself.

"I'll light the fire later if ye wish, *a ghrá mo chroí*. I want to see you in the moonlight now, for if there was ever a woman meant to be bathed in her beauty, it's you." Warm lips touched the back of her neck where he whispered, "It's always been you."

He handled her with reverent care, stripping her pants from her an inch at a time. And for every inch revealed, he kissed bare skin. When they were finally to her ankles, she was a trembling wreck of need and want, awash in desire.

"Turn around." His gruff command was tempered by tender hands.

She faced him and let herself be drawn into his embrace. Rising up to meet him halfway, that first kiss was tenuous, fragile. Her tongue darted out to taste his lower lip and he groaned, pulling her harder against him. She'd forgotten he'd had whiskey, neat, in the living room.

His cock pulsed against the cool skin of her bare belly.

When he sipped from her lips, then delved into her mouth, she couldn't stop the sound of need that escaped her.

"Ah, gods, Kennedy. Let me…" He laid her across the bed and urged her legs wide open. Crawling onto the mattress, he slid his hands under her ass and lifted her to his mouth.

Kennedy's eyes flew wide and she almost protested, but he moved in, swift and sure.

His first taste of her was bold, and she cried out.

"No' yet, *a chuman.*" He worked her gently, pushing her toward the crest only to deny her when she was seconds away. When he took her this time, though, she bucked in his grip and fisted the sheets.

"Please, Dylan."

"Come for me, lass."

He sucked her clitoris and Kennedy shattered, riding the orgasm out as wave after wave of pent-up emotions carried her away. There was no fear, no sorrow, no anger. She was simply his.

Dylan crawled up her still-quivering body and gently set himself at her entrance. "Ye're ready for me, *a ghrá.*"

She reached for him and, together, they worked him into her. He was so large she was stretched, pain and pleasure converging so that where one ended the other began, a never-ending circle.

He curled his hips forward and she arched her back, taking him deeper and squeezing her sheath around him. "Dylan."

He spoke through gritted teeth when he said, "I'll no' last long if ye keep that up."

"Love me." Those same words she'd issued a week ago were now more a plea. She opened her mouth to tell him, to admit she loved him, when he pulled away.

Flipping her over, he pressed her chest to the bed and lifted her hips. He fisted one hand in her hair, hauling her head back before covering her, his breath hot on the shell of her ear. "Ye'll take what I can give, Kennedy."

She tried to shake her head in denial, but his grip held her firm. Never imagining she'd take to being dominated, not like this, she found herself wildly aroused. "Do it," she groaned.

Dylan slammed into her.

Kennedy screamed, pleasure coursing through her core. The smell of the sea, the sound of the waves, the heat of the man—it was wild and raw and perfect.

He set a bruising rhythm. All she could do was close her eyes, a slave to sensation. She was his to love. A single tear scalded her cheek, and she pulled against his grip.

The sound of skin on skin was an erotic background to the heavy bellows of Dylan's lungs behind her.

I love him.

He changed the angle of penetration at the same time he nudged her knees impossibly far apart. "Come for me now, *mo dorcha áilleacht.*"

A second orgasm ripped through her, violent and demanding.

Dylan's roar of satisfaction echoed throughout the high-ceilinged room.

She slid forward, her mind hazy and confused when he followed her down, still buried to the hilt.

He pressed a kiss to her temple before whispering, "I'm far from done with you, *álainn.*"

And then he showed what it was like to be physically loved beyond mortal boundaries.

Kennedy lay sprawled on her stomach, more thoroughly ravished than she'd ever been. *Ever.* Dylan had taken her in ways she hadn't known were physically possible. Muscles she hadn't known she'd possessed ached, and she celebrated each pang of discomfort as a badge well earned. She lazily rolled her head to the side, the blaze of the fire warming her. Still, Dylan reached down and pulled the sheet over her. With that simple gesture she got the feeling he was beginning to pull away.

I love you. "Don't go," she said softly.

He sat, forearms propped on bent knees, head hanging low, his breathing just returning to normal. Turning his head a fraction, he lifted one shoulder. "I'm here."

She rolled over and went to her knees beside him. "I need you *here*—" she touched one hand to her chest, the other to his "—as much as *here*." She patted the bed.

He looked at the fire, face impassive. "Want and need are two different things."

Had he slapped her, she couldn't have been more surprised. Confusion bloomed, dark and thorny. *Want and need...* "Which am I to you?"

He glanced down at his fingers and began picking at a rough cuticle.

"Dylan?"

He rolled out of bed. Retrieving his leathers, he pulled them on and took up an almost identical position at the window—palm pressed to the casing, gaze on the sea, moonlight casting him in as much contradiction as his words had his lovemaking.

Tucking the covers around her, Kennedy chewed her bottom lip. If ever there was a time to tell him she loved him, it was now. While there was time. She opened her mouth, and he cut her off.

"Don't do it, Kennedy. Don't take this somewhere we both know it can't go."

Her mouth worked silently until she could finally whisper, "What?"

"I told you to take what I could give. Don't ask for more than that. I don't have it in me." He looked back, green eyes gone lifeless. "Not even for you, *mo chroí.*" He turned back to the window, clearly thinking to end the conversation.

She reached for a book on his bedside table and pelted him with it. "Liar!"

He exploded away from the wall, stopping himself halfway to the bed. "Do ye no' see? I canna let it go so far as to love you!" His words vibrated with centuries of unspent emotion. "If I allow myself to love you and you die? You'd be no different than my mother, and I'd be no different than the lad who couldn't protect her." His chest heaved. "I'm no different," he rasped. Dropping his chin to his chest, he leaned forward and gripped his thighs.

"You're surely not still blaming yourself for that?"

"And who else would there be to blame, Kennedy?"

"You were a boy."

"I was a boy whose element was aether! I could have dismantled him where he stood!"

She rose with as much grace as she could muster and went to him. Taking his hand in hers, she slid between him and the stone window casing. Rigid muscles refused to relax under her stroking. Hand over his thundering heart, she kissed his bare chest over and over. Small butterfly kisses that drifted over his torso until he began to yield to her. With a bottomless well of love, she showed him what faith looked like—touch, taste, smell. When he laced their fingers together, she gently pulled him back to bed. Stripping his pants, she laid back. "For one night, let it go. Just one night."

He allowed her to pull him down. Situating him so his head rested on her breast, she whispered words of past-due absolution so softly he couldn't have heard.

She held him there, listening to his breathing grow deep and regular as she stroked his hair. His arm snaked over her middle in sleep. As the moon sank toward the sea's horizon, she laid a gentle kiss on his brow and closed her eyes.

I love you.

Chapter 19

Dylan glanced at the clock above the living room mantel. "It's too early for this." He took another sip of whiskey then leaned forward as he stared into the broad flames of the fire. Last night had wrecked him. A choking tangle of emotions clogged his brain. Every time he thought he'd come to some sort of conclusion, one more memory would bombard him and drag him under sanity's surface. If a man could drown in want and need, he was doomed.

Want and need. The same things he'd said to Kennedy last night. Gods, what a fool he was to believe the two were so far removed from one another when it came to her. He wanted her with a burning passion. He needed her like his next breath.

The main door opened without a knock. *Gareth.*

The man stepped into the room, an unopened bottle of whiskey in his hand. "See we had the same idea." He looked like hell warmed over.

"You been to bed yet?"

"Nope. Stood outside your door last night to make sure you had help if the wicked witch rose to take her broom out for a round of fun and a nightcap." He sank into the sofa with a groan. "Feels good to park my arse." He toed off his boots and propped his stocking feet on the battered chest that served as a coffee table.

Dylan started to lift his glass to his lips but paused. "Hallway door or bedroom door?"

Gareth shot Dylan a wry grin. "Bedroom—from the moment it closed till ye yelled at her." The grin faded as he took a nip straight from the bottle. "She loves you, mate. Doona feck this up."

"And what would you know of it?"

"I know you've let history ride your back like a gods-be-damned rucksack for more than three hundred years." He held his bottle up to the firelight and rolled it back and forth between his palms. "Give this thing with her a chance, Dylan. Set the past down and walk away, man."

Dylan swallowed his vitriolic response and need to strike out. Restless and edgy, he sat up. "Aye? And what would you have me do when it comes time to strike her down?" Throat tightening, he set his glass down and stood. The urge to move, to be out of Gareth's direct and knowing line of sight lashed him like a whip. But where would he go?

Slumping lower in the sofa, Gareth rolled his eyes up and met Dylan's. "Someday, at some point, you'll find something that's worth letting go of the past and the guilt that follows along with it."

Dylan downed the last of his whiskey and silently held out his Glencairn glass for a refill.

Gareth obliged, filling it nearly to the rim.

Sipping, Dylan walked to the windows out of habit as his mind chewed over both the advice and the speculation. Voice low and gravelly, he asked, "Then what, mate? Swing the blade that ends the threat, as I've always done? Because if I acknowledge this…this…" He closed his eyes and drew a deep breath, whiskey fumes burning his nose and lungs. "I wasn't built for relationships, Gareth, and I definitely wasn't built for *more*." He looked back. "The Fates saw to that when I was hardly a boy."

The assassin's eyes slid closed and a frown pulled at the

corners of his mouth. "Why does it have to be so bluidy hard? Why can it not be a choice you make for you?"

"Some things are simply greater than personal choice. This is one of them as both duty and honor demand I do right by the Order." He set his glass on the bookshelf and turned back to the window, leaning his shoulder against it and pressing his forehead to the cool glass. "If I choose not to swing the blade, Chaos will be released, and none will survive. If I choose to swing the blade and execute the threat, one perishes and mankind survives."

Gareth snorted. "I truly hate the 'good of the many at the cost of the one' argument."

"Why?" Dylan asked, his breath fogging against the cold windowpane.

"Because it's almost always irrefutable." Leather creaked. "Kennedy. Good morning."

"Hi."

Dylan turned to find her standing in one of his long, linen poet shirts. She'd rolled the sleeves back several times and the deep V of the neck came to a point well below her breasts.

Hair a tumbled mess and feet bare, she was, "Beautiful." The word escaped Dylan before he could stop himself.

A faint blush stained her cheeks. "Hi," she repeated softly. Her stare was direct, open, but unsure.

Like a compass pulled to true north, Dylan moved to her with slow, unsure steps. His heart lurched. The pain that had at first been so persistent and had then become so fierce now made sense. *Love.* Centuries of going without the emotion left him unfamiliar and uncomfortable in handling it.

The door opened before he reached her, and the warlock strode in. He made a beeline for Kennedy, moving without Dylan's hesitation. "Morning, gorgeous." He hugged her tight, picking her up and setting her farther from Dylan in one efficient move.

"Hey," she said, looking to Ethan with something akin to hope and definitely related to faith.

Jealousy, wild and violent, moved like poison through his veins.

Ethan's eyes narrowed. "Something entertaining, Assassin?" His emphasis on Dylan's title made Kennedy visibly flinch.

Dylan stood straighter and shifted his balance. "Ready for combat, are you?"

Ethan relaxed, grinning. "I'm not going into combat with you, dumbass. It's a video game. Probably the only way I'd ever have a chance of beating you at anything." He chuckled. "Pretty funny to think you've lived far enough under a rock you don't know what a PS4 is, or even an iPad Mini."

"I've the PlayStation," Gareth said, his tone smooth and deep. "He has the Mini. He doesn't game much because he's too busy."

"Impressive." Ethan's snark sullied the air, taking the comment from jesting to just plain rude.

Dylan clenched his fists and the air around him wavered. "You're testing me on the wrong day, warlock."

"Fair." He took Kennedy's hand and led her to the second sofa, plopping into it with a casualness Dylan couldn't help but envy, particularly when Kennedy followed him down and snuggled under his arm. He yawned wide, jaw cracking. "So what's the plan?"

"Plan?" Dylan parroted. He felt so distinctly removed from reality, like life was moving ahead and forever leaving him two paces behind.

"You know," Ethan said in a Jersey accent. "A plaaaan." He squeezed Kennedy's cheeks.

She caught the look of confusion on the assassins' faces

and grinned. "*Better Off Dead*. My favorite movie." Color fled from her face as if chased, leaving her pale. "Ironic title, I guess."

Dylan hardly heard her last four words over the white noise roaring in his ears. *I can't do this*—won't *do this. By Danu, this is an act no man should have to endure. If the goddess had given me a clue, even one so minor as "It begins with the letter..." then I might know what truth I'm supposed to find before...*

His knees gave way and he sank to the floor, hitting hard. "By Danu." Staring down dumbly, Dylan let his hands fall to his sides, the knuckles resting on the well-worn Oriental runner that spanned the stretch in front of the windows. "I've found the truth."

Gareth was out of his chair and on one knee in front of Dylan before he could take his next breath. "What is it?"

Dylan's gaze slowly lifted and found Kennedy moving toward him in a rush, her slender body outlined through the linen by the fire at her back. "Dylan?" She went to her knees beside Gareth. Taking one of Dylan's frigid hands in her own warm ones, she rubbed briskly. "What happened? What truth?"

He stared at Gareth. "She's my truth."

"Yes, but how?"

Dylan glanced quickly at her then back to Gareth. "It's my choice."

"Oh, great Dagda." Gareth wobbled, bracing his fist on the floor.

Kennedy looked between the men. "What are you discussing?"

Ethan's legs filled his peripheral view on one side as he moved in close. "Huh?"

Dylan could only focus on Gareth. He knew his face had to be an uncharitable confluence of understanding—that Danu had shown him the truth from the very beginning.

That Cailleach believed Kennedy strong enough for the reincarnation. That she had likely cultivated Kennedy's lineage to ensure a host powerful enough to survive the ritual the first night that Venus, Mercury and Saturn had aligned since her incarceration. That he'd been given the key to stopping the events to come, but he'd remained entirely blind to what had been right before him all along. *Kennedy.* She, *she* was the truth he'd been meant to find. All that she was, all that she could be in his life. *His* truth. The one thing that made his life worth living and, ultimately, atoned for the sins of his past and made his life an adequate sacrifice.

Still staring at Gareth, he worked to speak through lips gone numb. "What do I do?"

The man's head snapped back as if he'd taken a shot to the jaw. "You're asking me?"

In answer, Dylan simply stared.

Kennedy reached out and stroked his face. "Dylan? Talk to me."

Gareth gave a barely perceptible nod.

Dylan rose on legs as sturdy as saplings and moved to the sofa. Fire had warmed the leather, and that warmth seeped into his bare torso, but his bones remained cold. Gareth offered him the Glencairn and Dylan took it, drinking three fingers' worth of whiskey straight from the bottle in seconds. Alcohol's numbing fingers warmed him from the inside out, reaching into the darkest nooks and crannies to leave him slightly lightheaded. The urge to get fluthered and let the final hours pass without acknowledging what he knew he had to do was far too tempting.

"Dylan?"

Kennedy's voice cut him to the quick. Setting the bottle down hard enough to splash amber liquid over the rim, he gathered the woman—*his* woman—into his arms. His lips sought hers with unapologetic need, his tongue delving into her mouth at her gasp. Squirming, she worked to press her body into his. He cupped her ass and cradled her shoulders, holding her across his lap. She tasted like peppermint toothpaste, smelled like sex, felt like home.

Dylan took the kiss deeper, sensing first her surprise and then her pleasure. Tucking his hand up under the hem of the shirt, he found her wearing nothing more than a thong. A rumble of approval sounded from deep in his chest.

Someone nearby cleared his throat with such uncomfortable desperation it sounded like a goose was being asphyxiated.

Kennedy pulled back, eyes wide and glazed. Her nipples pressed into his chest while her nails dug into his arms. "Let me know what I did to deserve that because I'll do it again as soon as you're done explaining."

Dylan grinned down at her, something settling into place—a piece of him that had been missing far too long.

Ethan spoke, low and earnest. "I owe you two an apology. I thought—" he ran his hands through his hair…twice "—well, I thought you might be using her." At Dylan's killing glare, the man shrugged. "I was wrong. Look, you've loved her for a few days. I've loved her for years."

Even Kennedy's fine movements stilled as he held her in his arms, a field mouse under a predator's shadow.

"Uh…this isn't some big secret, is it?" Ethan tugged at his wrinkled T-shirt.

"No." Dylan fought the itch between his shoulders and looked down at Kennedy. "She understands what I'm able to give."

She let out the breath she'd been holding, the rush of air reeking of disappointment.

Gareth opened his mouth to speak, but Dylan shot him a hard gaze. Changing the direction of the conversation, he set Kennedy beside him on the couch and dropped an arm over her shoulders. "I heard Aylish tell you he'd take you to the Library last night. Find anything useful?" He deliberately kept his tone cool as he surreptitiously swiped at the nervous sweat dotting his brow.

Ethan looked at Kennedy for several minutes before he answered. "Not much, baby girl. Seems like there's something to do with Samhain's planetary alignment this year that's going to give her the strength to reincarnate. She was bound by the Druids under the same sky, so clearly they're stronger, too. But from what I could gather? Their magicks are pretty much equal once the moon rises that night. The only way to stop her at that point is to…" He swallowed hard before burying his face in his hands.

Dylan unseated her when he surged off the couch. "Say that again."

"I'm not fighting with you, asshat." Ethan's words were muffled through his hands, but the emotion was clear. *Grief.*

"So this is it, huh?" Kennedy shifted to set her feet on the floor, twining her hands in her lap. "No way to get it over with soon—"

Dylan spun, grabbed Kennedy's hand and hauled her off the sofa. To Ethan he said, "Get your ass in here, warlock. I need you to help me stop this."

Ethan sprang up, eyes wet with unshed tears. "Whatever it is, man, you've got it."

"Good." Dylan jogged into the bedroom, pulling Kennedy along behind him. "In here." He gave her a gentle shove toward the bed before ushering Ethan in. Grabbing his claymore from behind the door, he started out. "Stay here for a second. Do *not* touch these doors."

Shutting and locking the door on their confused faces, Dylan focused and pushed, letting the aether burn through him. His will was its flame, his desire its fuel. The wood of his doors shimmered, mirage-like. Wood particles exploded with sensational force. The smell of sawdust permeated the room even as iron bindings were reduced to dust particles. The metallic tang of a blacksmith's shop overlaid the wood. Dylan moved through the aether and began to reform the doors, pulling the elements together to create a stone wall. It came together in a rush, settling into place without an errant seam. "By the gods, the warlock's onto something. The planetary alignment's ramping up the elements. Come with me."

Without questioning him, Gareth fell into step.

Dylan grinned, wild and feral. "I know the truth and know what I have to do."

Kennedy watched in awe as the doors began to shimmer in the fog-diffused midmorning light. They twisted and groaned under the force wrenching them apart. She moved a step closer only to find herself hauled back.

"Stay clear, Kennedy. He wasn't joking." His voice was hard, no longer miserable and distraught.

She glanced over her shoulder. "What's going on?"

"Aether," he said between gritted teeth. "His element. He's doing something to the doors, likely to keep us in here." When she started forward, furious, he grabbed her and yanked her backward, this time banding his arms around her. "I'm not screwing around, Jefferson. He's literally remaking the doors into something else. You get caught up in that shit, and you'll be dismantled on a cellular level, and come back like the doors. Wrong."

Her mouth fell open as the doors flexed and broke apart. Through the haze, she caught glimpses of Dylan. He was focused, eyes luminescent, entirely invested in what he was doing. And when the atomic mist shifted, she knew why the Assassin had been so determined. He'd walled them in.

Kennedy broke free of Ethan's grasp and raced forward, pounding her fists on the new stone wall that stood where doors had been. "Put the doors back, Dylan!" She railed at him, punctuating the curses with fists. *Futile.* She snarled at the wall. *And I don't* do *futile.*

"C'mon, Kenny. Sit down. We'll figure a way out of this."

She spun on him. "Don't you get it? One of two things is going to happen. He's either keeping me here until the appointed time, or..." She pressed her back to the wall.

"Or what?"

"Or he's doing something all 'save the girl,' as if I'm incompetent and can't help. If that moronic Druid was standing in front of me right now, I'd drop his ass to the floor faster than he could say 'bippity-boppity-boo' and show him *exactly* how capable I am." The urge to growl had her baring her teeth.

Ethan's lips twitched. "Bippity-boppity-boo?" His shoulders started to shake.

"Shut up. I don't know what you guys do when you do that voodoo that you do." She grinned.

None of this was funny, but if she didn't laugh, she'd cry.

A memory from her first tour in Afghanistan as a field medic came back. She'd found herself under fire as a Special Forces team performed an extraction. Even now, "terror" didn't begin to describe what she'd experienced. The guys had come back to the chopper with the two wounded soldiers, shoving them inside before they'd taken to the air amid a barrage of fire and counterfire. She had been working like a madwoman to get the guys stabilized when one of the wounded soldiers looked up at her. "Ginger," he'd said, "that was a hell of a three-hour tour." She hadn't known what to say or do until one of the pilots at the stick called through the headphones, "We're getting you off the island, Gilligan." Kennedy smiled, remembering. They'd been a team, working together, and that was what pissed her off about Dylan. "An island unto himself," she muttered.

"What island?"

She blew out a breath and looked up at Ethan. "Nothing. No island. I need to grab my sweats before we figure out how we're going to get out of here."

"My element is earth. I can't make things—" he waggled his hands as he thought "—change. We're stuck here until someone lets us out."

She narrowed her eyes. "You're never stuck until you're eight feet under and lacking a pulse."

A faint smile pulled at one corner of his mouth, curling it gently. "You going all badass on me?"

"When it's the only option I've got, it's the only choice to make. The army taught me enough about hand-to-hand and weapons to ensure I'd survive in basic combat. But I was a nurse first then, and I'm a nurse first now. I'll always be a war vet, though. Plus? I'm a woman." She paused, closing her eyes before blowing out a breath. "And I love him."

Silence greeted her admission, and she was a little more than half afraid to open her eyes.

"You sure, Jefferson? Because that changes things."

She opened her eyes. "I'm sure, but what does it change?"

He didn't answer her, instead tipping his head toward the window. "What are you willing to do about it?"

"I love him more than anything, but throwing myself from the proverbial balcony isn't my style." She wandered to the window and looked down. "We're at least forty feet up."

"Grab your sweats and some shoes. You're going to need a jacket, too. For that matter, so will I."

Feeling more lighthearted than she would have ever guessed she could under the circumstances, she started for the closet. "Be right back."

She went to the closet and quickly dressed. A small leather case poked out from beneath a sweater shelf. Curious, and feeling slightly criminal, she pulled the case free. The brown leather was worn, the patina of age darkening it to near ebony in places. She popped the lid, and several beautiful daggers, slim and deadly sharp, glinted in the overhead light.

Kennedy set the case beside her as she tied her shoes. In a last-minute decision, she grabbed the longest knife and clambered to her feet. "Might be theft, but I'm not going unarmed." Fear, cold and leaden, settled in her stomach. Of course, if Cailleach rose, she'd just given the bitch a blade. "But I can control her. At least enough to push her out of the way and do what needs to be done." Because Dylan was *not* going down for her. No way. If she had to, if all the cards were on the table and there was no other choice, she'd take her life herself.

She shoved the knife through the back pocket of the jeans, wincing as it sliced through the brand new—expensive— denim. "Sacrifices should hurt, I guess."

Satisfied, she grabbed one of Dylan's jackets for Ethan and headed out of the closet.

"I thought you said you could 'control' your element!" she shouted, fighting to keep her feet under her as yet another giant boulder slammed into the castle just below the bedroom windows.

Ethan stood, feet spread, hands at his side, palms down and fingers splayed. Sweating, he hardly spared her a glance, and then the rumbles stopped. Outside the stone wall Dylan had replaced the door with, voices were raised. They were too muffled to understand.

Voices outside could be heard, too, but they were quite a ways away and likely carried by the wind. No one was stupid enough to stand in range of the flying boulders.

"You've got to stop. The keep won't be able to stand the battering."

Ethan's hands relaxed, and he plucked at his sweaty T-shirt. "I don't know what else to do."

She paced, winding her hair into a loose topknot and tying it up with one of the random leather thongs Dylan kept on his bedside table. Hands on her hips, she stared out the window. Giving up wasn't an option. If only they had one of those emergency inflatable slides like an airplane... Turning slowly, trying to bank hope that this might work, she squared her sagging shoulders. "What about a land slide?"

Ethan eyed her suspiciously. "Um, that would probably be worse than the boulders."

"No. Not a landslide. A land. Slide. Two words. You pull earth up to the window and we either walk or slide down." Her stomach knotted as she waited, wondering.

"Huh. It's worth a try. But if this power surge continues to make things wonky, I might cover the whole building in grass," he muttered. "Open the windows so I can get some air, then move back. Far as you can."

Kennedy rolled each window open before moving to stand at the opposite wall, eyes trained on the warlock. *This has to work.*

Shaking his hands at his sides, Ethan dropped his chin and rolled his head back and forth, lips moving silently. He stopped with a suddenness that made the hair on the back of her neck stand up. Magick charged the air like static before a storm. Her skin tingled. The urge to slap at the prickly sensation was almost too much to stand. She managed to remain still, though barely.

Cupping his hands at his sides, he drew them together and up.

The ground rumbled, a great roar of protest.

Hangers clattered in the closet, and in the bathroom something glass hit the floor, shattering. The bed creaked and groaned, the massive structure moving several inches as the side tables slid several feet.

The smells of wet earth and grass permeated the air completely.

Flames roared in the fireplace.

Magick bit into her skin and left her with a thousand invisible wounds.

Sweat poured from Ethan's forehead and temples. His shirt stuck to his back.

And then it stopped.

Silence weighed heavily, like it waited for the warlock's next order and knew it would involve the earth's protests and Kennedy's pain.

"Ethan?" Taking a tenuous step forward, she laid a hand on his back.

"It's the best I can do without additional instruments." His voice was hollow, devoid of any warmth. When he turned and looked at her, his pupils were huge, leaving his irises devoid of color. There was no recognition in them. "I need rest."

"I can't," she said gently. "Come back to me, sweet cheeks. I have to go get Dylan. Remember? He's the one you sort of despise? Kidnapped me? His people brought you to Ireland for me?" With every question, she moved closer to him. "We've been best friends for years. You call me Kenny."

He blinked slowly, the darkness in his eyes folding in on itself until his pupils were pinpricks. "Yeah. I'm here. Just never call me 'sweet cheeks', Kenny, however, call me Thor, even though Chris Hemsworth isn't half the man I am."

"Right, big guy."

"That would be the Hulk." He smiled, clearly exhausted.

"Don't nerd out on me now." Kennedy couldn't stop

herself from hugging him. "Stick with me just a little longer and you'll get to see me kick that damn Druid's ass."

"That's an energizing thought." One corner of his mouth curled up.

Racing to the windows, she gasped.

Earth had risen up like a giant slide, stopping several feet below the windows.

"I wonder what the people downstairs are seeing?" Her voice was weak with wonder.

"Likely a whole lot of nothing and the occasional earthworm," Ethan answered, moving to stand beside her. He whistled, long and low. "Can't believe I did that."

"Why?"

"Not usually within my power level." He shrugged. "Gotta be the planetary alignment."

"Sure." She swung a leg over the windowsill.

"Hey, wait." Ethan took her upper arm. "Let me go first."

A radical crack and boom split the air, the percussion tossing her back into the room. She clung to the window casing, righting herself as the pressure eased. "What the hell was that?"

Ethan's mouth hung open.

"What?" she demanded, fear clawing its way up her back with slow, piercing progress.

"Biggest magick I've ever felt." He glanced at her and then the window, letting go of her arm. "You need to go. Now. Something's happened."

She turned and swung her legs over the edge, dropping to the upper swell of earth and pulling her lifted dagger. Gaining her footing, she started down the steep decline, at times forced to scoot on her butt. Little clods of dirt and grass tumbled around her. *Ethan's following.* She was both relieved to have him at her back as well as frightened for him.

Hitting level ground, she sprinted in the direction the

sound had come from. *He's okay. He's okay. He's okay. Please don't let him have done something horrible or irreversible.* Stumbling to a stop, Ethan plowed into her and they rolled in a tangle of limbs to the foot of a stone circle she hadn't known was here.

"No!" she screamed, shoving Ethan away as she sprinted toward Dylan.

He lay flat on the altar stone as if sleeping, his claymore running down his body even as it was gripped in his hands. But something was wrong. Something was *missing*.

She rounded on Gareth. "What have you done?" When he didn't respond, she shoved him and shouted, "Answer me!"

He grabbed her around the throat and squeezed gently. "Don't knock me out of position, Kennedy. We're the only anchor that can call his soul out of the Shadow Realm. Move me from true north and there's nothing left to hold him here."

"What has he done?" she demanded quietly.

Gareth let her go. "He…" His mouth worked wordlessly for a moment. Shaking his head, he said, "He used the aether to separate his soul from his body. Then we cast him to the Shadow Realm."

"You. Did. What?" she asked, low and vehement.

"It's the warlock's fault." Gareth shot Ethan a scathing look.

"Hey. You guys brought me here and asked for help. I *never* suggested he send himself to Hell."

Kennedy stared at Gareth through narrowed eyes. Her chest heaved as she fought to catch her breath. "What, exactly, is he doing in the Shadow Realm? And don't spare me, Gareth."

He met her stare, eyes cool yet still compassionate. "He's facing Cailleach. The warlock suggested Cailleach's power would be strongest with Samhain's moonrise while our powers are already stronger as the planets pull together.

She needs the alignment. We, apparently, need only the general proximity to see the effects." The bitter words were nothing compared to the way his arms trembled.

"Gareth." The word boomed across the grounds, and the man winced. Aylish stormed up to him, stumbling when he caught sight of Dylan. "Oh, Great Father, no." Spinning on his heel, he ordered one of the Elders to gather the others to take up the subpositions of the compass and to gather every man in the keep to guard the formation. Then he turned to Kennedy. "You need to leave, lass."

"Screw that," she spat, clenching her dagger tighter. "I'm not going anywhere without him. I love him, Aylish. Like hell I'm going to leave him. I never got a chance…" She fought the urges to scream and cry and rage, swallowing them down and saving them. "I never told him. He needs to know."

"I'm sure he does," he said gently.

"No offense? But that's not good enough."

Gareth grunted and gripped his sword tight enough his knuckles whitened.

Kennedy spun and found a dark stain spreading across Dylan's thigh. "What? What happened?" She raced toward him, only to find herself yanked back seconds before she reached him.

"He's been wounded. It's the first and won't be the last." Aylish's hands shook as he held her. "Anything you do to his body, his soul will feel. You must do nothing—*nothing*—to impede his ability to defend himself, Kennedy." Aylish's words were low and violent, even as a shallow gash appeared on Dylan's bare forearm.

She turned to one of the men she recognized from Gareth's debacle. "Get those medical chests out here and bring Angus. He and Ethan can help stabilize Dylan without harming his ability to defend himself." Whirling back, she looked between Aylish and Gareth. "I'm no Cinderella, gentlemen, and Shakespeare wrote the only Romeo and Juliet. I don't intend to let this become a tragedy. Get me down there."

"Like hell!" Gareth snarled as Ethan and Aylish shouted their own denials.

Stepping in front of Gareth, she fisted his shirt in one hand. "Get me down there, Gareth. I'm not playing around."

Gareth went stony.

She turned back to face Ethan.

Dylan jerked again, and blood wept from a deep cut on his biceps.

She hoisted herself onto the slab and crouched on her knees, stroking his face. "Dylan, get your ass back here. If you can hear me, get back here *now*. I'm done messing around, Druid. I won't lose you." She laid a hand on his wound and was sick with the level of damage that radiated through her palm. "Give me the bag, Aylish. I have to do something."

Dylan's father moved to her side and turned her, drawing her into his embrace. "It's too late, daughter mine."

"In a wise woman's words, it's not too late until you're eight feet under and not drawing a breath." Ethan scrubbed his hands through his hair. "Or something like that."

Those fatherly arms that held her, loved her in a way she'd coveted all her life, were her undoing. The dam of emotion she'd kept at bay broke free and rushed forward, carried on a devastating wave of fear. She clung to Aylish and shook as he stroked her hair and murmured to her in a voice his son had inherited. *Inherited...*

Pushing at Aylish, she shoved off the altar stone. She hadn't been thinking. "You do it. Send me down there." She lay next to Dylan and took his hand in hers, lacing their fingers together. "Do it."

"He'd not want this, Kennedy." Aylish moved to stand over her.

Then came the voice she had trusted for so many years. "If you won't do it, move over. I won't try it for him, but for her?" Ethan's eyes met hers. "Anything."

She grinned up at him. "Hand me that short sword. I'm nobody's Juliet."

"Kick her ass, baby." Ethan handed the sword to her and watched as she laid it vertically on her chest and gripped the hilt, mimicking Dylan's broadsword. Pushing his sleeves back and kicking his shoes off, Ethan tugged off his socks and curled his toes into the earth. He turned his face to the sun. Then he began to chant.

She braced herself and waited. Long seconds turned to interminable minutes that continued to pass like a lazy summer breeze—slow and without any discernable effect. "Ethan?"

"Something's wrong." He tried again, ignoring her cry of distress when a deep wound appeared over Dylan's abdomen. "Kenny…" His voice was tight with grief. "I can't. Cailleach is sucking energy down through the earth. It's like it's being funneled to her. I can feel it happening, but I'm not strong enough to pull against her to any effect. I can't even slow her down. There's nothing I can do."

"No," she whispered. Rolling onto her side, she cupped Dylan's face. "You hold on," she said through her teeth. "You. Hold. On."

Rolling off the altar stone, she landed on her feet before turning on Aylish. "You fix this. He's your son and I love him and you won't steal the lifetime I might have to love him. Send me. Now." When he hesitated, she whispered, "I'd rather die with him than live another minute without him."

One look between her, the mortal in front of him, and Ethan, the warlock closing in on him, seemed to make up Aylish's mind for him. He moved in quickly and urged her to the altar beside Dylan's body even as another wound appeared over his sword arm. "Bring him back to me, daughter."

"Get ready, bitch," she whispered, nodding before closing her eyes. "You hurt him, I hurt you. You cut him, I cut you. You try to kill him, I'm *going* to kill you."

Chapter 20

Materializing in the Shadow Realm had been a shock. Dylan had done it. Made it to Hell. Now it was a matter of determining if he'd ended up in the right prison cell. He needed to find the goddess and launch a preemptive strike, take her down before she realized what he'd done. If he could release her soul in the Shadow Realm, it would be bound here forever. Likewise, he had to prevent himself from being killed. What happened to his spiritual body would translate to his physical body. If he was mortally wounded here, he was finished, as damned as he believed himself.

Waves of shale ran in every direction and made stealthy movements impossible. Every step rattled and echoed as ragged rock slid down every swell he climbed and decline he traversed.

Souls of the dead clung to the walls, wraiths bound to torture at the hands of those gods of the Shadow Realm. Or, in this case, gods *bound* to this plane.

Dylan ignored the shiver that made his tailbone curl, that prehistoric response to…fear. *Stop it. Stay focused, arsehole. It's like any other mission—get in, get done, get gone.* He slipped and rode an avalanche of shale to the edge of a narrow, dark crevice. Using the momentum, he leaped across the chasm and clawed his way up the next rise, more mountain than hill.

Standing to survey his surroundings, Dylan's mouth

fell open. A shimmering, translucent wall locked him in. Across the giant cavern he could see similar watery walls, behind which each god was trapped. And there, just in the corner, stood Cailleach.

She turned to him, a faint smile pulling up one side of her mouth. "I wondered if you'd come."

The goddess was too far from him. He needed her close. "I called to you through your host, but you didn't answer. It occurred to me that meeting you here might be advantageous."

"Advantageous, indeed." She moved toward him, her form flickering between the beautiful young maiden, the mother and the hideous crone.

The strobe effect made Dylan's stomach lurch.

"I see your distress, Assassin. You're accustomed to my appearance in the host. But this—" she swept a hand over her body "—is the reality of my damnation. Never to choose one form, but forever locked in eternal discord within myself. It's slightly…maddening."

"I can't imagine."

"No, you can't." She moved toward him.

He itched to pull his broadsword free. But instead Dylan widened his stance and crossed his arms, placing his hands closer to the dagger sheaths strapped there.

Ethereal and hideous at once, Cailleach moved toward him without seeming to walk.

Is she bluidy gliding? Fecking hell, she is.

She settled several feet from him. He hadn't noticed she, too, was armed. "Expecting trouble?"

A faint smile colored her pale lips. "Only you."

"Fair enough." He sank to his heels. She was so slight, he hardly had to tilt his head to see her. "Seems we're at odds, Cailleach."

"Only because you're too ignorant to put the pieces of

my offer together. Mortal minds rarely grasp the full im-
plications of dealing with gods." She moved closer.

"You were clear in wanting a consort."

"Ah, but you see such a limited view of *consort*, Assassin." Again, she moved closer.

Dylan's hands flexed.

She arched a brow. "Anxious?"

"Realistic."

"Smart man. I've always preferred them smart. So tell
me, then. What do you think a consort does?" Her con-
descending grin told him she expected a crude answer.

He delivered. "Fight as well as they fuck."

She stepped closer, and Dylan raised a hand. "No closer.
Not yet."

"Not yet means soon," she purred, running her hands
down her sides. "I can wait. Aren't you curious about what
your role as my consort would be?" Her eyes blazed with
sexual hunger and a feral, presumptive possession. "You
see, as consort, *my* consort, we will control aether. You'll
be my personal phoenix, Dylan. With the aether, you will
help me remake the universe from the ashes of Chaos.
You'll become a demigod as you rebuild worlds under my
direction. All planes of existence will be reconstructed,
and I'll rule them with you at my side. We'll be worshipped
as the highest of high."

Dylan ran his free hand over his mouth as he tried
to sort his thoughts. One thought broke free of the rest.
"You've cultivated Kennedy's female line. Why?"

She propped a hip out and planted her hand on it. "None
of your business."

"Did you kill the women as they aged?" he demanded.

Her eyes narrowed. "I'll answer you this once, but you'll
maintain a deferential tone. I didn't kill the women. Their
minds were weak and they succumbed to the pressure of
my…demands."

"So you killed them."

"Encouraged hybrid vigor, survival of the fittest—that type of thing." She looked down at him. "Does this disturb you, you who have stolen so many lives?"

Hatred boiled in him, but he didn't know who it was for—himself or her. She didn't lie, and he had no defense.

The pieces came together in that moment with an emotional thunderclap. Dylan had come to fight for Kennedy's right to live, for the right of the worlds to go on untouched by Cailleach's maddened hand. Now he found himself adding one more victim to the mix. *Him.* The goddess had singled him out, as well. A sinking horror rose up in him, and the question was blurted out before he could stop himself. "My mother. Did you…?"

"You were a boy with too much potential to be coddled. I needed you stronger, hardened, *honed.*"

Magick coursed through him, unchecked. Dylan's hands shimmered so hard they were nothing but a blur.

"Ah, ah, ah, Assassin. You'll want to control that."

When he didn't rein in it and while his hands were too warped to reach for a weapon without changing it, she struck. Pulling her sword with blinding speed, Cailleach scored his thigh, deep and hard. The pain shocked him, and his magick extinguished. He rose slowly, forced to use the uninjured leg alone, drawing his blade as he went.

She circled him, eyes shrewd. "You've drawn a weapon against me. That's an act punishable by death."

"Sure an' as your right, but the death won't be mine, you crazy bitch."

They came together in a clash of steel that rang through the cavern and caused the damned to scatter up the walls like spiders. She swung out.

He batted her blade away with his own.

They circled and struck, circled and struck, until both

bled freely. Magicks fouled the air, their dark taint lost to the vast, black cavern.

Dylan drew shale up and formed walls to back her into, but she evaded or knocked them down. He drew shale up and morphed it into a cage.

She shattered the bars.

On and on it went, magicks devolving into crude and rudimentary spells flung out to cause the most damage possible.

The next time they passed close to each other, she closed in on him. Faster than he'd assumed she'd be, she scored his biceps when she lunged. Still, he didn't complain. She'd aimed for his heart.

He sidled up the incline and swung a wide arc, shattering her collarbone but missing the taking of her head.

She screeched and swiped out with a wee dagger he hadn't seen. He didn't feel the cut to his lower abdomen. *Not good.* "Stop fecking aboot, woman. You want me? Then come!" His bellow caused shale to fall from the cavern roof.

Cailleach grinned. "You, Assassin, just damned yourself, and for what? A woman?" She lunged and he blocked. "She does hold an interesting talent, though." At his blank look, she laughed merrily. "You don't know? That's divine. I think I'll hold on to her soul for a while, let her experience the horrors to come. We'll find the key to the aether. Nature operates in pairs—male, female, yin, yang, light, dark. You're one of two." Her mouth foamed like a rabid animal's. "I'll release my brothers and sisters and we'll destroy the Druids before any others." Blade low and across her body, she swung up with stunning strength at the same time she slammed her dagger upward.

Dylan deflected her sword blow and swept a hand out, cutting her across the throat. *So close. So gods-be-damned close!* He was so focused on beheading her and ending this that he almost missed her dagger. Jerking backward, Dylan managed to avoid the killing blow, but the tang caught his chin. Stars burst like fireworks as his head snapped back. He fell, fighting to find up from down and keep his sword. Shale clattered madly around him, cutting him a hundred times if it cut him once. He hit the valley between rises hard. Every bone in his body shifted on impact, and his sword chattered across the blackened floor.

The metallic tang of blood filled his mouth. He was in trouble, and he knew it. Large flakes of stone continued to land around him, the dust clogging his nose and collecting as fine grit in his mouth. Ribs aching, he clutched them and rolled over. The deep cut in his thigh bled freely. Thank the gods it had numbed out with trauma shock.

Cailleach stood a good twenty feet from him. The Arcanum, even the Elders, had underestimated her strength prior to the moonrise.

He pushed to his feet, spitting blood. Relative certainty settled over him, despair leaving a bitter taste in his mouth. He would die here today. It would mean his soul would be irretrievable, bound to the Shadow Realm forever. If he had his way, though, he'd be taking this bitch with him. The initial strategy of strike hard and fast had failed, and miserably. *Time to reassess.*

Cailleach flipped her hair over her shoulder, the movement coquettish. "Are you clear on where we stand, Assassin?"

"Aye. It was foolish of me to attempt a preemptive strike." He took her measure and found her wanting. *Him.* Fighting a shudder, Dylan stood straighter. "I'll change tactics and see what you're willing to negotiate."

"It's clear you're not interested in negotiation, *Dylan.*" His name was a verbal sneer.

"Better to live, I'm thinking." He limped to his sword and snatched it up. Heat burrowed into him in the mind-numbing cold. With a shout, he dropped his sword and looked down to find his hand blistered.

"A small warning, Assassin." Cailleach started down the steep incline. "As is this." She threw out her hand and a power surge like none Dylan had ever felt slammed into him.

He was tossed backward, unable to do anything but try to tuck and roll as he landed. A plate of shale found his open thigh wound and embedded itself deep. Dylan screamed as it struck bone. Dust filled his eyes and they wept tears of protest. One arm was broken. Lifting his good hand, he tried to pull the shale free. It wouldn't budge.

"Such a vain man, thinking you could defeat me simply because I'm a woman." Cailleach's low-lidded gaze filled with heat. "You think because your mother died so easily, all women are as easy to dispatch." She raised her hand to him, a small black tornado forming in her palm.

"Good thing I'm not quite so fallible." Kennedy's voice echoed through the room.

Kennedy wanted to scream when she saw Dylan lying before Cailleach, prone and vulnerable. He bled from so many places she wasn't sure what was superficial and what was not. Tear tracks carved through the gritty dust that blackened his face. The whites of his eyes were red, the irises flaring when he saw her.

She ignored it, turning her attention back to Cailleach.

"Foolish girl," the goddess snapped. "You'll stay out of this. Your time is nigh, and I won't have you fouling up millennia of planning due to some misbegotten idea of love or loyalty."

"Misbegotten?" Kennedy said, her lip curling in an imitation of Dylan's most derisive snarl. "Who's the foolish woman between us? I'm thinking anyone who discounts either love or loyalty, let alone both, is the fool."

Cailleach raised her hands, and Dylan shouted a warning.

Kennedy dropped low as watery magick flew overhead. Rolling to the side, she scuttled down the hill. Intent on making it to Dylan, she sank low and loped forward, clenching her weapon.

Burning pellets rained down on her, and she dove forward in the most awkward somersault ever accomplished.

"No!" Cailleach's screech created a maelstrom of falling shingles and dust.

Ignoring the barrage that could impale her and the stuff that was going to give her black lung, she pushed on. Then she saw him.

Dylan had curled on his side to protect himself but still clawed his way toward her with fierce determination.

Kennedy rushed up to him, grabbing his good hand.

His back arched and he hissed.

She dropped his hand.

"Again," he ground out.

"Again?"

The hair on the back of her neck rose all at once, and Kennedy flattened herself over Dylan, barely missing the goddess's magickal offense.

Offense. "Dylan, we have to get out of here, back to the Arcanum. They can help."

He shook his head. "Can't."

"*What*?"

"Have to kill her here. She'll be too much for us if she reincarnates." His breathing was labored. "Grab my hand again."

"I'll grab your hand, you fucking irritating Irishman." She did, hauling him through the maze of valleys the shale hills and mountains made. Every time she rounded the corner, the goddess was there atop the next knoll. When she backtracked, so did Cailleach. "Damn it!"

Crouching low, she took Dylan's face in her hands. "If

we have to kill her here, we're going to have to do it together."

"You." He coughed and blew out a mouthful of black,
tarry stuff. When he tried to move his broken arm, she
could only gape. "You held on to your damn *sword*?"

"Must take her head. Just like if it was you." Pain made
his eyes unfocused. "Take my hand and push."

She picked up his good hand and pushed. He winced,
so she dropped it.

"Nay, lass. *Push*. Mentally. I believe you're an amplifier. Felt it when you first touched me moments ago." He
held up his shaking hand again.

She took it gently. "What's an amplifier?"

"You're a magnifier for magick. It's what she meant,
that I hadn't figured it out yet. The yin to the yang. You're
drawing on all the elements, including aether." His eyes
flared wide. "Oh, gods. You're the balance to my element."

"What? What balance?" she asked, only half listening
to him as she scanned the peaks of each rocky hill for the
crazed goddess.

"Later. Good, firm grasp, Kennedy." He grasped her
hand. "Push at me from the very center of who you are."

Her deepest fear surfaced. *Who am I? Not daughter,
not nurse, not lover, not medic, not enough. Never enough.*
The connection she felt with Dylan was as stagnant as
shallow pond water.

"Faith, Kennedy," Dylan ground out between gritted
teeth. "Trust me in this."

She nodded, her searching eyes blind to her surroundings.

He squeezed.

"I don't suppose it would be appropriate to start sing-
ing 'Send Me an Angel' right about now," she muttered,
scooting closer to him.

Dylan's mumbled reply was lost in a cascade of rock and dust.

Cailleach stood over them, her image flickering ever faster. Hands raised, she shouted a command in a language so ancient Kennedy's bones ached.

Terror gripped her, and in the back of her mind, she heard the rattle of gunfire from memories that were never far enough away. Dylan's hold on her hand tightened until bones ground together, pulling her back. Their eyes locked...and she pushed.

Dylan's eyes rolled back in his head, and his back arched.

Raw, undiluted pain rolled through Kennedy, and she screamed.

A voice whispered through her mind. "Let go. Live."

"Screw. You." The words were lost in the roar of sound.

Dylan sat up, eyes wild, wind blowing around him. Left arm dangling at his side, he twisted to his knees before standing, never letting her hand go.

She clung to him, fighting the air that beat dust into her eyes with every pulse. Leaning around him, she hauled his broadsword up and let it rest, tip in the gravel. "What now?"

He glanced at her. "You canna touch her, Kennedy."

"No shit." She smiled. "But I can beat on her, right?"

"Braw lass." He smiled. "Up you go, then. I've your back until you reach the top. Then I'm up after you."

"Last one to the top buys the drinks?"

"Deal."

She started forward with the sword in her left hand, dagger in her back pocket again. Only a quarter of the way up, she was panting. "*This* is what Cross-Fit got me?" Still, she pressed on. Magicks would wing overhead, sometimes coming close enough to split the air above her and leave behind the smell of burning ozone. An idea began to form.

It would be a gamble, and she'd have to get close enough to test her theory, but it might end this thing.

Cresting the rise, she found Cailleach waiting for her.

"Come to meet your death early, did you?" She stepped closer. "You're in luck. I'm feeling amicable. Kill the Druid and I'll let you coexist with me."

"Are you insane?" she gasped, bending forward to catch her breath. Never once did she take her eyes off the goddess, though. *Dumb? Maybe. But too stupid to live? Never.*

Cailleach's eyes narrowed. Pulling her sword free, she tossed the scabbard aside. "You seem in need of a lesson, not unlike your Druid lover."

Lover. "Look, bitch. I've been through two tours in the Middle East. This place is an air-conditioned cocoon compared to that hell. Now bring it—" she motioned forward with her free hand "—or swing it." She switched the sword to her right hand and twisted it back and forth.

Cailleach was on her before she could think to respond. Claws ripped through her shoulder.

"You want to play that way?" Kennedy seethed at having been caught off guard.

When Cailleach swung her sword free and brought it against her in a wide arc, Kennedy deflected. The vibration of metal ran through her like an electrical jolt. Hands numb, she struggled to maintain the sword, nearly fumbling it as she parried the goddess's lunge. Training— military *and* kickboxing—finally engaged, and Kennedy delivered a bruising kick to Cailleach's midsection.

The goddess stumbled back, gasping for breath.

Kennedy rushed forward. Part of her realized her hind-brain had taken over, was in the driver's seat and simply using her body as a weapon. The conscious part simply cheered and threw confetti.

Cailleach attempted to ward off Kennedy's jabbing

thrusts, but she was too slow once. Just once. And that was all Kennedy needed.

She ran the goddess through.

"Like spearfishing for deities," she said through gritted teeth.

Cailleach flailed about, trying to dislodge the blade from her middle even as she bled freely. Cupping her hands, she began to conjure black smoke that funneled upward in a rapid spiral.

"You *don't* mess with my man, and you don't *ever* underestimate *me*." Gripping Cailleach's throat, she pushed with the core of who she was—as soft as that sense of self remained.

Cailleach's smoke grew wispy as her eyes grew large. "You cannot amplify one and nullify the other."

Kennedy's heart fell but her tone was matter-of-fact. "We're a little too close, you and I. Same object can't occupy two places at once. An amplifier can only amplify what comes through it." Kennedy yanked the sword free and watched dispassionately as Cailleach tried to drag herself away. "You used me so often, you left a little of yourself behind each time. I was terrified it was happening, changing me. I *felt* it happening. Turns out it's for the best, because now I can draw on it and amplify it myself."

Kennedy raised the sword, and Cailleach held up a beseeching hand. "If you kill me, binding me here, you too may be bound."

"So be it." The sword fell as Dylan shouted.

The goddess's head rolled away clean, and Kennedy waited.

Nothing happened.

A strong arm came around her, pulling her into a familiar hard body. "You've got to get out of here, Kennedy. I doona think we'll be safe much longer."

The light was fading as the goddess's soul bled from

her body. Damned souls all around crept forward, ravening mouths open and hungry.

"I don't like this." She backed into Dylan, and he twitched before stepping back.

"Where'd you find my *sgian dubh*?"

"Um, closet. We can talk about my filching it later. Let's go."

"Lay down."

"Not the best of times for this, Dylan." Adrenaline was washed away in a sea of exhaustion. She was too tired to fight with him.

"Now."

She pulled the dagger free and lay down.

He followed her to the ground. Clutching her hand in his, he said, "I'm going to ask you to push for me one last time." When she started to protest, he brought their joined knuckles to his lips. "For me, Kennedy."

She closed her eyes and nodded.

"On three. One…two…*three*!"

If Kennedy had ever thought she'd known pain before, she'd been wrong. She was ripped apart and remade a thousand times in the space of a single heartbeat. She opened her mouth to scream but there was no air.

And then it was done.

Gasping, tears streaming down her temples, she opened her eyes and found blue sky overhead. Ethan's face filled her vision, but that wasn't who she was looking for.

Rolling to her side, she found Dylan lying still as stone, just as when she'd left him.

He'd sent her back alone.

Kennedy screamed, throwing off any and all attempts to help her. She scrambled to her knees, looming over him as tears dripped freely from her nose. "You listen to me, Dylan," she rasped, choking on so much emotion she wondered that she could breathe at all. "You listen." Taking his cheeks in her hands, she sobbed as his whiskers rasped against her palms. "Don't you leave me. *You come back.* Come back to me," she pleaded.

His lips were soft under hers, pliant, not like the firm lips that took kisses and gave pleasure. She kissed him over and over, pleading with all the gods she'd ever heard him name, that one might hear and answer. But no one came forth.

Her wild eyes found Ethan's, and the pity there destroyed her. "No," she pleaded. "He was alive. I was just with him." She turned, looking for Aylish. Finding him next to Gareth, she threw herself in his direction, falling to her knees before scrambling to her feet and reaching him. "Send me back there! Don't you leave him down there to die!"

"Kennedy—"

"No!" she screamed. She looked at Gareth, and time coasted to a stop. He stood staring straight ahead, tears coursing down his face. His shoulders shook as he tried not to let go. Kennedy spun in a circle, looking for anyone who would help her defy the odds and the gods and help her save him.

No one would look at her.

A single tear traced slowly down Ethan's cheek as he stared at the sky.

The Arcanum stood at the four points, none of them willing to relinquish his soul to the Shadow Realm. And she couldn't stand it.

Dagger still in hand, she walked back to the altar on numb legs. This wasn't happening. She hadn't set aside her fears of not being good enough, loveable enough, instilled over a lifetime of criticisms from her father and given herself up to this kind of love only to lose it now. Crawling up on the stone slab, she couldn't stop the sobs that took her over. She curled up on Dylan's good side, holding his cooling arm around her.

She fought to remember his smell, so very much like the wild Irish coastline with an underscore all his own. It was lost to the sea air, and she didn't want to let it go.

Their last night together came back to her. She'd told him she loved him a hundred times over, always in her head, never brave enough to say it out loud. She'd take it all back, tell him a thousand times, tell him until he pleaded with her to stop, all so he'd know now, when it mattered most.

"I'm Juliet after all," she whispered brokenly into his still chest. "Damn you, Romeo. This wasn't how it was supposed to end."

Letting go of his hand and trying not to wince when his arm fell back, she took her knife and sliced her palm. Taking his broken arm, she gently pulled it toward her. The blade scored his calloused flesh easily, and she prayed he didn't feel anything. Pressing their palms together, she laced their fingers. Tossing the knife to the dirt, she used her free hand to clasp their hands closer. And then, with everything she had, she pushed.

Nothing happened.

She brought their joined hands to her cheek. Dropping her chin to her chest, she let the tears fall. They dripped onto his linen shirt, silent as snowflakes.

"Dylan…" Her voice broke. She cleared her throat. "I love you," she said roughly.

Gareth broke, going to his knees. Every other member of the Arcanum followed suit.

Kennedy shook her head and closed her eyes, unable to watch them tell her what she knew. He was gone.

"Please…" she pleaded one last time. When he didn't respond, she let their hands fall apart before lying down, her cheek on his chest. "I love you. I'll always love you. No one will ever take you from my heart, you noble bastard."

"I…love you." His voice rumbled, faint but there, under her ear.

She responded by falling off the altar.

"Kennedy?"

His voice was the most beautiful thing she'd ever heard.

Shouts of jubilation sounded all around her. Aylish went to his knees, face buried in his hands as his shoulders shook.

Dylan closed his eyes as she clambered back to his side and rained kisses all over his face. "Did ye have to choose me broken arm to pull on?"

"Did it work?"

"I felt you… I never wanted to leave you, *mo bonnie gabhar asal.*"

Laughter erupted around her.

"What did you just call me, love?"

"What you've always thought I was calling you, my beautiful woman. A bonnie goat's arse."

She threw back her head and laughed.

Dylan rolled his head to the other side, ignoring Ethan and Angus as they began to work on his effusive wounds. "Da?"

Aylish looked up, his tear-streaked face raw with grief. "I thought…"

Dylan swallowed hard. "Me, too." He pushed the physicians back and tried to sit up, making it inches before collapsing.

Aylish stood over Dylan. "*Mac.*" Son. And he embraced him gently, their fractured past lost to the first steps toward healing.

Letting go of his father, he grumbled that the "sadistic bastards" could get on with their care of him. The Arcanum crowded around, each laying a hand on some part of his head and issuing fervent blessings to the gods. But Dylan's eyes were only for her.

Kennedy moved in close, taking his good hand in hers.

"Your hand will scar," he murmured.

"It'll match yours."

"I'd rather a more lasting commitment than a scar, Kennedy Jefferson."

Her heart galloped away with her common sense. "Yes."

"You'll be my swineherd?" Mischief twinkled in tired green eyes.

"If that's what it takes to be with you. Yes."

"Be my wife."

Everyone froze. Midinjection, Ethan looked up at her.

"Only if you're promising me forever."

"Wouldn't have it any other way, Kennedy. I wouldn't have it any other way. Given you've retained a piece of the goddess, forever may be far longer than you think."

"May Danu will it so," she whispered, laying a gentle kiss on his lips.

He glanced at Ethan and frowned. "Get on with the bluidy drugs, would you?"

Ethan grinned. "This? It's an antibiotic *and* painkiller. Didn't want to waste time. Bad part? It's going to hurt like hell." He started to depress the plunger, never wavering when Dylan let out a grunt.

"I love you, Dylan O'Shea."

His eyes found hers as they grew soft and unfocused. "And I you, Kennedy Jefferson," he said, lacing their fingers together. "And I you."

* * * * *

MILLS & BOON®

Why shop at millsandboon.co.uk?

Each year, thousands of romance readers find their perfect read at millsandboon.co.uk. That's because we're passionate about bringing you the very best romantic fiction. Here are some of the advantages of shopping at www.millsandboon.co.uk:

* **Get new books first**—you'll be able to buy your favourite books one month before they hit the shops

* **Get exclusive discounts**—you'll also be able to buy our specially created monthly collections, with up to 50% off the RRP

* **Find your favourite authors**—latest news, interviews and new releases for all your favourite authors and series on our website, plus ideas for what to try next

* **Join in**—once you've bought your favourite books, don't forget to register with us to rate, review and join in the discussions

Visit **www.millsandboon.co.uk**
for all this and more today!

MILLS & BOON®
n o c t u r n e™

AN EXHILARATING UNDERWORLD OF DARK DESIRES